THE ALBION CHRONICLES
Book 3

Battle for Brigantia

Back in the
Day
Happy reading
x
Welly Flosher

Also by Nelly Harper:

The Albion Chronicles:
Queen of Betrayal
The Girl of Two Worlds
Seven Druids

******

The Jet Necklace

The Albion Chronicles

Book 3

Battle for Brigantia

By

Nelly Harper

The Albion Chronicles – Book 3
Battle for Brigantia
Published by Goblin House
www.goblinhouse.co.uk
Paperback
ISBN: 978-0-9932748-7-9

For Sam, Becky & Ciaran
I could not love you more.

Pronunciation guide

Anniel	An-yeal
Beltatucadros	Bella-too-kad-ross
Bodach	Bo-tach
Cailleach	Kai-lee-ach
Callimai	Cal-i-may
Dimmi	Di-mee
Dun da Lamh	Doon da Larve
Faela	Fay-el-a
Ioho	Ee-oh-ho
Kydas	K-eye-dass
Martaani	Mar-tar-nee
Nantosuelta	Nan-toe-soo-elta
Naraic	Na-rake
Nighean	Nyee-uhn
Samhain	Sow-wain
Shael	Shay-ell
Schiehallion	Shee-hal-eeon
Vacomagi	Vack-o-mag-eye

1

For Carrick, the journey across the spine of Albion had not been an easy one. As expected, Martaani had numerous lookouts hiding along the way. Keeping well out of sight of the main route they were no threat to the usual travellers but Carrick was under no doubt that whoever the spy at the Carvetii village had been, he was bound to have been thorough. Everyone who had been travelling south in Kariss's party was certain to be targeted should they be seen. So, despite the threatening sky to the southwest, Carrick had taken a risk and opted for the high route; crossing over the tops of the peaks, where the going was extreme and the weather could change in an instant.

Snatching only a few hours of sleep at a time, he had found the going even more strenuous than anticipated. The wind had worried at him constantly, sending dark, angry clouds hastening towards him. The hilltops were no place to be caught in a storm but, try as he might, he had not been fast enough to outrun the weather. Before long, his visibility had been reduced to only a few feet in front of him. Even the tussocks of grass had become obstacles as he stumbled his way forward. Without any landmarks or stars to guide his way, he soon became lost. When a huge boulder had loomed up out of the mist he had taken refuge behind it, sinking to the saturated ground with a mixture of relief and frustration. His reprieve from the wind was instantaneous but despite this the pain in his right ear had, if anything, grown worse and more insistent. He had rubbed at it, cursing to himself at his predicament.

Then he had remembered the advice Torwain the druid had given him: Cernunous could always be relied upon to help him remain hidden. Realising that the god must have sent the fog to cover his movements, Carrick was filled with inspiration. Without waiting to question his thoughts, he had jumped up from his sanctuary behind the boulder. Willing Cernunous to keep the wind direction steady, he had used it to guide his way. Eventually, he had won out into the rain shadow on the leeward side of the hills. Staggering from exhaustion, he had collapsed in the dry bracken at the edge of the forest. It had taken him three days to cover a journey ordinarily done in one.

Torwain had found him there the following morning. After leaving Kariss, the druid had travelled as fast as he could, making his way back up towards Stanwick, where he could create the most havoc. He had been following the tracks of some legionnaires when movement at the edge of his vision had made him freeze. The legionnaires could wait. Lowering his body nearer to the ground, he had turned away from the path and crept towards the edge of the trees.

The raven was agitated, hopping from branch to branch before swooping down to peck at the two wolves beneath her on the ground. Wolves did not usually bother ravens but today she was not for sharing her find. The body on the ground would have made a good meal for them but Torwain was apt to share the raven's view.

He raced headlong at the wolves, waving his arms in the air and hissing for all he was worth. The creatures recoiled in shock and the druid was able to grab Carrick and drag him closer to the trees. Wolves were not usually dangerous to man but any predator would be foolish to ignore such an easy meal. They gathered at a safe distance, watching. As Torwain gathered kindling and set about lighting a fire, the larger male dropped his head, turned, and sloped off. The female followed. Man was best avoided.

The raven and Torwain watched them go. Torwain sent up a silent prayer to Cernunous, to guide them well away from this area before someone decided a wolf pelt would be preferable to a woollen cloak.

Beside him, Carrick was beginning to stir. Torwain fished in his friend's bag for his water pouch. He dribbled some of the liquid onto Carrick's lips, letting it trickle slowly into his mouth. He had no idea how long Carrick had been lying out here in the open but he suspected it must have been a long time, to have attracted such wary predators. Slowly, Carrick regained his senses. He groaned at the stiffness in his body. Trying to stand, his legs buckled beneath him. He was going nowhere.

'Tholarg is not far from here,' Torwain told him, 'but you will not make it there today. You need rest.'

Carrick tried to argue but no matter how determined his mind, his body was not going to cooperate.

'Lend me your cloak,' the druid said. He had left his own clothes behind with Kariss, preferring to reside in as natural a state as possible, but he knew that his nakedness was not appreciated by others. 'I will leave you food, fresh water and an ample supply of fire wood. Even in this state, you will be safe enough until I return.'

Carrick pulled off his cloak. Just that small action was enough to make his head spin. He leaned back and almost at once he was asleep again.

When he woke, he was alone. The sun was already well down in the sky; he must have been asleep for a long time. The fire had burned down low but kindling soon brought the flames alive. Beside the fire, Carrick found a pot already filled with water and what looked like limp nettle leaves. The bitter plant was just the thing to strengthen his exhausted body. He stirred the contents and found to his surprise that there was meat in the bottom of it. He had just finished his second helping when Torwain returned.

'I have told Tholarg that you will catch up with him in a day or two,'

Carrick nodded his thanks. He was unaccustomed to needing help yet this was the second time since they had left the Vacomagi lands that he had been forced to accept it. It did not sit well with him. They sat in silence for a few minutes. Carrick, aware that he was acting ungraciously, broke the silence. 'Where did you get the pot and the meat?'

The druid winked. 'I relieved it from a nearby legionnaire camp, they had left it sitting there all alone and unguarded.'

Carrick gave him a thoughtful look. 'Why are you here, anyway? The spring cannot be this close to Stanwick or we would have all travelled together.'

The druid shook his head slowly. 'It seems that the priests Martaani has with her have somehow latched onto my presence. I serve Kariss better now by causing mayhem in the smaller camps the Romans have set up around Stanwick. I have the legionnaires chasing shadows. They have no idea how I am finding their hideaways.' He grinned, flicking his head towards the path. 'The men whose tracks I was following when I found you are her messengers. They have led me straight to numerous of their hidden camps. I return a day later and...' his voice trailed off as he shrugged and winked. Torwain's secrets were his alone; Carrick did not need to know how he was managing to confound the soldiers.

'It is lucky that the northern nations are so restless amongst each other,' Torwain continued. 'For they separated themselves out into smaller camps as soon as they arrived, the Caledones taking the position nearest to Stanwick since they now have Enda amongst them. It was felt that she would be better away from the rest of the Epidii warriors. It would not do to have her exposed as Kariss's decoy by an unwitting friend. There is little point in them withdrawing now The Gathering is so close but Tholarg has sent word to the outlying groups to tell any new arrivals to keep themselves under cover.'

Carrick gave a snort of derision. 'It would appear that I have struggled for nothing, then.'

Torwain shook his head thoughtfully. 'I do not believe so, my friend. The gods were with you over the spine, or you would not have been able to carry on. There must be need of you here.'

Carrick shrugged. His pride had taken a serious blow. One of the people he had left behind had managed to not only beat him here but to also save his life, and complete his task for him.

Torwain added more sticks to the fire; the flames dwindled for a few moments before the wood caught light, hissing as the heat seared the last of the dampness from the wood. It might have been almost

Midsummer but down off the hills the rain was once more a feature and the night promised to be cold and miserable.

'I know how you feel, you know,' Torwain told Carrick when the silence stretched on. 'When Cernunous told me that the Roman priests had their eyes on me, I thought I had failed in my mission, too. Yet if I had not been warned away, I would not have been here to find you.' He smiled, 'There is always a reason, if you look hard enough.' He picked up his slingshot; he had passed some ducks on his way back. Hopefully they would still be there.

Carrick watched the druid leave, shuddered, and thought longingly of his remote cottage, with its comforting, blessed solitude. It seemed such an age since he had left. It would be another age before he returned. He wished that he had Torwain's sense of optimism but he had seen too much of the harsher side of human nature. It had scarred him. Maybe he had been stupid to think he could be comfortable in the presence of others again?

He was not part of this world. Long ago, he had chosen to withdraw. Ever since that time, he had only left the security of his woodland when Alpin had need of him. This trip was the first time he had integrated himself with others in many long years. He had allowed himself to care again; to shed the reclusive, taciturn man that life had driven him into becoming.

He had not thought he would care for anyone else again but they had somehow got past his defences. He thought of Naraic, and wondered if his own son would have been someone he could have been as proud of. The thought gripped at him, fingers of pain grabbing at his insides as he remembered. Years of pain had taught him to banish such thoughts the instant they appeared. No good would ever come of them. What was done could not be undone. Lord Alpin had been the only link to his past. The only one to know what had happened. He too had never spoken of it, as if he had known that there were no words that could ever do it justice. Carrick closed his eyes tight and sighed. He would miss his friend dearly.

He thought of the other place, the one only he knew about. The one he had always intended to disappear to when the great man was gone. Where no one would ever find him. It was habitable - just. Provided the weather was favourable. He hoped the autumn would be calm, to give him more time to get the place fit for the winter. First, though, he had to meet up with the warriors, to help Kariss take her place at the head of the Brigantes. He would not abandon his new friends until their task was done.

2

The Wendell contingent arrived at Stanwick two days before Midsummer. Faela had travelled with her brother, Taratus, and their men whilst Taratus's pregnant wife Shael and their children remained at home. The journey had been tense; Taratus had sunk into a black mood, which darkened the nearer they came to the capital. He had argued against Faela coming. The rows became more and more heated but Faela would not be swayed. She longed to see her cousin Kariss again and she was mindful of what Umar had told her. She had confided in no one about their conversations although as promised she had thought long and hard over what the gods could have meant about her importance. Nothing came to mind. Still, she had kept her eye out on the road for the brightly-clad druid, only to be disappointed that he was nowhere to be seen.

Hidden amongst her belongings was the keepsake box that had belonged to Wendell's old druid, Kel. She had taken one look at it and been enveloped by an overwhelming feeling that Umar should have it. She had no idea where the thought had come from but she did not question it. Druids were powerful men; they worked in ways far beyond the understanding of ordinary people.

The roads were rutted and hard to negotiate in places, made worse by the high volume of travellers and the incessant rain. The bare earth had long since been reduced to sludge and puddles; mud sucked at hooves and feet and splattered everything in sight. What was not covered in filth was soaking wet and bedraggled.

Once at Stanwick they were settled into their rooms and able to finally get cleaned up. Being members of one of the leading families, they had accommodation at the fort itself, although their men had to find whatever room they could, either in the town or else in the camp that had grown up outside the palisade. Faela searched for Umar as promised but no one had seen a druid in unusual madder robes.

Taratus waited until his sister was out of the way then he too left the fort. Taking care not to be seen by anyone important, he ducked into the narrow alleyways heading east. The poor weather had made people miserable; they kept indoors as much as possible, leaving much of his route deserted. Taratus found his journey easier than at previous times; no one was interested in what was going on outside in the relentless wet. He slipped into the guest quarters, unseen.

As he had anticipated, Martaani was not pleased.

'You have failed me again.' She sat by the fire, steam rising from her wet clothing, filling the air with the smell of damp wool. In her hands she twisted a strip of leather thong, the only outward sign of her anxiety. Her words tremored with restrained temper, it would not do to raise her voice too much in the confines of the town. They had not long since returned from viewing the ceremonial area where The Gathering would take place. It had not put her in the best of moods.

Martaani glared at Taratus. Time was running out.

'How is it that you, her only relatives, have had no contact with her whatsoever? Do you really expect me to believe it?' Martaani's words were laced with derision.

Taratus had expected no less. 'If there has been contact, I have heard naught of it. My sister no longer trusts me, and my brother is far away.'

'Ah yes, your brother. Tell me again where he has gone. You are always so vague when I ask.'

Taratus shuffled uncomfortably. He had told her many things but he would not betray his little brother. 'He has gone away, I know not where. He is in training, for his craft. He does not speak with us now. Not for years.'

The Pontiff smiled. It was a sight to send shivers down Taratus's spine.

'Years, you say? There is only one... craft -' he emphasised the word '- that calls for such devotions, is there not?'

Taratus did not answer

'I say your brother is a druid. He is gone to these conclaves in the woods, the so-called nemetons. Has he not?'

The last words jabbed at Taratus like a finger. He felt his stomach drop but looked the priest firmly in the eyes and said, 'My brother would not tell me where he was going. We... we argued, badly.' He shook his head. 'It was stupid, we argued over his becoming a smith. It is dangerous work, mixed with magic and powers we cannot understand. I felt we had suffered enough at the hands of the gods. In truth, I do not know where my brother went. I suspect he has gone to learn the skills needed to transmute earth into metal. The only person who will know is my father.'

They had established, all those months ago up at Eildons, when he had first met Martaani, long before anyone knew she had reached Albion, that his father had gone to Mona, Lord Hightern giving him command of the island after Taratus's mother passed away.

Martaani waved her hand in dismissal. 'Very convenient. What of your sister?'

Taratus relaxed a little. Here he was on safer ground. 'My sister befriended a druid who came to Wendell. They spent a number of days together before he left suddenly on the day our own druid, Kel, died.'

'That is strange, is it not? Surely this new druid would have stayed and performed his burial.'

Taratus shrugged. 'I do not claim to understand the ways of druids. This one was just passing through. We did not exchange more than a handful of words between us. He was strange, though. He looked more like a warrior and wore bright red robes instead of the usual muted tones. He seemed a bit mad, if I am honest. His name was Umar, an eastern name. Presumably he was from the Parisi.'

The Pontiff jumped to his feet. 'Why would a warrior druid be visiting your sister at this time?'

Taratus shook his head. His wet clothes were uncomfortably cold now. He moved closer to the fire. 'I have no idea but he frightened her to start with. I think he was just a roving druid. We get them occasionally, it is not unusual. My sister is not hiding anything. Trust me, I would know.'

'Well, that is just it, is it not?' Martaani said. 'Do we trust you?' Her eyebrows raised.

Taratus held up his hands. He did not want this to descend into an argument. 'Look, Kariss is bound to turn up here sooner or later, she cannot hide forever. I am sure she will come to us. I will watch my sister; she will not get the chance to meet with her without my knowing.'

'See that you do.'

With that, Martaani dismissed him and Taratus found himself back out in the rain. The sky looked as if it might be brightening. He did not want to be caught in the wrong part of town. He rushed back to his room.

'Where have you been?'

He jumped, startled at the sudden voice. Trust his sister to notice he had gone out. He ignored her question and made to push past her.

'Taratus, wait. I do not care what your problem is with me. I am past worrying about it but it is Lord Hightern requesting your company, not me.'

Taratus cringed at both her tone and her words. 'I am wet. Give me a minute to change.'

Faela turned on her heel. Let him follow, she thought. She was already seated, talking with Cartivel when he arrived.

'Ah, here he is at last,' Lord Hightern said with a smile. Taratus bowed his head; his hurriedly brushed hair was still damp, though the sun was now shining through the gaps in the thinning clouds.

'I have a headache, my Lord. I was out walking to try to clear it.'

He took the seat that was indicated to him and a servant brought him wine. There was no fire burning in the grate to warm him and fill the air with the comforting smell of burning applewood but the floor had been strewn with herbs and the sweet scent wafted up whenever anyone walked on them. Taratus looked around him. The opulence of the room was understated, though still apparent. The goblets they were drinking from were bronze, decorated with berry motifs, as was the flagon containing the wine. At the hearth stood a pair of fine wrought-iron fire dogs with bulls' head terminals, holding a stack of logs. The chairs were decorated with silver and bronze inlay; as a child, he had tried to follow the lines of similar patterns but he had always lost his way as they looped over and under each other with no beginning and no end.

They passed the next half-hour chatting about family and various fort-related news. Then, ever wary of Martaani's spies, Hightern lowered his voice.

'Have you any news of Kariss?'

Taratus and Faela both shook their heads.

'We had hoped she would come to us,' Faela said. 'But we have not seen her. I was hoping she would be here when we arrived.'

'There has been no word for a while now,' Cartivel said, rubbing his leg. He had damaged it in a hunting accident years earlier, putting paid to his active war-leading days. It still bothered him occasionally, mainly when the weather was cold or damp. 'We know she went up to see Lord Alpin, and somehow managed to leave there safely.'

At the doorway, the double layer of guards watched for signs of anyone approaching. Martaani had a habit of appearing without warning, expecting instant admittance.

The visitors looked puzzled; word of Alpin's demise had not yet reached them. Cartivel quickly explained what little they knew of the massacre at Dun da Lamh.

'Then it is as well she did not come to us. We would not want the same thing happening at Wendell.'

'Taratus!' Faela glared at her brother. He looked slightly abashed but was unapologetic.

'You cannot blame a man for considering the safety of his wife and children, not to mention his people. They must come first. It will do our cousin's cause no good at all if everyone who harbours her is put to the torch.'

Lord Hightern watched the exchange with growing sadness. He had hoped the rumours about Taratus were false but the man was not projecting himself as loyally as he should. Nor, though, had he shown any definitive signs of betrayal. Hearsay and a brusque, selfish manner were not treasonous in themselves. He noted Cartivel's appraising look. As a leader of the army for many years he had seen every kind of warrior; from the truly dedicated to those intolerant of violence. There was not much that escaped him; it would be interesting to hear his thoughts.

Corio entered the room just then and talk of Kariss halted while he greeted the guests.

'I was deeply saddened to hear of Kel's passing,' the druid told them. 'I would have come down to Wendell myself but...'

Faela smiled, 'We understand. You are needed here.'

'I trust his passing was peaceful?'

'Indeed. He had been failing for months but Umar was with him when he went so he was not alone.'

'Umar...' Corio's face had paled, '... was at Wendell, with you? Is he here now?'

Faela shook her head, 'He was called away but he told me to look for him here. Do you know him?'

Taratus looked sharply at his sister; this was news to him.

'We have had cause to meet in the past,' Corio pulled at his beard. 'Can I ask, why does he require you to seek him out?'

Faela was about to answer but just then her brother groaned and jumped to his feet, sending his seat shooting backwards. 'Forgive me... head... pounding,' he stammered before rushing from the room.

'My brother has been acting very strangely lately,' Faela explained. 'He complains of headaches a lot, I think they make him sick. He often rushes off like this. Maybe you could take a look at him?' she asked Corio.

'That would be a good idea,' Corio agreed. There was much about that young man he would like to discover but first he must learn all he could about Umar. It could be no accident that he had turned up just before midsummer.

Faela explained all that she knew, holding nothing back. It was good to be able to confide in someone again. 'I still have no idea what my link to Kariss is, though,' she admitted.

Corio wondered how much he should say. Lacking his goddess to guide him, he was unsure. Without speaking to Umar, he had no idea if Faela's role was for Brigantia's benefit, or its downfall.

'You must find him,' he urged, 'and when you do, tell him that I need to speak with him. I have not heard of him here as yet. Is he still... bright?'

Faela laughed, thinking of Umar's red robes. 'He certainly is. He should be easy to find.'

The town looked hazy in the afternoon sun, the heat of which drove the moisture from the thatched roofs so that it hung like mist over the houses. Out in the woods, the warmth was slower to penetrate. Umar felt a chill as he stepped underneath the gloomy canopy. He had been unable to approach Faela as she made her way back through the imposing gateway because he was not the only one watching the growing number of Brigantes arriving for The Gathering. The Augur was also in sight, standing back in the shadows, sweeping his beady eyes over the makeshift camps beyond the wattle-and-daub houses. Stanwick was a small, compact town, consisting of the fort and a large number of houses squeezed into the space within the surrounding palisade. Whilst the fort itself kept a number of small houses available for visitors, these had already been filled, by Martaani and her leading men. Those with no relations in the town were having to make do with the camps outside. Now that the weather had finally improved, these people had moved out into the open area between the surrounding woodland and the palisade walls and at last their numbers could be realised. The Augur was letting nothing show on his bland face but he spent a long time watching.

Umar did not want to cross paths with the Augur yet. He had dealt with him before, in his time overseas. It was a shock to see him here in Albion. He knew him to be a sly, devious man and no stranger to war. He had seen him kill indiscriminately, using the foulest of methods. His presence here with Martaani added yet another layer of menace to her challenge for the throne. Umar shivered, forcing the memories of their last meeting away. He turned away. He would have to find Faela tomorrow.

A little to the north east, the northern warriors were making ready for The Gathering, the Epidii and Caledones closest to Stanwick. Farther away were the Damnonii who had also answered the call; they had mustered a huge force, even larger than the Caledones. Their king, Loth, was a conscientious leader, well aware of the dividing nature of his lands which stretched from east to west above the Votadini and the Selgovae. He would not stand by and let any nation, be they to the north or the south, use his territory to invade another. As soon as he had become aware that Martaani had crossed his lands to launch her attack on Drost's village on the Tai; not only crossed it, but actually camped within his borders, he had sent out his call to arms. The Damnonii were a fierce nation, their presence was unnerving but at the same time reassuring. If anyone had to meet the Damnonii for battle, it was far better to be fighting on the same side.

Smaller camps of the Cerones, Taexali - with a handful of Vacumagi amongst them - and Venicones dotted between these larger ones. Each keeping to their own, co-ordinated by Carrick and Tholarg. This was not yet a united army.

Carrick, almost recovered from his exertions over the spine, was kept busy stopping the various nations from fighting amongst themselves. There had been numerous petty squabbles, not helped by a standing argument between the Epidii and the Cerones. As neighbours, the two bickered constantly about their borders. Carrick soon began to see what Torwain had meant about his presence being needed here. Not only was he part of Kariss's inner circle, he was also a northerner; the combination made him the only person in the camps that each nation respected. He urged Uurad and Gartnet, the Cerones leader, to tell their men to save their angst for the Romans. Gartnet - a short, weighty man with small, beady brown eyes - answered his pleas with his usual derisory snort.

'Just because he has put up the lass's decoy does not mean he has more weight in this fight than I do.'

Carrick rounded on him. 'Keep your voice down, man. Do you want the whole place knowing our secrets? How do you know about that, anyway?'

Gartnet snorted again. 'Bah! The whole camp knows of it. Yon Epidii have mouths like gaping sea beasties. Uurad is no more able to control them than he can run on wet kelp.'

Uurad's face bloomed red and before Carrick could respond, he had knocked the Cerones leader to the floor with a right hook to the chin. Gartnet rubbed his jaw and laughed.

'Touched a nerve there, did I?' He grinned, picking himself up. 'You should have seen this fool, lad,' he told Carrick. 'Flat on his arse he went o'er a wee bit o'seaweed.'

Uurad looked as if he would explode.

'Enough!' Carrick yelled at them. 'Are you here for Albion, or not? Because if you are just here to carry on your own petty arguments then you might as well go home. Kariss needs men she can trust, not ones who refuse to control themselves. If you cannot be here for her then think of the gods. Would you lose their land for the sake of gaining a little more for yourselves?'

Uurad and Gartnet turned to Carrick in shock. Too late, Carrick remembered that he was talking to kings. He could not take the words back now. For a long moment, the air was filled with tension, then Uurad let out a roar of laughter and clapped Carrick on the back.

'I've got to hand it to you, lad, you're not short of courage.'

Gartnet had not been shouted at like that in many years; the words cut deep. 'I do not know this lassie, Kariss,' he said through gritted teeth, 'I am here for the gods, I do not pretend any different.' He threw a look in Uurad's direction, 'Keep him away from me, and his men from mine, and the gods will have no reason to doubt our loyalty.' He turned and stomped away.

Carrick let out a breath he had not realised he had been holding. He glanced at Uurad, who was watching Gartnet's retreating back, shaking his head

'I suppose I should be grateful he came at all. His men will fight well,' Uurad said. 'We are so used to fighting amongst ourselves; it is hard to remember we are on the same side now.' He winked at Carrick. 'At least I put him on his arse this time.'

Carrick shook his head and smiled. The man was incorrigible.

The problems kept on coming. A man from the Caledones accidentally shot and severely wounded a Damnonii warrior whilst out hunting. They had been tracking the same deer, each unaware of the other's presence. Retaliation had been swift; Damnonii warriors had crept into the Caledone camp that evening and set upon the perpetrator, beating him senseless before his friends could come to his aid.

Luckily, the Damnonii backed down. They had done what they had set out to do. They withdrew to their own camp and the wary Caledones stayed in theirs.

Three Venicone warriors, who had tagged onto the Damnonii warband, had seized one of the Epidii women and dragged her into the bushes to take their pleasure of her by force. She put up a healthy fight, managing to put her dagger into one of them, killing him instantly. Uurad was incensed. He stormed up to Loth, demanding justice. Loth was not one to condone the rape of warriors. He turned on all Venicone warriors, expelling them from his camp forthwith. Carrick could see danger in this move, though. The men were now bitter, and very resentful of their treatment. Such men were apt to change sides to get revenge and the Venicones were already a worry. They bordered the Votadini lands and the two nations enjoyed close trade links. The last thing Carrick wanted was to send the few Venicones who had volunteered to join them running to the Romans. He had a quiet word with Tholarg; the Caledones also enjoyed good relations with the Venicones. Tholarg agreed to take the men into his camps providing they understood that the next woman they attempted to rape would be free to serve her own justice.

There were numerous other spats. Nothing less could be expected with a force this size. The warriors had marched long and hard to get here. They were tired, footsore and itching for a fight. Carrick was starting to have his doubts as to whether they would ever settle down into a unified army.

3

Torwain crept through the trees. He had been stalking a group of legionnaires since midmorning. They were walking at a good pace but making no attempt to be quiet. Torwain was intrigued - why did they feel so confident? Legionnaires never walked well in woodland but they usually kept their voices low and any noise to a minimum.

A fox bolted from the undergrowth. The direction was wrong; it was not the legionnaires who had frightened him. *The cunning one is afraid and running*, Torwain thought. His eyes darted around him. Where was the danger? He could see nothing but the message could not have been clearer - *Run!*

He turned after the fox but his foot caught in a tree root and he stumbled sideways, straight into a concealed pit. As his body broke through the branches covering the opening, he cursed. He hit the ground with a thump that forced the wind out of him. The legionnaires let out three shrill whistles and within minutes the pit was surrounded by men.

Torwain struggled to get his breath back. He could not think properly. How on earth had he missed all the signs?

The men seemed in no hurry to get him out so he sat back and forced himself to concentrate. He remembered seeing a scolding squirrel run up a tree not many minutes before, its red coat flashing amongst the grey trunks. A weasel had darted across their path before that and, on hearing their approach, three roe deer had crashed through the bushes. None of them should have been there if this many men were hiding close by. A thought came to Torwain and he stilled, almost as if his body ceased living for a second before thumping back into life. The priests! They must be close by and cloaking the legionnaires somehow.

He closed his eyes. Cernunous had warned him, he should have been more vigilant. Should he call out to the gods for help? He decided against it; that might be exactly what the priests wanted. His hand reached up and touched Cernunous's torc around his neck. The metal thrummed with life, it gave him reassurance.

High above him, a chiffchaff called out, repeating its name over and over until it got confused and chaffed when it should have chiffed. It stopped suddenly. Torwain looked up. A new face had appeared. Long and thin, with a strong, determined jaw and a high forehead. The man sneered down at him. Torwain closed his eyes. In his mind, he grew a sturdy set of antlers, with sharp, lethal tines; his fingers grew talons; his toes, claws. Surrounding it all, to further shield himself, he imagined a protective bubble. When he was ready, he faced the priest.

'The men were beginning to think you were a ghost,' the Pontiff laughed. 'It is a pity I have no lion here to put in that pit with you. I don't even have a handy lynx nearby.'

Torwain thought of Carrick and the injuries he had sustained from the lynx before Naraic had been taken. He pushed the thought away.

'What would you like in there instead?'

Torwain remained silent.

Someone threw a bag into the pit. Torwain flicked his eyes towards it. The bag sounded angry, the buzz of whatever was inside warned him to prepare. He strengthened his mental shield, took a deep, calming breath, and waited. An arrow thumped into the bag and the droning grew even louder. Torwain crossed his legs and waited patiently. Two, three, arrows hit the bag before it burst open and a swarm of furious hornets escaped. Torwain closed his eyes and forced himself to remain still. Overhead, he could hear laughter.

All his years of training paid off. The hornets ignored him, flying upwards instead, searching out movement. Only when he heard the curses of the legionnaires as they were repeatedly stung did he open his eyes. He did not allow himself a smile, there would be more to come.

Adders were thrown into the pit. They darted around, trying to find cover, curling up into protective coils when they reached the broken branches that had fallen in with Torwain. *Are they supposed to heal me or weaken me?* Torwain thought. Snakes had long been associated with the healing arts; he was not sure if the Romans made the same connections but he was sure they must. He looked up again and saw the priest walk away. The man was clearly playing with him, thinking to heighten his fears before facing him properly. He could hear more noises now. The legionnaires were busy. The sound of hammering was clearest of all. Torwain wondered what they were building - it concerned him far more than hornets and adders.

He was still sitting in the same position when the Pontiff returned to the pit. 'Time to come out.'

Torwain looked at him but remained silent. Two legionnaires leaned over, holding out hands to haul him up. He ignored them. The Pontiff laughed again. 'That will not save you.'

He ordered one of the men down into the pit. The man jumped down warily, his sword pointing at Torwain. 'Move.' He jabbed at him, forcing him to his feet. Torwain took a step towards him and the man backed off, throwing a nervous glance up at his comrades.

They are scared of me.

Torwain took another step, and another. The Roman scurried backwards. The Pontiff shouted at him, calling him a coward. Torwain took advantage and grabbed for the bag. He picked it up and swung it at the man, feeling as he did the sting of a hornet between his fingers. The bag hit the man full in the face, giving Torwain just enough time to grab one of the branches and lunge at him. Adders recoiled and one pulled back its head, making ready to strike. The branch caught the man in the stomach. Its broken end was sharp, piercing the skin and sinking deep into his body. He gave a grunt and fell to his knees and the adder struck, biting him on the arm. More adders bit him and the man cried out. The Pontiff yelled at his men and two more jumped down, grabbing Torwain and pinning his arms to his sides. He was manhandled to the edge of the pit and hauled out.

A stake had been hammered into the ground, another piece of wood lashed to it to form a cross. Torwain was dragged across and held up whilst nails were hammered into his hands and feet. The pain was unbearable. Torwain tried to keep silent but failed. He bucked and fought the men but that only made the pain worse.

They left him hanging there. The Pontiff watching him as if by doing so he could learn his secrets. There was not only pain in the nail wounds and throbbing from the hornet sting. The pressure on Torwain's wrists and arms was immense. He could feel that his right shoulder had dislocated. He tried to take a deep breath to calm himself but found that in this position he could not. He needed Cernunous but still he refused to call him. The world reduced to that of only pain and for a few minutes he wallowed in it. Then he opened his eyes and saw the Pontiff studying him. Years of deprivation had taught Torwain resilience, to endure what most could not.

This is no different to a freezing cold night in the middle of February without a fire, he told himself; walking naked through a patch of nettles; raiding a bees' nest to steal some honey. You do not need deep breaths to be calm. He took another short breath. *Calm*, he told himself. *Calm*. He kept up the mantra until he felt himself relax slightly.

The Pontiff walked towards him, taking his time. The smile on his face was cold. Torwain kept his gaze steady, looking at him as if he were an interested spectator. Inside, he was furiously reinforcing his shields. The injured man was being taken from the pit. The priest barely cast him a glance.

'Are you king of the druids?' The Pontiff reached a hand out to touch the torc and his hand recoiled as if burned. He struck Torwain hard across the face. Behind him, the injured man screamed as the branch was pulled from his body. The Pontiff flicked his head in the man's direction. 'There are plenty more where he came from. Will Kariss fare so well without you?'

He walked around the stake. Torwain could feel all his body hair standing on end. His chest was tight with fear and his throat felt the first tangs of acid. He swallowed. He would not be sick. He forced himself to think of peaceful things - waterfalls, gently babbling rivers, the warmth of the sun on his bare skin. He inhaled and smelled the woodland. He needed to keep his wits about him, death was never a certainty - however impossible the situation may appear. He had seen it time and time again, the hare escaping the wolf; the fish escaping the bear. He just needed to keep alert to any opportunity he could utilise. He could not allow fear or pain to take over. He must fight to the very end.

The Pontiff looked him up and down, sneering at his filthy, naked body. 'At least you saved us the trouble of removing your clothing.'

Through the pain, Torwain smiled. If the Romans thought his nakedness would shame him, they could not be more wrong. It gave him power and strength, and he intended to use every ounce of them. He was the stag of this forest; the Roman might seek to challenge him but despite Torwain's hidden fear, he had no intention of relinquishing his dominion.

The Pontiff hit him again. His head was thrown to the side, jarring his dislocated shoulder. He did not curse or cry out. His years living wild had taught him that silence was not only safety but also the difference between hunger and food. To make a noise was a sign of weakness; he would not give the priest the satisfaction. Besides which, he thought he had seen a flicker of something in the priest's eyes. Could it really be?

'You thought to make a fool of us.' The Pontiff spat at him, thinking back to a previous journey and the empty dead raven left for him to find in the middle of the night, the terror he had felt at the time. He struck the druid again. 'You will not win. We will win, for we are superior to you in every way.' The Pontiff stalled; despite his loathing for the druid, his train of thought kept veering to places he had no intention of visiting. He struck out once more, seeking to chase the wayward thoughts away. He was a priest, a Pontiff no less, he would keep control. He took refuge in words. 'Where are your precious gods now, druid?'

Torwain answered him with silence. His insides roiled with fear but again he had seen that flicker. The Pontiff goaded, 'Do they see you hanging there?'

Silence.

'Will they whisk you away through time to save your scrawny neck?' The Pontiff looked him up and down again. Torwain was sure he had seen it that time, was it a weakness? Something he could use? He took a slow breath. It was a risk, it could make things worse… or it could fluster the priest into making a mistake. He could feel the torc around his neck, its vibrations growing stronger. He looked the Pontiff deep in the eyes, his mouth turning up slightly at the corners. 'My body is not scrawny though, is it?'

These were the first words he had spoken. The Pontiff blinked. Undeniably, the druid's body, though slender, was corded with muscle. Through the dirt and the sweat he could see the ridges on his stomach, the hard muscles of his arms, the strength of his thighs. The Pontiff swallowed, turned, and stalked away.

There were only three legionnaires with him now. The other two had taken the injured man away. They stood in front of Torwain, taking turns to prick at him with the tips of their spears. The Pontiff relieved himself behind a tree, taking the time to order his thoughts. The Augur had demanded that he be present when they finished the druid. Really, he should send someone to fetch him. Looking over to where the legionnaires were laughing and jeering as their spears drew blood, he felt a stab of annoyance. The druid was his to torment, not theirs. He should have his fun first, before the Augur came and they lit the druid up like a human candle. He strode back over and barked an order. Immediately they ceased their actions and left the pair alone.

'Why are you not afraid? You have no god with you now, I would know.'

Torwain held his tongue.

'My gods are taking over. Blocking your senses and hiding my men in your blanket of trees.'

Torwain could feel the other man's disdain, the Pontiff was building to something. He readied himself for pain, his earlier thread of hope still present in the back of his mind.

'You were quite correct before, of course. You do have a strong body. One that will give us so much more pleasure as we entertain ourselves with your suffering.' Again, the Pontiff looked at Torwain's body, his sight drawn like a magnet. A frisson of fresh fear gripped Torwain. He had heard much of the Romans' torture methods. He closed his eyes for a moment, fighting the urge to call on Cernunous for help. The torc pulsed and his mind filled with the sight of himself as a powerful stag, dominating all around him. Was it a message? But how could it be? There was no way Torwain could dominate anyone when he was nailed to a cross.

He had been so focused on the Pontiff that he had failed to notice what the legionnaires were doing until he smelled woodsmoke. The Pontiff saw the flicker of realisation in his eyes.

'Do you like fire?'

He ran his hand over Torwain's torso, feeling the raw strength contained in the druid's lithe body. He felt a stirring deep inside him. It shocked him that something he considered so disgusting and dangerous should suddenly arouse him. He had always liked his men slender and strong, abhorring uncleanliness. He looked into Torwain's eyes, reading the recognition there. He pulled his hand away sharply. Torwain smiled; his thread of hope had gained substance.

Sex was not a shameful act; it was a glorious celebration of the human body. It only needed to be between a man and a woman when procreation was involved. Not that the feelings were requited in this case; Torwain could no more wish to be intimate with the Pontiff than he could turn his back on Cernunous. The Pontiff, however, did not know that. Torwain smiled at him, thinking the most arousing thoughts he possibly could. The pain was not helping but he persevered, willing his body to respond.

'I like fire. I like how it turns flesh red, not once but twice,' the Pontiff rushed on, taking a burning branch from one of the legionnaires. 'Once when it comes close to the skin.' He held the brand towards Torwain's chest and the skin glowed red as the flame reflected on it. Torwain turned his head from the heat and stubbornly concentrated. He thought of the prowess of a mighty stag, its need to dominate driving it to mount both the male and female deer in its herd. He smiled again at the priest, who dropped his eyes to Torwain's manhood. It was starting to rise.

Flustered, the Pontiff pushed the burning branch angrily onto Torwain's skin. The druid's teeth ground together as he forced his scream inwards. The Pontiff pulled the brand away, leaving a vivid red mark, 'And again when it touches it.' His breathing was heavy now, his skin flushed.

The pain seared through Torwain, he could smell his flesh burning. It stalled his thoughts but again the torc pulsed and the mounting stag flared into his mind. It took every bit of resilience and training to drag up the most erotic thoughts he could muster. He could feel the stag in his mind, urging him on until he hung on the cross proud and erect.

The legionnaires looked at him in astonishment. The Pontiff looked with desire. His voice was thick as he continued, pointedly refusing to comment on it. 'It matters not where the flame goes, the result is just the same.' He touched the branch to Torwain's arm, his stomach and his thigh. He could not bring himself to touch it to the druid's groin. He had known of men who enjoyed pain, but not to this extent. Hidden beneath his robes, the Pontiff was also erect. He had never witnessed such virility. His body was flooded with longing, he licked his lips. Throwing the torch to the ground, he turned to the legionnaires, ordering two of them to fetch the Augur.

The remaining legionary held out a knife and grinned at the Pontiff, 'Cut it off.'

Torwain felt his stomach contract as the priest took the blade but he held firm to his plan. As the Pontiff stepped towards him again, Torwain looked at him with longing. They locked eyes. The rest of the world melted away and in that moment it was just the two of them connected by that look. Power was coursing through Torwain's veins, his arteries pumped it stronger and stronger. Pure animal instinct had taken over, his need to dominate the Pontiff blocking everything else out.

'I should sever this,' the Pontiff said, his voice barely more than a husky croak. His lips were dry, his skin electric and his insides molten. Torwain parted his lips, the Pontiff dropped the knife, grabbing instead the back of Torwain's head and pulling the druid's mouth down onto his own. He did not hear the shocked gasp of the legionary behind him, who shifted uncomfortably, not knowing whether to be aroused himself or disgusted.

The druid and the Pontiff broke apart, lust now dominating the priest in every way. Behind them, the legionary scuffed his foot against a stone. The Pontiff snapped back to reality, horrified at himself. Shame won over his lust. Averting his eyes from the proximity of the druid's body, he bent and grabbed the knife. Again, he thrust it towards Torwain. Just then, the crossbar of the crucifix snapped and Torwain's arms dropped like stones, sending pain lacerating through his dislocated shoulder. The wood hit the Pontiff, sending him flying to the floor. The moment was broken and Torwain was unable to keep hold of his arousal.

The Pontiff's temper was unprecedented. He scrabbled to his feet and stormed towards the legionary, shouting and cursing, calling him every kind of incompetent imaginable. The man wanted to answer him, to accuse the Pontiff's lewd behaviour of putting too much weight on the crucifix, but it was more than his courage would allow.

'Tie him to the tree,' the Pontiff yelled, spittle flying from his mouth.

The legionary rushed to obey. He ripped the nails from Torwain's feet, releasing them from the post. Heedless of the pain it caused, the man dragged him to the nearest tree. Torwain struggled but his arms were pulled behind him around the tree trunk. The pain was unbearable; he hardly felt the nails being pulled from his hands.

They were the only ones left now, the others would not be back for quite a while. One man between the Pontiff and his downfall. He could not let news of his failure reach the others; the Augur and Martaani, especially. He had a reputation to uphold and it did not include any weaknesses, let alone those of the flesh. He must be seen to be in command of his senses at all times, it was the only way he could maintain his position. Killing the legionary would cause many questions; it must be done with care - something he could blame on the druid and his magic. His eyes fell on a cluster of white flowers with their tall, tell-tale purple spotted stems. Hemlock.

Close by, he spied ransoms. Their flowers were just finishing but the leaves and bulbs would work to cover the unpleasant, musty smell of the poison. He set to work digging up the roots of both plants whilst the legionary was still busy with the druid. There was already a pot over the fire; the water was just coming to a boil. The Pontiff added his ingredients, stirring them thoroughly. He threw in some elderflower to sweeten the mixture.

The legionary had finished tying Torwain to the tree and was teasing him with his sword when the Pontiff made his way back over to them. The sight of the naked druid stirred his arousal once more. It both unnerved and excited him. He licked his lips as if to taste him again. They would have an hour or two alone before the Augur arrived. Long before then, he would have removed the druid's tongue so that he could not betray him. The Augur would have no trouble believing that it was the only way to stop his deathly curses.

'There is a warming drink in the pot,' he told the legionary. 'It will drive the damp from your bones. I will watch this filth for now, I have already had mine.'

The druid raised an eyebrow. His gaze burrowed into the priest's, drawing him closer. 'Hemlock does not take long to work,' he whispered.

The Pontiff froze. He knew! All at once he remembered just how dangerous druids were and why he hated them so much. He struck Torwain again and again and began to feel that he was gaining back his control. Staggering from the effort of the last hit, the Pontiff had to reach a hand out to steady himself. It landed on Torwain's dislocated shoulder and the druid cried out in pain. The Pontiff felt a surge of power and at last he could smile again. He swung around as the unsuspecting legionary returned. Leaving him guarding the prisoner, the Pontiff sat by the fire. He must keep a grip on his control of the situation and not give in to his desires. For that, he needed to speak to Felicitas, goddess of success.

Felicitas, however, had other plans. She could feel the presence of Cernunous, seeking to have his druid win power over the priest. The gauntlet had been thrown down. Did the god not know who he was dealing with? Failure was not something she would tolerate. She came to the Pontiff hand-in-hand with Voluptas, goddess of pleasure. Together, they whispered in his ear, firing his wilted libido. He tried to fight them, to call upon Jupiter to control his mischievous goddesses.

In Rome, he had managed to keep his sexual desires at bay, though they had always been his greatest weakness. Whenever he felt the need, he would leave the city, seeking out those areas where he was not so well known. He knew the places where he would be accepted with open arms and no questions, where he could allow himself to revel in whatever proclivity took his fancy. Never, though, had he experienced such raw animal appeal. The virility of the druid was exhilarating. His prowess as impressive as any he had ever seen before. The goddesses fuelled his lust, filling his mind with images he found himself craving. He knew he should resist, fight off the urges that were overwhelming him, but the pleasures they promised were too enticing.

The legionary was starting to fidget and look uncomfortable. The Pontiff called him back to the fire. The man struggled to walk. He staggered and fell, his dilated pupils causing him to wince in the strong sunlight. The Pontiff stepped over him, ignoring his pleas for help. He walked back to Torwain as if pulled by some invisible force.

'Wet your hands,' Torwain whispered as the Pontiff bent towards him. 'My burns are on fire, I need you to touch me.'

The Pontiff did not stop to think. He licked his hands and covered the burns in turn.

'I need my hands.' Torwain looked at him longingly. 'I want to feel you. You can keep my feet tied, I cannot run. Do you not want to feel my hands on your body?'

The Pontiff pulled out his knife, he slid the tip of the blade along Torwain's collar bone. 'Do not think to fool me,' he said. 'I am not stupid.'

'If you do not cut the rope, you can tie me back up afterwards.'

The Pontiff frowned and Torwain wondered if he had gone too far. He was breathing rapidly. The Pontiff mistook it for arousal instead of pain and his excitement intensified. Putting the knife between his teeth, he soon had the ropes undone. Torwain cried out as his right arm fell uselessly to his side. Ducking his head as the Pontiff came to kiss him, Torwain tugged at his robe instead. The Pontiff lost a few minutes divesting himself of his clothing. Torwain made no attempt to escape. His heart clamoured in his chest as he appeared to wait patiently until the priest was naked. Ducking the Pontiff's kisses again, Torwain reached for him, pulling him close, pressing his groin into the Pontiff's hip and kissing his neck. The Pontiff groaned. He had never felt such a powderkeg of emotions. The goddesses had filled his mind with images of him dominating the druid but in truth that was not the role the Pontiff enjoyed most. Excitement exploded everywhere the druid's hands and lips touched and not for a moment did he regret untying them. He was so lost in pleasure that he failed to notice he was the only one enjoying himself. He felt his legs going weak and Torwain sank to the ground with him. His feet were still tied to the tree and he fell awkwardly onto his dislocated shoulder. Pain lanced through his body but he forced himself to keep going; it would be over soon.

The weakness in the Pontiff's legs was growing stronger, pulling at him insistently. Suddenly, realisation hit him. With a roar, he dragged himself away from the druid and grabbed at a rock. He swung it hard onto Torwain's temple, knocking him unconscious. When the druid came to, his hands were once again tied to the tree and the Pontiff was scrabbling back into his clothing. Torwain's heart sank. He had been so close.

The Pontiff retched as he cursed his own stupidity. The druid had played him well. In his excitement, he had quite forgotten to wash the poison from his hands and knife. He doubted that he had ingested enough to kill himself but it would certainly make him insensible for many hours, if not days. He needed to think quickly whilst he still could. The Augur would demand answers. At least he had not freed the druid.

Torwain watched him crawl back to the fire and tip out the contents of the pot. His plan had failed but it had given him some time. He worked at his bindings but the pain in his shoulder made him unable to twist his hand to work the knots loose. Finally, he sent up a call to Cernunous; the Pontiff could do him no harm now. Almost at once he heard a sound behind him and felt someone tugging at the ropes around his wrists.

4

'Hold still.'

Torwain felt a knife being eased between the rope and his wrists and stifled a cry of relief and pain as the bindings finally gave way and once again he fell to his knees. He looked up to see Carrick standing over him.

'Is he the only one here?' Carrick gestured in the direction of the Pontiff.

Torwain nodded. 'For now, but others are coming.'

'Here, take this, cut yourself free whilst I finish him off.' Carrick tossed his dagger to Torwain and made his way towards the prone figure of the priest. Halfway there, he heard the unmistakable sounds of approaching men. Dropping low to the ground, he rushed back to Torwain. They melted into the trees just before the Augur, flanked by a number of legionnaires, entered the clearing. The omens had already alerted the priest to trouble. He had not waited for the Pontiff's messenger.

The Augur's eyes went in turn from the Pontiff, writhing on the floor and struggling to breathe, to the broken crucifix and then the cut ropes at the base of the tree. The air was thick with the after-taint of gods. Whatever had happened here had not been entirely the Pontiff's doing. He flicked a hand and sent the legionnaires racing into the woods then slipped the bolas from his pocket, surveying the sky with all the intensity of a cat watching for a mouse. At his feet, the Pontiff clawed at his throat.

Focused on watching for a bird, the Augur did not notice the clouds rolling fast across the sky. He threw the bolas. His shot was good and a pigeon dropped to the floor a few feet away, just as the first large spots of rain began to hammer down. Within moments, the Augur had the bird slit open. Its innards slid easily from the carcass but were instantly washed away by the intensity of the deluge. The Augur kicked at the remains in his fury, just as Bodach rumbled his anger overhead.

By the time the legionnaires returned empty-handed, the Augur was trickling cooling rain water into the Pontiff's mouth. He had no idea if the priest would live or die but he at least had stopped tearing at his skin. Little did the Augur realise that this was because of the paralysis that had claimed the Pontiff's legs, working its way up into his arms. The Augur was not a healer. He suspected poisoning but he could not be sure that the druid had not used some form of magic.

The Augur would lose no sleep over the other priest's death but he would do his best to save him nonetheless. He wanted to know exactly what had occurred here and the Pontiff was the only one who could tell him. Whatever had happened, it proved just how dangerous the druid was if he could fool the Pontiff. They had been right to target him. Still, no druid should be suffered to live and after what he had seen, the Augur was even more determined to eliminate every last one.

Two of the legionnaires set to work making a bier they could drag the Pontiff home on whilst the others dug a crude grave for their dead comrade. The intensity of the rain had not eased, the soil was heavy clay and the work hard and messy - they wasted no time with burial formalities.

Torwain and Carrick plunged through the trees, the sounds from Bodach covering the noise they were making. As they splashed through a stream, Torwain tumbled to his knees. He shook his head; his shoulder was agony but it was the pain in his feet that had caused him to fall. He could run no further. He pointed to a large oak. It should hide them well enough. Most of the trees here were birch, too spindly for them to climb, but the oak had a thick, gnarled trunk and plenty of greenery. He staggered over to the tree and positioned himself carefully... waiting. As soon as Bodach crashed overhead, he rammed his shoulder into the tree. His roar of pain was drowned out by the thunder but in his haste he had not got his positioning correct and the shoulder remained dislocated. Carrick pushed him to his knees and took hold of his arm. With a quick twist, the joint popped back into place. Torwain cried out. The thunder was still rumbling on but anyone close by must have heard him.

They were not quite high enough to be safe when two legionnaires appeared below. Not daring to risk any further movement, Carrick and Torwain froze where they were, relying on the deluge to protect them. The legionnaires moved forward slowly, peering all around themselves, clearly having heard something, but never once did they think to look up. One of them stopped close by. He flicked his saturated hair from his face and cursed. In the tree, Torwain and Carrick were also soaked to the skin and uncomfortable but the rain was doing an excellent job of keeping them hidden so they were only too glad of it.

The Romans moved on but the tree was safe so Torwain and Carrick remained there for a long time. Perched on a thick branch, his back resting safely against the trunk, Torwain inspected his feet. The wounds where the nails had secured him to the cross were red and angry. Those in his hands were only slightly better. He held them out for the rain to wash away the worst of the mud - it was all he could do for now.

Only when Bodach had rumbled his last and allowed the rain to move away did they finally judge it safe to leave.

It was good to feel warm and dry again. The sodden fire had been re-lit by the time the two had arrived, bedraggled and in a sorry state, at the Caledones' camp. Clothes had been fetched to cover Torwain's nakedness, his wounds had been treated and his burns dressed. Whilst his body was starting to relax, his mind was not. He sat worrying; something was nagging at him, desperate to be remembered.

Adders!

The adders were still in the pit, they would never be able to get out on their own. The bottom would probably be flooded but there were enough branches in there for them to at least get out of the water. Cernunous would never forgive him if he left them there but with his bound feet, Torwain could not go himself. He called out to a passing man and begged him to go and lower a branch down into the pit to release them. The Romans would be long gone by now, there would be no danger.

Torwain tipped his head back and looked at the early evening sky, sending up his thanks to Bodach. He was not sure he was ready to face his own god yet. He felt uneasy, sullied by what he had been forced to do. Enduring the hated priest's hands on him had been bad enough at the time but he could still feel them cloying at his burnt skin. For a moment, he worried that the hemlock was working its way through his skin but his body had been well and truly washed by the rain. He shuddered, feeling his skin crawling over his bones. His mind was crawling, too. He heard a foot scrape and jumped as someone sat down next to him.

'I imagine that whatever you went through was not pleasant,' Carrick said, holding out a cup of strong wine. 'Though I admit, I am impressed at how you managed to kill one Roman and almost kill their Pontiff whilst you were nailed to a cross and then tied to a tree.' He half smiled. 'You need not look so worried. I saw only the end of your ordeal. I have seen men reduced to a shadow of their former selves by such treatment whilst imprisoned. Never, though, have I seen one turn it around on their captor as you did. Tell me. What happened to him? How did you manage to poison him when you were tied?'

Torwain raised his eyebrows. Of all the things he had been expecting, that was not one of them. He looked at Carrick anew; there were depths there that would take years to plumb. Not that Torwain had any intention of prying.

'Actually, he poisoned himself — unintentionally, of course.' For the first time since his escape, Torwain managed a smile. 'I merely encouraged a spark, and then fanned the flames.'

He explained what had happened. He had forgotten how cathartic some conversations could be. Carrick was a good listener and it had been many years since Torwain had explained himself to anyone. As he talked, he found himself feeling lighter, the worms of disgust shedding themselves from his skin. Somewhere along the way, Cernunous slipped into his core. Torwain felt him stretching out like fingers, reaching for every part of him. By the time his tale was told, he felt more in control of himself.

Carrick did not speak right away, taking the time to weigh his words carefully. 'I can only imagine how intense a battle of the wills would be between yourself and the Pontiff. You were at a disadvantage but you still managed to turn the situation around and defeat him.' He paused and took a sip of his own wine. 'Domination is the power trip of weak men. If they are not careful, it can leave them wide open to manipulation, as the Pontiff found out to his cost. You played him incredibly well and it saved your life. You should be proud, not sitting here looking like you need to crawl under a rock.'

'It almost saved my life,' Torwain corrected, 'It still took you to release me; I would never have got myself free in time.'

'I was just returning the favour.' Carrick grinned and held his cup up. 'To good friends saving each other just in time.'

Torwain nudged the cup with his own. From somewhere deep inside him, Cernunous called.

The sun had dropped and the sky had turned a fiery orange as Torwain rode bareback the short distance through the trees. Cernunous was waiting for him. He held out his hands and two snakes slipped down his arms and onto the druid. They wound their way all over his body and Torwain felt his skin come alive again in their wake. When he was strong enough, he slipped from the horse.

'The taint of the Roman gods has left you now,' Cernunous told him as the snakes coiled themselves contentedly back around his biceps. 'The priest's touch inadvertently cloaked you in it. It was not disgust at your actions which was causing you to feel so oppressed. It was their energy working to steal yours. Even after escaping the Roman's clutches, their gods still held you prisoner.'

With his mind unburdened, Torwain was finally able to focus on the thought that had been nagging at the back of his mind since he had first noticed the glimmer of interest in the Pontiff's eyes. 'Why did the Pontiff not have more control?'

'He was not acting alone.'

'Did his gods have a hand in his behaviour?'

'Indeed. They might have been able to hide the legionnaires' presence in the wood from you but because you are wearing my torc they could not overpower our connection. There is no way the Pontiff would have been able to touch it, let alone remove it, so they needed some other way to defeat us. I felt their presence strongly just before the Pontiff gave in to his desires, but forgive me; I only realised their true reason for having the Pontiff touch you so, when your mood began to be affected.'

Torwain ran his fingers over his torc. 'I felt you with me, encouraging me to take every advantage I could. I would never have thought of it otherwise.'

'They will have felt me there, too.' Cernunous's voice as usual reverberated both inside and outside Torwain's body. 'Their senses are much stronger than that of the priests. I believe that is why they attempted such an impromptu plan. Unfortunately, the Pontiff will live, and he will be all the more dangerous to you for it. He will blame you for his failings.'

Cernunous reached out and stroked the neck of the horse. It whickered with pleasure. He held out an arm to help Torwain remount. 'Do not remove the torc, the gods cannot sever our connection so long as you wear it. Of course, it does not guarantee your survival, you understand?'

Torwain nodded and Cernunous faded away. The horse turned its head towards the camp and slowly, carefully, picked its way through the wood.

5

It was pitch-black in the box, making it almost impossible to tell any difference between having his eyes open or closed. Then, if he craned his neck, he noticed that there was a tiny crack of light down by his feet and he could see the dusty air swirling and playing in the bright rays. For a while he watched, wondering - did motes only exist in shafts of light? Or was such a dance being played out everywhere, unseen by human eyes? The cart jolted and once more his head thumped against the floor. He groaned. It was a weak sound, for he was a weak man now; he had been captive for a long time.

Day and night he had been cramped in this coffin-like box inside a covered cart. Three or four times they had let him out to relieve himself in a pot. He barely had time to stretch his aching body and force down the morsels of food he was given before they were gagging him again and shoving him back inside. Not once had he been allowed to exit the cart itself. He almost longed for his usual confinement; a cold stone room with the same pot in a corner and rat-infested reeds for a bed on the hard floor. At least there he had not been gagged. He could taste a metallic tang; he must have bitten his tongue again. By the time this journey ended, he would be black and blue.

He knew they had kept him somewhere in the Votadini lands. He had recognised the accent from the odd times that he had heard an Albion voice. The rest of the time, he had only heard the Mediterranean lilt of his Roman guards though even they were better than the harsh tones of Martaani.

She had visited him a number of times, usually flanked by her praefectus, Proculus. If the two were not lovers then the praefectus certainly was in love with her. That much had been obvious from the outset. Proculus looks at Martaani, he thought, the same way I looked at... He stopped himself; he must not think of her now. To do so would plunge him into a pit of despair, he missed her so much.

Martaani had made it very clear - anyone close to him was in danger. So he had steeled himself under her interrogations. Making out that his wife was just a woman, disposable and easily replaceable. That opinion had gained him a severe beating but he would tell any lies, and stand any amount of blows, to keep her safe. Martaani had been relying on his connections to further her cause. Hoping to play on his fears to get information. The less regard he could show for anyone he cared about, the safer they would be.

He had lost all sense of direction very quickly within the confines of the box but he was certain that there were only five legionnaires guarding him. By the feel of things, they were heading through some difficult terrain today. He had heard plenty of cursings from the guards outside and the cart had been stuck, presumably in mud, a number of times.

The cart lurched again, much worse this time. There was the accompanying sound of splintering wood and he thumped into the side of the box as the world tipped sideways. A few moments later, blinding light dazzled him as the lid was removed. A guard ordered him out, dragging him from the tilting cart. Impatiently, he was pushed across the muddy, rutted path to a stand of alder with their feet almost in the edge of a fast-running river. There he stumbled and fell, his legs useless after the cramped conditions of the box. The guard laughed at him sprawled in the mud then kicked him into position and bound his hands and feet around the trunk of one of the trees. He left him there, sitting on the sodden earth, unable to move. Back at the cart, they set about trying to mend the broken wheel before darkness fell.

This lower-lying land was taking its time to recover after the recent rains. It was waterlogged, the road covered in a layer of mud inches thick, hiding deep ruts and pot holes. The turbulent river had long since burst its banks and bore no resemblance to its usual calm flow. Here and there, the river had come so far over that the road had been almost obliterated. The far bank had fared much better. There the land was sloped, rising well above the swollen river.

Kydas sat hugging the alder, trying to imagine the land in a calmer state. He soon realised exactly where they were - not far from Stanwick - but clearly not heading for the capital. His body ached and the wet seeped up into his clothing but the joy he felt at being back in his homeland surpassed any discomfort. The fresh air on his face was a welcome relief after the stifling conditions inside the box. He could tell by the sunlight that it was late afternoon. The guards would be anxious to get underway as soon as possible but judging by the tone of the voices at the cart, the repair was not going to be an easy one.

Another voice found its way to Kydas, startling him, for there was no one else around.

Fearn speaks to you.

It took a moment for him to realise that the voice was audible only to him. He felt the tree he was wrapped around almost shudder and wondered if he was going mad.

Fearn greets you and offers you his strength and protection.

Kydas jumped as the voice sounded again. He had not been hearing things. In the past he had heard the druids talk of communing with nature, with trees in particular, but he had never believed it to be literal. He could not deny, though, that he needed strength from somewhere. Protection, too. When they got to where they were going, he was in no doubt that Martaani would be waiting for him.

You must listen to me now, Fearn said, more urgently. *You do not have long to get away.*

Kydas frowned. Early on he had attempted to escape many times but always he had failed. He saw no way he could succeed now. He wanted to tell the tree this but how did one talk to a tree?

You do not need to talk to me, I hear your thoughts. There is no hope where you are going. You must leave. Now. There is no time to ponder. This challenge will take everything you have and more. Breathe deeply now. Take strength from me. Just as the water makes me stronger, let it make you so.

Kydas thought of his wife and did as he was bid. Here at long last was his chance to get back to her; maybe his only chance. With every inward breath, he felt his determination blooming again. His limbs were still weak but it ceased to matter so much. It was as if he were breathing in sustenance. He began to feel revitalised, desperate to be away. His hands scrabbled at their bonds, working the leather around until the buckle was within reach. It was lucky that the guard had tied him this way and not with his arms behind him, or he would never have had the dexterity to work himself loose.

'Sit still,' one of the guards ordered, coming over from the cart to give him a kick. 'Any more movement and you will go back in your box.'

Kydas waited until the guard was busy again. This time he was more careful, keeping one eye on the legionnaires and stopping every time they looked his way. They did not bother much. None of them were expecting him to make a break for it; he was too weak to manage anything remotely resembling an escape.

When the moment is right, you must run down into the river. There are stepping stones beneath the flow. Holly guards each end.

Kydas could see the holly bush only a few steps away. He closed his eyes. Could this all be true, or was his mind playing tricks on him?

Trust in me now, Fearn told him. *The goddess Brigantia is fighting for her land; she will not see you drown. Why else do you think you are here?*

Kydas had never considered himself such an important cog in Brigantia's wheel. Yet Martaani had.

Kariss herself is nearby. Kydas's mind filled with an image of a woman sitting amidst a mass of bracken. His insides leapt, he knew the place. It was only a short distance away. He should be able to run that far. At that moment, the buckle finally gave way and his hands sprung free. His guards had not noticed. Carefully, he reached down and unbuckled his feet.

Are you ready?

Kydas breathed in deeply. He was. Behind him came the sound of more splintering wood as the axle snapped and the cart crashed over, crushing three of the guards beneath it.

49

Go!

Kydas ran. He plunged into the river by the holly and sure enough felt firm stone beneath his feet. He worked his way forward at an angle, towards the holly on the far side, his feet feeling blindly for each new stone. The water was deep, almost up to his thighs. He slipped in places as the torrent pushed at his weakened legs. Behind him, he could hear the cries of the injured men and the shouts of those working to free them. He had been forgotten for now but he knew that would not last. His leg muscles were burning. It would have been the easiest thing in the world to let the current carry him away but somehow he kept going. The pressure of the current eased as he neared the far side; still he stumbled as his foot hit the submerged bank. He grabbed at roots and hauled himself out of the water only to collapse in a heap behind the holly bush.

Every second, he expected to hear a shout and the sounds of pursuit but the remaining legionnaires were still distracted, trying to rescue their comrades. Kydas paused only long enough to catch his breath and let the pain in his legs ease slightly. He could not let himself think of his wife; instead, he forced himself to concentrate on Fearn's image of Kariss. His wife was there with him, though, hovering around the edges of his psyche. Like a ghost tempting him to acknowledge her presence.

Just as soon as he got safely to Kariss, he told himself, then he would be able to think of her. The thought acted like a stimulant, pushing him forward when his body screamed at him to rest. The trees began to thin the further he went from the river, letting in more and more light. The ground cover bloomed in response. Late bluebells hung their wilting heads amongst wood anemones and lesser celandines. Here and there ox-eye daisies stretched their heads ever upwards. It was a sight to uplift the spirit, yet Kydas barely noticed. Kariss was not far now and still he had heard nothing from behind him, could he really make it?

A noise to his left startled him. Before he could turn his head, he was bowled to the ground. A man sat astride him, knife pointed to his neck.

'Who are you?' the man demanded. 'And what is your business here?'

Kydas bucked and fought, using every last ounce of energy, only stopping when he heard a woman's voice. Her accent was strange but clearly she was from Albion. She stepped into view and all his fight evaporated.

'Kariss,' he managed before exhaustion took hold and he slipped into unconsciousness.

Water splashing on his face brought him back. It took him a few moments to get his bearings. He was still laid on the ground but now he was surrounded by Kariss, the man who had attacked him, a boy, and a dog.

'You moved,' he said to Kariss. 'I expected to find you still up on bracken heath.'

'How did you know we were up there?' she demanded, flicking a worried glance at the man beside her.

'Fearn, the tree, told me. He showed me where you were and helped me escape. I don't know how he did it, but he told me Brigantia herself was helping. The cart collapsed just when I broke free and I managed to get away without them seeing me.'

He realised he was gabbling and stopped. 'My name is Kydas, I am from Wendell, where you were born. A long time ago, the Romans took me, they have been holding me prisoner ever since. Is it midsummer yet?'

It was Naraic who found his voice first. 'It is midsummer's eve. Did they torture you, too?' he asked, holding up his maimed hand.

Kydas grimaced as he saw it. He pulled up his tunic to reveal a torso covered with burns and poorly healed injuries. 'The bruises were terrible,' he said, 'but at least they heal the quickest.'

Naraic shuddered. Kariss looked horrified, 'Did they do this because of me?'

'Not because of you,' Anniel scolded gently. 'You have to stop thinking like that. They do it because they want to win. It would not matter who it was standing in their way.' He turned back to Kydas, 'I am Anniel, Kariss's husband, son of Alpin, from the Vacumagi.'

Kydas smiled at him. 'Have you got any food?'

Naraic found him some cold meat from their last meal, 'I am Naraic, I was Kariss's guide north and this is Cloud. There is also Garth and Umar but they are...'

Cloud interrupted him with a low, curdling growl, his top lips curling up to reveal his sharp canines. A stone whistled past everyone to hit the dog squarely on the head. He dropped to the ground. Naraic didn't even have time to reach him before a strange noise from Kariss stopped him in his tracks. He turned to see a legionary's arm tight around her throat.

'Well, well, well, lose a minnow, catch a trout,' one of the Romans sneered. 'One more move and I hurt her.'

There was nothing any of them could do other than submit to being bound, gagged and forced to the ground.

'You would not be surviving now, if you had not brought us to this pretty peach,' one of the guards told Kydas, kicking his leg hard. The legionary eyed Kariss up and down. 'Martaani is going to have a grand old time with you,' he laughed before speaking in his native tongue to the two others. One of them raced away. 'We camp here tonight. Tomorrow there will be no need for you to go to Stanwick.' He laughed again.

Kydas watched as they gathered wood together for a fire. He did not want to look at the others. They must be hating him right now for leading the enemy straight to them. In his desperation to get away and find Kariss, he had forgotten all about the tracks he was leaving behind.

A nudge to his back made him look around. Anniel looked as though he were smiling at him, though it was hard to tell beneath his gag. Kariss too looked anything but angry. Naraic had eyes only for his dog, who still lay prone on the ground, a few feet away. Anniel nudged Kydas again and looked towards the legionnaires. He nodded his head twice, flicked his head in the direction the other had gone and nodded again, then shrugged. Kydas frowned. He nodded his head at each of the legionaries as Anniel had done, adding two more with a shrug of his own and a pointed look at Cloud. He couldn't remember if he had told them of the accident with the cart. Everything had happened so quickly.

They lay there for hours. Darkness came but they did nothing more than catnap. At some point, Cloud regained consciousness and managed to crawl to

Naraic but one of the legionnaires kicked him away and he slunk off into the woods.

Garth eased his way across yet another patch of flooded ground. There was no way he could avoid leaving a trail behind him but he could at least make it as difficult to follow as possible. His heart was racing. More legionnaires could be anywhere and he did not want to stumble across them in his haste. It had been no easy thing - to leave the rest of his party behind as captives. He would have tried to rescue them but acting alone he could not be sure that one legionary would not kill Kariss whilst he dealt with the other.

He had been scouting the area when the legionnaires had attacked. The noise of the scuffle had brought him rushing back but he was too late to be of any use. He knew there was no one else in the immediate vicinity so the legionary he was just in time to see leave was probably heading for Stanwick. Garth needed to act quickly; he had to try to stop the man from reaching help. The legionary had moved quickly. He was long gone by the time Garth had made his way around the camp and picked up his trail.

Umar had been to check on Stanwick. He was making his way back to the camp when a solitary legionary came into sight. Umar ducked behind a tree and watched him pass. The man was clearly in a hurry; he was soaking wet and covered in mud, nothing like the neat appearance the Romans usually favoured. It crossed his mind to kill the man but he was a poor specimen and it would only cause trouble.

Umar had decided not to use the hidden ways to make his way back to camp but instead to stay close to the main path. He could still keep out of sight and it would give them a better idea of how busy the area was likely to be for their journey tomorrow. Today the path was in regular use but this was the first Roman he had seen. It was a shock when a short way on, he saw Garth, looking almost as bedraggled.

'There was plenty of activity around Stanwick,' Umar told him as they hurried back to the camp. 'I could not get near to Faela, I will have to watch for her tomorrow at The Gathering. Martaani was there, I caught a brief glimpse of her. She was surrounded by guards - anyone would think she was expecting an attack herself.'

The noise of the swollen river sounded ahead. Garth was surprised when Umar headed straight for it.

'You will never get across here. You need to go a distance downstream, there is a way over using boulders and a fallen trunk.'

'Indeed?' Umar called back over his shoulder. Ahead of them lay a rutted road running adjacent to the river. As they neared it they could see that is was blocked by an upturned cart. One legionary was busy trying to remove the broken wheel. Approaching with caution, they could just make out the body of another still trapped underneath. Close by, a muddy horse grazed on rose bay willow herb. There was no one else in sight.

Umar looked at Garth and raised his eyebrows. This time, he had no qualms about killing. As far as he was concerned, open hostilities had been declared the moment Kariss was captured. He picked up a twisted branch and, using it as a staff, he started forward.

The legionary heard them at last. He struggled to his feet and limped towards them, asking for help.

Umar let him get close then swung the staff with all his might. With a bone-shattering crunch, it connected with legionary's head and down he went. There was no one else in sight so they shoved the fresh body half under the cart. Garth unhobbled the horse, removed its harness, and chased it away down the path.

They had no time to waste searching the cart. The messenger would have reached Stanwick by now; already riders could be on their way. At the river, Umar made for the holly bush, hitched up his robe and stepped into the water. Garth followed without question; druids had their own ways of knowing what most men did not.

As they neared the camp, Cloud skulked out of the bushes. Dried blood stained the fur on his head and his tail was tucked down between his back legs but it wagged a little at the sight of his friends.

They were relieved to find there were still only two legionnaires. The pair were sitting together by a small campfire, a little way off from their prisoners. Umar pointed at Kydas and pulled a questioning face. Garth shrugged his shoulders; he had not noticed the stranger before, tied amidst the others. He held up a hand and counted down from five to one. They charged in.

The legionnaires had no chance to put up any sort of resistance. Umar felled one with a mighty swing of his staff, Garth finished the other with his sword. Neither had a moment to make so much as a noise.

Then there was no time for talking. They stripped the bodies of anything that might be useful, before weighting them down with rocks and hurling them into a nearby bog. Slowly, they disappeared from sight.

By the time everyone had been cut free there were only a few tell-tale bubbles left on the surface.

It was nearing midnight when they reached the stone circle beneath How Tallon. It was not such a long journey but even with Garth's help and the use of Umar's makeshift staff, Kydas had struggled all the way. Months of confinement had wasted his muscles and sapped his energy. Umar hid their tracks as they went, ever cautious for the sounds of pursuit, but he heard nothing. Inside the circle, they found dry wood piled ready for them and two brace of coney laid on a rock. The gods may not be able to show themselves but they were certainly still helping them.

They left Kydas to rest whilst they prepared a fire and cooked the meat. The rabbit was good. Between mouthfuls, Kydas told them more about himself. At the mention of his wife, his eyes cast down in sadness, but Umar let out a great yelp of delight.

'Ahah!' he cried, jumping to his feet and punching the air. He stood dancing from foot to foot, pointing at Kydas. 'I knew it; I knew there was a reason. The goddess did not play me false.'

Kydas looked around at the other faces in bewilderment. Kariss was the first to make the connection. 'You are Faela's husband? My cousin - the one who the gods picked out for Umar here to...'

'They marked her out as someone who could alter the balance between Martaani and Kariss,' Umar interrupted, his excitement getting the better of him. 'We could not work out why. Faela had no idea, but...' He slumped back onto the ground, suddenly dejected. 'Why would she lie to me?'

'My wife does not lie. She is the kindest, most honourable woman you could ever meet. She will be the best mo...' Kydas's face flushed. 'What of the baby? Is it... he... she... is Faela healthy?'

Umar was not listening; he hit himself on the forehead with the palm of his hand and jumped to his feet again.

'She did not lie. She did not know. She never knew what had happened to you. How could I have forgotten? Kel told me all about your disappearance. They searched for weeks, Faela especially, but not a trace of you was ever found. No one ever considered Martaani might have you.'

A tear leaked from Kydas's eye. He made no move to wipe it away. All this time, he had forced himself not to think of Faela and how she might be faring. It had been the only chance he had of holding onto his sanity.

'If no-one ever knew, then what was the point in holding you?' Anniel frowned. 'What use is a hostage without any leverage?'

'What did they torture you about?' Naraic subconsciously rubbed at his hand as he asked. He was starting to look at the missing digit differently. Instead of a constant reminder of the terror he had gone through, the wound now gave him strength. He had faced the hatred of Martaani and survived. There were not many people who could say that.

Kydas took a moment to compose himself before answering. He looked apologetically at Kariss. 'You, mostly,' he said at last. 'They wanted to know if you had been in contact with anyone at Wendell over the years. Martaani was certain that you would go straight there when you returned from the north. It was too risky for her to target the fort itself, so she made them keep me alive as bait. If all else failed, Martaani believed that she could make Faela betray you to get me back.' He frowned. 'The way they spoke, the things they knew, they must have been talking to someone at Wendell. But if no one there knew I was a prisoner, how did they get their information?'

Kariss twisted a piece of grass between her fingers, 'I believe that would be Taratus.'

'No!' Kydas shook his head, 'There is no way Taratus would betray us. He might be bull-headed at times but he loves Brigantia.'

'He has been seen, up at Dumpender Law and at Stanwick,' Anniel said softly. 'We have heard about it from a number of sources. We even sent our own spy into Stanwick to speak with Lord Hightern. He returned with the news that Taratus had been seen sneaking into the Roman quarter only a few days before.'

Kydas closed his eyes. His head was spinning and his stomach roiled. His nerves were fraught and it had been a long time since he had eaten such rich food. He made it outside the circle before he was sick. Afterwards, Kariss helped him back to the fire and covered him with her cloak.

'You need rest. You are safe now. Sleep. Tomorrow, if all goes well, we will find Faela and you will have your answers.'

Kydas hadn't the strength left to do anything more than nod. For many moons he had longed for freedom but now that it was here he was overwhelmed by it. So many worries warred for his attention: his wife; his child; Taratus. For the first time since he had been taken, he began to feel unsure. He had been gone a long time and all that time Faela had thought him dead, or herself abandoned. Had she found another to take his place? And what of their baby? Umar had not mentioned it; had it not lived? Dead before birth or sometime after? Maybe it was deformed in some way and the druid was loath to tell him?

As if all that were not enough, there was the possibility that his good friend, the brother of his wife, was a traitor. He could not envision such a thing. Taratus was as loyal as any man could be. Besides which, Kydas knew what many did not; that Taratus had always held a secret love for Kariss.

Loyal he may be, but he was no saint. Shael had been available, Kariss had not. Their one-night dalliance had shocked Taratus by producing a pregnancy. After a few days of drunken self-loathing, during which he had made his confession to Kydas, Taratus had accepted the matter. He settled down with Shael and made the most of the situation. As a couple, they had found love and happiness. Taratus had never again mentioned his childhood plan to wed his cousin but Kydas could not believe that he would ever turn against her so completely.

Sleep took him eventually and his worries transferred into his dream state. He woke shortly after with a start, wondering for a moment where he was. The muted voices of his new companions drove away the nightmare. They floated across to him, wrapping him in safety, as he drifted back to a more peaceful sleep.

'Martaani is bound to have sent plenty of men,' Garth said.

Umar screwed up his face, 'I am not so sure. To do so is bound to raise questions. The men with Martaani are her personal guard, here with her for The

Gathering. What good reason could she possibly give as to why she would send some away now? She is bound to have more hidden somewhere and a few of these are who she will send but my thinking is that she will wait until The Gathering is finished before doing anything noticeable. The last thing she needs is for anyone to become suspicious.'

'Then why did we need to rush away?' Kariss was still trying to get rid of the memory of the bodies sinking into the mire. She may have lost most of her squeamishness over the food she ate, but the killing of men was something she hoped never to harden herself to.

'We do not know how many other groups are already out in the woods,' Garth explained. 'And we have no idea if the man who left went straight to Stanwick or went to get help from elsewhere first. By leaving no trace of what happened, it will hopefully be assumed that your captors simply moved you to another place.'

Anniel had been very quiet but now he spoke.

'Martaani will be expecting Kariss not to show up; she will be off her guard. We should take advantage of that.'

Kariss looked hopeful, 'What do you have in mind?'

'I think that you should not go to Stanwick in the morning. You should wait and go straight to The Gathering at noon, but you should not show yourself until the last moment. That way, Martaani will believe herself to have won; she may expect some unrest from the crowd, but she will not be expecting any challenge.'

61

It was Naraic who saw the problem with that. 'If Kariss does not show then there will be no need for the vote to go ahead. Martaani will be named heir.'

'What about Enda?' Kariss had not forgotten the brave Epidii warrior who had agreed to stand as her double. 'Could she not stand in for me to begin with?'

'Martaani must know there is a decoy, or she would not have attacked the Carvetii village,' Naraic reminded her.

'That could play right into our hands. If she is prudent, she will keep her own council on the matter,' Anniel said, grinning. 'She will know that once Enda steps up to speak as Kariss, she will be able to denounce her as an impostor and win the vote by default.'

Garth was more cautious, 'We must hope that Martaani thinks the same way.'

Anniel clapped him on the back. 'We will be in the crowd watching, my friend. We shall know if the ruse goes another way. So long as it is Kariss who speaks and not Enda then no rules will have been broken.'

Kariss still looked worried, 'So much for Lord Hightern's suggestion of arriving with a full guard.'

Umar pointed a finger at her. 'Never do the thing everyone expects you to do. Keep them guessing, that way they have less chance of outmanouvering you.'

Kariss could not deny the sense in his words.

'We must get word to Uurad tonight. And Enda must be made aware that she is not to speak until Kariss announces herself, no matter what happens.' Anniel was thinking fast. 'Umar, I think it would be best if you go. As a druid, you will not cause such a concern if you are seen travelling in the dark.'

Umar almost smiled. 'As a druid, I would hope that I am never seen travelling unless I intend to be.'

Anniel acquiesced. He looked around at the little group. 'Are we all in agreement?'

They nodded.

It was another hour or so before they had their plan refined. It would not be much longer before the sun was rising, they needed sleep. Umar gathered his things together. 'Until tomorrow.' He nodded at them and took his leave.

6

There was a wide open circle to the east of Stanwick, where the trees were kept from encroaching. It was here that the people of the capital held their celebrations. The site had been chosen because of the yew tree growing at its edge. Ioho was ancient, with a bole so huge it had split into three parts. Its limbs, so heavy that they could no longer reach for the sunlight, grew down and back into the ground. From this decay new shoots had sprouted, giving the impression that the tree was creeping its way across the ground. This cycle of death and rebirth was greatly enhanced by the sinewy appearance of the twisted new trunks.

Unlike Eburos, the oldest yew in Brigantia, which was known only by the druids, Ioho was sacred to all the Brigantes. He was their symbol of renewal, of continuation and strength, and every leader since Venutius had been blessed beneath his boughs at the start of their reign.

Before sunrise, Corio was waiting. He faced Ioho in the east, and behind him in a wide arc stood the inhabitants of Stanwick. Front and centre sat Lord Hightern, flanked by his personal guards, Viroco and Volisios. Next to him sat Cartivel, his wounded leg elevated on a stool. Beside Cartivel sat Bodvoc, still maintaining his invaluable senility. They made a sorry-looking trio but looks belied the sharp minds that hid beneath their decrepit appearances. None of the Roman contingent were present.

Corio felt freer than he had in months. Inside the palisade, the priests had stifled his powers, turning him into an impotent bystander. But not today, out here away from the fort. Today, the sun rose earlier than any other day, to shine its glory down on the waiting Brigantes. Today, Bodach would soar in the heavens, Verbia would flow through the river that curved its way past the ceremonial site, and the goddess Brigantia would renew her connection with her people. He could feel the auspices of the day grow with every intake of breath. Every exhale threw out the asphyxiating binds of the Romans. Later, if all went to plan, as the sun reached its zenith, they would gather here again and he would call forth Kariss and Martaani. He had no doubt that Kariss would be declared. The golden torc of supremacy would, of course, remain with Lord Hightern for now, but Corio would place a lesser torc about Kariss's neck: gold, as her new, regal status demanded.

He felt the urge to turn and scan the crowd behind him. Was Kariss there? Had she made it? In the last few days, Martaani had left the fort a number of times but as to why, Corio was firmly in the dark. He inhaled deeply and resisted the temptation to look. Only time would tell. It was getting lighter now and tones of pink had started blending with the violet sky. Bodach's warning, but to whom?

To the south of the ceremonial circle, a large fire burned. Three young druids walked around the circle. Above their heads they spun long, double-ended torches. The flames appeared to join together to form circles of light. There was much joy and excitement in the crowd. This was a day to rejoice in the sun.

The first glimmers of that fiery orb appeared over the horizon, just to the left of Ioho. Corio raised his arms high and wide.

'Hail to the sun.'

'Hail,' the crowd repeated.

'Hail to the sun,' he called again, and again the crowd replied. Three times this was done. Still, the torches twirled.

The colour of the sky deepened until it was a blazing inferno of red and orange. Corio had already planned what he intended to say but this warning could not be ignored. He paused for a moment to gather himself then, casting aside his prepared speech, he spoke.

'Oh Bodach, father of the sky, we feel your presence and we heed your warning. On this day of all days, we accept the dangers in our land and we pledge ourselves to drive them out.'

A cheer rose up behind him. He allowed himself a smile. It would appear he was not the only one going with an impromptu reaction to the unusual sky. Aside from their recognised responses, the crowd was usually silent during his address, but this was no ordinary midsummer morn and he took no umbrage from their reaction.

'Let those who fail to honour the gods today be struck down.' The crowd cheered even louder and he had to raise his voice to be heard above them. 'Bodach, consort of the great Cailleach, we feel you high above us. Your moods and your anguish impact on us each day. Today, we return that gift. Today, we stand firm! Today, we fight the canker in our midst. Today, WE give you the gift of life.'

Behind him, the crowd erupted. The torches twirled ever faster and the fire seemed to flare and burn with renewed vigour.

Corio turned to face everyone. His eyes alighted on his predecessor and he was greeted with an almost imperceptible nod of his head. Next to Bodvoc, Lord Hightern was clapping and even Cartivel had a smile on his face. Jubilant, he turned his back once more and resumed the midsummer celebration. A hush fell over the people.

'Mighty sun,' he called, 'we see your face rising to light our day. See you our fire here? This fire on earth, as you are fire in the sky? In the darkness of our nights, you travel to the otherworld, and so connect the world of the dead with the world of the living. Today, as those spirits walk amongst us once more, we light this fire in your honour. And in so doing, we also give you life here on earth.'

The sun had now cleared the skyline and Corio turned to address the yew. 'Ioho, most every part of you is poison to us. You symbolise death and endings, yet as your branches return to the ground to rot, new life springs forth. Showing us that to fear death is to fear renewal. The red flesh that hides your deadly seeds is food to us, showing us there is nourishment to be found in the most dire of places. Your message could not be any clearer to us than today.

'Today, as the sun stays in the sky, lighting our path longer than any other day of the year, we ask you to give up the spirits of our ancestors, to let the dead walk amongst us, so that we may learn from the lessons they have to teach us. Just as they taught us at Beltaine and will again at Samhain. We beseech you, open that bridge to the otherworld and let the ancestors cross.'

The young druids stopped twirling and came to stand with torches held horizontally in downstretched arms. Two on one side and one on the other, they lined a path from the tree so that the dead would find their way. The people moved apart from one another, giving the spirits room to move. A few sank to their knees, lost in memories of loved ones recently departed, but for most this was a joyous time. They closed their eyes and tried to feel a breath of wind, or loving caress that would tell them their mother, father, child or lover was close by.

Corio was reluctant to call down the gods whilst the Romans were nearby, so the ceremony was not a long one. Whilst everyone made their way back to their homes, Corio led Lord Hightern over to Ioho. The king wanted to sit for a few moments with his hands on the venerable yew and contemplate his own transition to the otherworld. Anxious as he was to leave his nation in safe hands, he was tired. For many months he had felt death hovering by his shoulder but he had refused to turn its way. Brigantia needed him to cling to life until this day was done.

Ioho did not speak to him. He saw no pathway to his future, no words of reassurance to light his way. Yet the feeling of comfort remained with him, as it always did of late when he thought of his coming death; the essence of tranquillity clinging firmly to him even without the mighty Ioho's assistance. Lord Hightern had never communicated with the gods himself so he was not perturbed by the tree's silence. In truth, he was not sure what he had expected. The archdruid was the one to speak with the gods and spirits.

'We cannot look into our own passing,' Corio advised him as his guards carried him back to the fort.

Privately, Corio was worried; he wished he could speak to Bodvoc. Lord Hightern was not the only one to have heard nothing from the yew. Ioho had never failed to talk to him before but today it was as if the tree had turned his back on them. The sky was still flaming, taking its time to dilute the invading red hues and return to the usual summer blues. Corio was not convinced that he had interpreted the warning correctly and Ioho's silence only re-enforced his unease. Without the gods for support, he felt like a blind man feeling his way forward.

A sudden shiver ran down his spine and he looked up to see the Augur staring intently at them. The priest's mouth curled in amusement as he watched the King of Brigantia being carried on his decorated chair. As soon as he realised that the druid had seen him, the hint of a smile vanished, replaced by his usual mask of indifference.

The Augur held his ground as Corio drew level with him. His accompanying auxiliaries, though, stepped forward as if ready to protect him if the druid were to strike. Corio met the man's eye unflinchingly. With a slow turn of his head, he dismissed the priest as if he were nothing more than a shadow. He suppressed another shiver; the Augur was an unnaturally cold individual. He would have taken great delight at seeing the ceremony performed without Corio invoking the gods.

Throughout the morning, people flocked to the ceremonial site from all corners of Brigantia. The leaders of the northern warriors were all present: Tholarg, Uurad, Loth, Gartnet, and Drest of the Taexali. They had only a small contingent of warriors with them, the rest staying well out of sight. Enda was amongst them, still dressed as Kariss. A loud murmur rumbled around the nearby crowd as folk shuffled nearer, to catch a glimpse of her. She smiled at those closest to her, eyes alert, wary for any danger in the crowd.

Around Enda, the warriors were sharp-eyed, keeping a hand on their loosely sheathed swords. Even here, they were taking no chances. Under the branches of Ioho, a hooded druid scanned the skies, watching for the slightest of signs. Tholarg kept him in sight at all times. Behind them, scattered in the trees, were yet more warriors, ensuring that no one could sneak up on the druid whilst his attention was diverted.

The bulk of the crowd appeared unaware of all this intrigue. They were far too interested in the coming event to notice such subtleties taking place on the sidelines. No one knew quite what to expect. Already the royal party was running late and the ceremony was in danger of being delayed. It had not gone unnoticed to those present at sunrise that archdruid Corio had not invoked the gods. Not even mentioning the name of the High One, Brigantia. Never before had there been a ceremony where their goddess had not been called.

The noise level dropped as, one by one, people noticed their leader, Lord Hightern, being carried to where a dais had been erected, the strain on his face apparent for all to see. Once he was settled into place, the rest of his worried retinue took their seats. Martaani, dressed in Tyrian purple robes, was amongst them. She looked straight ahead as she took her seat to the left of Lord Hightern. On her face, a look of imperious calm hid the glimmer of expectant success glinting in her eyes. Kariss was nowhere to be seen. Her seat remained significantly empty.

The crowd looked around as the rest of the royal party settled. Many eyes turned to Enda. Tholarg glanced again at Ioho but the druid gave a quick shake of his head. Tholarg closed his eyes for a moment, swallowing his concerns. He nodded to Uurad, who began walking Enda slowly through the crowd, accompanied by four warriors. As far as they were aware, no one at Stanwick had ever seen Kariss; they would be fooling both Albion and Roman alike.

They had never discussed what would happen if Kariss failed to show up before it was time for her to speak. All they could do was stall and pray. Uurad scanned the crowd for any sign of a familiar face. The only person meeting his eye was a tall, brightly-robed druid, who never so much as glanced at Enda. The druid just had time to give a barely perceptible nod before he was jostled to the side as the crowd pushed forward and Uurad lost sight of him. He glanced over his shoulder to where Tholarg still stood but heads were now in the way and he was unable to pass on the message. At the dais, Enda stepped up to her chair, bowing her head to Lord Hightern and then to Corio and Bodvoc in turn. Giving only the briefest acknowledgement to Martaani, she took her seat. Martaani inclined her head in return, her smile showing fully now. *She knows!* Uurad realised with a cold splash of dread. He took his place at the edge of the dais with his men, waiting for trouble.

Corio stood and raised his hands for silence. It was almost instantaneous.

'A great sadness is upon us,' he called, walking around the dais so that all present could see him, even if those straining their ears at the back could not quite make out his words. 'Lord Hightern, great leader and father of our nation, is no longer the healthy man he was. The time has now come to begin passing the mantle of leadership on.' He paused, letting his words filter through the crowds. 'As you all know, there is no clear successor to smooth our way. The most eligible heirs are the two women seated before you. Kariss, born in Brigantia at Wendell, daughter of Lizzelle; who in turn is daughter of Margeof, cousin to our own Lord Hightern's mother. And Martaani, born overseas, but whose lineage is assured right back to Queen Cartimandua herself. Today, we decide their fate.'

At Martaani's name, a rumble of dissent sounded amongst the audience. Corio wisely hid his appreciation of this, instead holding up his hands for silence. 'I have no wish to influence you one way or the other, for this decision is yours and yours alone.'

The crowd hushed again.

'Our High One, Brigantia, has already spoken of her choice. As have the other two who make up the Great Goddess as a whole - Verbia and Cailleach. That choice is Kariss.' A loud cheer went up. Corio had to raise his voice. 'Martaani, on the other hand, brings with her fresh new gods, not seen in this land since Cartimandua's time.'

'Where is Brigantia?' someone called from the crowd. Other voices joined in assent.

Corio held his hands up for calm, conscious that this must not descend into a riot. The vote must go according to the laws, or Martaani could still seek to gain the throne on appeal.

'People, please,' he called, his voice drowning amidst the din.

A loud whistle sounded shrilly, cutting through the noise like a blade through butter. Viroco whistled again and silence descended once more. This time it was Lord Hightern who spoke. His voice was too weak and faint for anyone but the very closest to hear him so Viroco's booming voice repeated what he said, word for word.

'My people, I ask for calm. We will listen to both these women with the respect due to their position. There will be no more outbursts. Those that do not keep to the peace will be ejected from this gathering and their right to vote revoked. We are as we act, and I insist that you act in a manner to make us proud. I want to remember this day in my next life and smile, knowing that you, my people, made the best choice, the right choice for Brigantia.'

Hightern was not so decrepit as to be unable to command a crowd. Such was the respect afforded to him that the people hung their heads in shame. Only when Corio spoke again did they look towards the dais once more.

'We will hear from our overseas guest first.'

If there was a slight inference to the word guest, no one remarked on it. Martaani stood, her head high, her back straight, and walked to the edge of the dais. She scanned the people below her, faces she would never respect. Then she smiled. Her cold face transformed and her beauty shone for all to see. She shook her mane of long black ringlets - if hair was power, then all would be left in no doubt as to who was the more qualified to rule. Her voice was clear as it rang out, though her accent appeared to slur the top of the words slightly. Every face stared up at her, mesmerised.

'Beautiful people of Brigantia. I implore you. Do not look at me as the foreigner who knows nothing of your world. Instead, look at me as a fellow Brigantian, born overseas. I cannot help where I was born but I have returned to you at my first opportunity. Tutored always in the ways of Albion, I have made it my life's work to learn everything I can about our great nation. Can you not tell this by my grasp of your language? By my respect of your traditions? By my adoration of your spirit?'

In the crowd, backed by his auxiliaries, Proculus watched. Her ability to lie so convincingly amazed him. Only a few hours before, she had lain in his bed scorning everything about this place. She had called the people's observance of their religion sickening, their reliance on the druids pitiful, and their gullibility laughable. She would be formidable when she took over. He glanced around him. These people had no idea what was coming.

Up on the dais, Martaani cut an impressive figure, as beautiful as she was dangerous. In the friendly guise she was portraying, it was almost impossible to see the pernicious woman she really was. Many of the crowd seemed impressed, their mood changing towards her. This was not what they had been expecting.

'I understand your worries and concerns,' Martaani called. 'Lord Hightern has been a prodigious leader. He has led this nation with a strong heart and a sharp mind. He has kept you in greatness and he will always hold the highest place of honour in our hearts.'

The people cheered and Hightern nodded his head cautiously. This was not going the way he had expected. He had seen Martaani play the kind-hearted, concerned woman before, and it chilled him to see it now. If only the people could see how brittle this facade was. He longed to stand up and tell them, but he had no say in this. The laws were very clear.

'I see the nation of Brigantia as the greatest in the whole of Albion. We have the strongest and bravest people; true Brigantians with fire in their hearts and a determined love for their nation. Skilled craftsmen and women, dedicated to their work.'

People began nodding their heads in agreement. No matter how prepared they were to hate Martaani, they now found themselves warming to her compliments.

'Our children thrive like no others on this isle. We are the largest nation; we should be foremost in Albion. I say we will be foremost in Albion. Others will look to our ways and copy us in their thousands.'

Martaani paused here, letting her words settle. Inwardly, she smiled; people were the same the world over. Give them enough compliments, raise their level of self-importance, make them feel great, and you had their attention. They were like sheep; easily distracted. They could be steered in whatever way you wanted, once you got their focus on something they could believe in.

'How long have we been the greatest nation? Hundreds of years, yet other leaders seek to address you as if they were your equals. They are not your equals.' Her voice rose now. 'We will show Albion how great we are.' Again she paused briefly, not wanting to give the audience time to remember their concerns about her. 'We will build better, warmer houses for your families; fortify the towns; introduce bath houses; arenas for entertainment; all will be welcome. Life will be for celebrating once more. Your hard work should be rewarded and it will be. I want you to feel appreciated, to know how much you mean to me.

'I will bring in new foods for you to grow and eat: onions, cabbages, peas. We will pave the streets, so you need not wade through mud anymore. Roads will be built, making travel easier and safer. We will even bring in waterways, aqueducts to carry fresh water into the towns. Life will be safe once more. I have heard of all the troubles lately, unruly behaviour, lawlessness. This must stop! I intend to police Brigantia properly and bring the perpetrators to justice.' Her impassioned speech stirred more people into agreement. This was not the hateful person they had been led to expect. She understood them.

Those who knew better looked on with growing unease. Uurad scanned the crowd desperately, hoping still that Kariss would arrive, but it was looking less likely by the minute. His heart sank further. All their planning, that long march south. Had it really all been for nothing? Enda sat impassively, looking neither right nor left. Uurad could see a slight flush to her cheeks, the only outward sign of her nerves.

Martaani had the people right where she wanted them. She rounded off her speech quickly before anyone remembered about religion. 'Do not let your fears control you. They are unjustified. Do not let those who would hold you back dictate how you must act. Change can be frightening but change for the better is exhilarating. You deserve better, you deserve all that I have promised. You deserve to have freedom of thought, freedom from fear. In short, Brigantes, you deserve to be great again.'

She took her seat once more.

Under the branches of Ioho, the druid still searched the sky. Tholarg could wait no longer. He gestured to one of his men. The warrior slipped away from the ceremonial site, to ready the men for trouble. The druid closed his eyes and willed a sign to appear.

All is not lost.

The words whispered in his mind like a breeze ruffling the new green leaves of a beech tree. Torwain felt his hope ignite. He opened his eyes again and searched the skies. There, to his utmost relief, came the signs he had been waiting for.

On the dais, Corio had stood again, thanking Martaani for her words. He turned to the woman he believed to be Kariss. Next to her, Bodvoc rubbed at his ear. The movement caught his eye; it was enough to give Corio pause for thought. Something about the movement was unusual, but what? Conscious that everyone was watching him, he played for time, looking individually at everyone on the dais, making it seem like an intended part of proceedings. He was just taking in the last face when he realised. Bodvoc's hand was not shaking; it was as steady as his own. He looked back at the old druid. Sure enough, he moved his hand again. This time, he tapped his leg and pointed a finger. Corio turned to look.

A raven dropped down onto the topmost branches of Ioho, unnoticed by the people. At the same time, overhead, the mewing cry of an eagle could just be heard. Corio glanced at Bodvoc again; he was smiling at a face in the crowd. A woman stood there, dressed in shabby attire more suited to a man than a woman. Her hair was tucked under a scarf but as soon as she pulled it off, Corio knew who she was. He stepped back to give her room to mount the dais.

'My friends,' she called to the stunned crowd, 'I am Kariss, wife of Anniel of the Vacumagi, who was named as Lord Alpin's blessing. You have all heard of me, no doubt.'

7

Kariss turned to Lord Hightern and bowed her head. Corio held up his hands in a futile attempt to silence the uproar amongst the audience. Kariss swept her gaze across the sea of faces; she saw their disappointment. They had expected a heroine, not a rag-taggle woman who looked no better than a beggar. She caught snatches of their conversations and was dismayed to hear how taken with Martaani some of the people were. It was clear that a good number no longer expected much from her. Another whistle rang out from Viroco and the air hung with pregnant anticipation. Kariss took a deep breath, she had only one point to make.

'People of Brigantia,' she cried. 'Where are your gods?'

The crowd shifted uncomfortably.

'Brigantia did not come to you this morning as you welcomed in the sun. Why? She was not even called upon to renew her connection with you. Why? Have you forgotten your gods so quickly?'

Kariss stared out at the crowd, the sea of faces looked ashamed now. People glanced down as she looked at them, unable to hold her gaze. The silence was only broken by the thin wail of a young child, quickly hushed by its mother. Kariss had spent weeks worrying about this moment, not knowing if she would even be able to stand up and face everyone. Now the time was here, though, her nerves had left her. She no longer thought about how she would be received, about whether she would be able to convince everyone that she was the right choice.

She had felt the absence of the gods the moment she had arrived. It had reminded her straight away of London. Cold, meaningless existence, filled with greed and emptiness. Instantly, something inside her had shifted. She had the chance to stop that future becoming a reality. It propelled her on.

'Who did you implore when the rain would not stop? When you needed food on your table or a loved one saved?' She could feel the hatred emanating from Martaani at her back. She closed her mind to it, concentrating only on the people in front of her. 'Your gods have not forgotten you, but they had to keep their distance. The Romans are a threat to them all. They bring their own deities, their own religion, and their own priests to order it.' She glanced around her, 'I notice that those priests have not seen fit to show themselves today. Remember what your forebears told you? How the druids were persecuted and slaughtered on Ynys Môn.' She looked to Corio with a sad smile, 'Our druids are hated by the Romans. Already, they are being targeted by their priests and blocked from hearing Albion's gods.'

A shocked gasp rose up from the listeners as Corio's flushed face nodded, confirming the words. In the yew, Cailleach ruffled her feathers. From the corner of her eye, Kariss noticed the movement and recognised the signal.

'I may not look like a leader to you right now.' She looked down at her attire and shook her head before raising her arms skyward. 'But appearances are deceptive. The only thing you need to know is that I bring the gods with me.'

Overhead, thunder crashed and the eagle soared. The raven took to the air and flew, cawing her raucous cry over the heads of the crowd. She landed on Kariss's shoulder. 'We stand side by side. Strong in the face of those who would deprive us of our heritage.'

The Roman watchers were tense now, preparing themselves for problems as the crowds erupted.

It took a number of whistles to bring the audience under control again. Enda gave up her seat to Kariss and returned to Uurad's side, relieved to be away from the animosity of the woman she had been sitting beside. Martaani was now the one to sit uncomfortably. The raven had not left Kariss's shoulder as she had taken her seat. The vicious, thick bill was only inches away from Martaani's head but when she turned to sneer at it those sharp, beady eyes had looked at her with such a knowing stare that Martaani's insides had twisted with shock. It was as if this bird truly was the black goddess herself.

Once more, Corio was on his feet. He was readying the people for the vote. Martaani forced her attention away from the bird to listen.

'Those of you who cast your vote for Martaani, shout out now,' he called. A few voices sounded but were soon cut short as the people nearby glared them into silence. 'Those of you who cast your vote for Kariss…' he got no further. The deafening cries of the crowd drowned out his voice.

Martaani froze in her seat. Anger and humiliation warred for priority. She stole a glance sideways at Kariss but all she saw was the raven's beak opening wider and wider, as it let forth its own cry. Fear was not an emotion Martaani allowed in herself but she felt it now. She looked around her and caught sight of

Proculus moving towards the dais with a handful of his men. With all the dignity she could muster, she rose from her seat and left the dais. Proculus took her arm and they slipped through the crowds, leaving the Brigantes to celebrate their stupidity.

Only those who had been sitting closest to her saw her leave. No one made a move to stop her, though a small group of Epidii warriors followed at a distance. At the edge of the crowd the warriors were joined by some of the guards set by Tholarg. Unnoticed, the warriors formed a ring around The Gathering, faces outward, alert for any approaching danger.

As Kariss took to her feet, the raven cawed loudly again. The sound was drowned out by the cheering Brigantes but the vibrations of it cleared the air on the dais, shattering the heaviness that Martaani's presence had created. Even in the woman's wake the air had remained coagulated and oppressive. Corio felt his essence lighten, unbalancing him for a moment so that he almost staggered. He was calmed by the feeling of a broad, motherly smile in his mind. The wren was hidden in the branches of Ioho, too small to risk the jubilant crowds. It would not have mattered which guise she had chosen for The Gathering, Brigantia would still have been overwhelmed by the reactions of her people. Her tiny eyes sought out her druid, eager to see the moment that he realised their connection had at last been re-established.

It had been harsh yet necessary to keep the Pontiff's block in place. Albion was a small, dissected land compared to the vast swathes of the Roman Empire. Only stealth, cunning and a swift final blow could defeat the greater army. The gods were in no doubt that these islands could hold out against a prolonged campaign. Allowing themselves to assume the weaker-looking position was their way of easing the Romans into a false sense of superiority. If they appeared easily mastered, the Romans would have no need to send for re-enforcements.

Forgive me, my friend, she spoke in his mind. *You played your part in this well. Your position was not an easy one.* She did not need to hear his response; she already knew what he would ask. *You would have been the first person the priests targeted had we not succumbed. I would not have you harmed if I could help it. There is still a great deal for you to do. Kariss needs all the strength she can gather around her now. Allow her only until midday to enjoy her success then you must bring the leaders together and plan for battle. Martaani will not be leaving quietly.*

Corio gave a firm nod of his head in answer to her, his attention taken by the raven flying away. As he watched the bird land back on the yew, he noticed the tiny brown body of the wren next to her. He smiled inwardly at the incongruousness of the bird forms they each chose to inhabit. The Goddess Brigantia, High One of the Brigantes, a diminutive figure now next to the gnarled and aged form of the hag goddess Cailleach.

Corio wasted no time. He held both his arms skyward and silence fell over the crowd as he called out to Brigantia.

'Deae Nymphae Brigantia, hear me and see us now. This day, your people have made their choice. They have chosen Kariss as the next leader of our great nation. This day, we acknowledge her true born right to the throne, and honour her standing as Lord Hightern's heir.'

Lord Hightern was on his feet, holding out a golden torc. It was the one Kariss had already seen about her neck in the vision Coll had given her. It seemed such a long time ago since she had woken under the old hazel tree on Long Water island; was it really only a few moons? She blinked back her emotions. There was no doubt in her mind now that she would be leading a host into battle soon. She was frightened and strengthened at the same time. She barely heard the words spoken to her as she bent and let the king place the torc around her neck. Dimly, she heard cheers, they sounded far away.

This is your destiny, child, she heard Brigantia's voice say, bright and clear despite all the noise around her. *Remember where your strength lies… breathe… and know we will always be here for you. As you must always be there for your people.* Then the goddess was there, standing next to Lord Hightern, smiling. She stepped forward, embraced Kariss and placed a kiss on her forehead 'Be strong, Kariss.' She stepped back, still unseen by anyone else.

As if surprised, she cast her head quickly sideways before melting back into the ether. The noise of the cheering audience rushed back to Kariss and with it came the harsh call of the raven. The druids all looked up to see her flying overhead agitated. Then both they and Kariss heard Cailleach and Brigantia call out together.

Run!

A heartbeat later, one of Tholarg's warriors yelled from the edge of the crowd. 'Romans! Soldiers coming, masses of them.'

Confusion followed. On the dais, Corio was the first to react. 'Quickly, get Lord Hightern to safety.'

Bodvoc grabbed at Corio as he passed, 'Take her to the Straiph.'

Corio had no time to puzzle over Bodvoc's words; he turned away and called out to the alarmed crowd. 'There is danger coming. Run, leave this place now whilst you still can.'

Only a fool ignored a druid's warning. The people ran. Within their midst, Umar urged them on, all the while trying to hurry in the direction from which the raven had flown.

Anniel and Garth pushed their way through Uurad's remaining guards who, along with a number of Stanwick warriors, now formed a protective ring around the dais. They dived onto the platform to Kariss's side, swords already in hand.

Anniel thrust one towards Kariss, 'Here, you will need this.'

'There was a warning from Brigantia,' Kariss told them, ignoring the sword, 'she said to run.' Corio looked sharply at her but said nothing.

Panic was rising as the sounds of screaming began filtering through the stampeding people. Her people, Kariss thought. She wasn't just here for the gods; she was here for them as well. She felt sick with fear, just like when she had faced her old tormentor back in England - the man who became her landlord and tried to rape her. The gods had helped her then and she must trust that they would help her now. 'But how can I run yet? I must see the people safe first.'

'You must. Now is not the time to ignore the gods,' Garth growled, trying to usher them from the dais.

'There are plenty of warriors to help,' Anniel said. 'If anything happens to you now then Martaani wins. Do you not see that? If she takes you out before you are queen, she takes your place. Here.' Anniel thrust the sword into her hands. 'You may still need this.' He put a hand on Corio's arm. 'We need you with us.'

Corio nodded, his mind reeling with everything that had happened. Ahead of them, people were starting to turn back, creating pandemonium as further back people still surged forward. An image filled Corio's mind of the wren and the raven, standing safe on the tree. Ioho, he thought, and suddenly Bodvoc's words made sense. He signalled to the others to follow him and pushed his way towards the yew. Torwain was still there beneath its boughs and he joined them as Corio led the way past the tree, forcing through briars and heading to a cluster of blackthorn. Garth hung back to make sure they were not followed but no-one else came near the bramble barrier. He sent up a silent prayer of thanks and ran to join the others.

He caught up with them as they rounded the stunted, thorny trees. Ahead, Corio dropped to his knees and crawled forward. Everyone else followed closely. Long, vicious thorns hidden amongst the dense branches threatened to bar their way but somehow they managed to make it into the centre of the ring of trees without mishap. Once there, they found that they could sit upright, closely packed together in the small space.

'Forgive me,' Corio whispered, pulling on his beard. 'I should have thought of the Straiph straight away. Bodvoc planted them when he first became archdruid for just such a happening. He has a number of such places hidden around the area. No one will find us here; there is only the one way in.'

Torwain looked about himself in naked admiration. He had never seen such a hideaway. Outside, the sounds changed from screaming to the clash of sword upon sword. It was over quickly enough but they did not dare leave their sanctuary. Eventually, they heard the sounds of men searching close by. At the unmistakeable lilt of a northern accent, they began to relax; the Romans must have been defeated. Corio held a finger to his lips and they sat in silence, listening.

They didn't glean much; the men were searching for any Roman soldiers hiding in the woods surrounding the ceremonial site. They soon passed them by, but still Corio waited. It was not until they heard the sound of a wren singing its little heart out amongst the small, narrow leaves that he let them leave.

Back at the fort, they gathered in the great hall. The guard had been tripled around the town; no Roman was getting back inside now. Beyond the palisade walls some of the northern warriors were busy setting up a new camp. There was plenty of wood and thatch, and small, makeshift houses were soon erected amongst the tents. The rest remained further away, out of sight for now, ready to receive any new forces that might arrive.

Old Cartivel joined them in the hall, in place of Lord Hightern. The excitement had taken its toll on the leader and Corio had insisted that he rest.

'It was a swift, well planned attack,' Tholarg told them. 'Like the jaws of a bear, they came at us from two sides, hoping to trap us in the middle. It is lucky we surprised them by having men surrounding the area. They had not foreseen that, and it slowed their attack, giving most the chance to escape.' He paused, glancing towards Kariss. 'Once they realised you had disappeared, they made a hasty retreat.'

Anniel squeezed her hand. Kariss felt sick. For the first time, she had tried to ignore the advice of the gods, and had Anniel and Garth not convinced her otherwise she would have endangered the very people she had been trying to protect. She took a deep breath and vowed never to think she knew better again.

'We fought them right back into the surrounding woodland but the trees soon become too dense for such combat,' Uurad said. 'I have left warriors patrolling there to make sure they do not return.'

Angry voices disturbed them from the passageway outside the hall. Umar's booming voice insisted he be let inside but the guards were under strict instructions. Garth strode over to the doorway and spoke quietly to them. They removed their spears immediately and Umar entered. His robe was torn and blood dripped down his face from a deep cut on his temple. He staggered over to the table, took stock of who was there, and frowned.

'Lord Hightern?'

'Resting,' Corio answered, 'as I believe you should do, my friend. You look done in.'

Umar shook his head and for the first time seemed to notice the blood as it speckled the wood in front of him. He took a linen rag from inside his sleeve and dabbed at the wound, wincing slightly. 'I encountered one of Martaani's priests in the woodland to the north of here. I wish I could say I had finished him off but we were interrupted by Martaani and her personal guard. It would not have been prudent for me to stay and fight. As strong as I am, I could not have taken them all on.' His hands gripped the table, white knuckles the only tangible sign of his annoyance at leaving a fight unfinished. 'The priests and servants were waiting, ready for flight. There was a certain amount of disarray; they could not understand how Kariss had escaped their grasp.

'They have a place, a fort; Trimontium, they called it. Before I was seen by the priest, I had been close enough to hear his conversation with one of the guard. They were waiting for news of the attack, of whether they would be heading back to Stanwick in triumph or north to this Trimontium.' He gave a harsh laugh, 'The priest said the people of Albion were a cunning and sneaky people who could not be trusted, not even in Votadini lands, apparently.'

Most around the table raised their eyebrows at that titbit of information but Galan was incredulous. He had arrived down in the area only the night before, with a small contingent of men. Others, he had assured them, were waiting ready for the call. 'I have already learnt to my humiliation what sneaking, treacherous peoples these Roman scum are. How dare they accuse us of the same, when we are only protecting our own lands?' A sudden thought crossed his mind. 'How is young Naraic? I have not seen him yet.'

'We thought it best to keep him out of harm's way. He is in a safe place, looking after another victim of Martaani's cunning.' Anniel looked at Garth, 'Will you go to How Tallon and bring them both back here after we are finished? You will need to take men and a litter with you.'

Garth nodded his agreement and the talk returned to what had happened at The Gathering.

'Do we have any idea how many of our people were killed?' Cartivel asked.

Kariss closed her eyes, asking the gods for strength. She would never get used to this - to learning how many had died in her stead.

Tholarg answered him. 'It is too early to tell, but it was evident the Romans were only targeting those on the dais; once they realised everyone had got away, they made a hasty withdrawal. But for the warning Uurad's man was able to give, it would have been much worse. It appears only those who ran directly into the soldiers' path were in danger.'

'It was not everyone on the dais,' Cartivel corrected. 'We were not quick enough to avoid the first soldiers, but they gave us no mind. It would not be in Martaani's interest to have anything happen to Lord Hightern just yet. Not now Kariss has been declared his heir.' The words he didn't say hung heavy in the air.

8

It was cool in the hall after the bright sun outside. Kariss felt a frisson of cold run up her bare arms; she rubbed her hands up them, feeling goose bumps. She had not managed to relax much since the brief meeting earlier. Whilst everyone else was resting, she had been talking with Brigantia.

'They had not invoked their gods or made any attempt to protect themselves,' the goddess told her. 'Had they done so, we would have been able to give you more warning.' She sighed, 'Martaani is a volatile woman if she acts on impulse as much as on planning. I am afraid of what this might mean.'

Kariss played with the torc around her neck; she was feeling its weight more and more. 'Martaani was fuming, she was certain that I would not be there, that the crown would be hers by default.' She thought of Dei, and of Anniel's family, 'We know how vicious she is when she is angry. It is then that she reacts swiftly and without thought for the consequences. I wonder if she even realises that it was her own actions in the north which united the warriors against her. I had nothing to do with it.'

Brigantia's face lightened. She could see the depth in Kariss that Cailleach had always insisted was there. She carried with her no ego, or self-importance. Instead, she had humility and kindness in her soul; it would carry her far. Outside the room, people were beginning to stir; Lord Highern must be ready for the war council. She leant forward and placed a kiss on Kariss's forehead.

'You must ensure that you protect the druids; without them, we will be lost. I fear for them. They will cling to their faith no matter what we tell them. We do not want it to be their downfall.' With those words she faded from view, leaving Kariss pondering her options. She had already given a lot of thought to the druids. The massacre at Ynys Môn had been horrendous not only because so many druids had been slaughtered but also because it had happened on sacred ground. The druids may feel that they were safe, hidden away inside their nemetons, but Kariss knew otherwise.

In the hall, tables had been dragged together. Lord Hightern sat with Cartivel and Corio on his left and Kariss and Anniel on his right. Behind him stood Viroco and Volisios. Around from Corio sat Bodvoc, with two men Kariss had not seen before. Opposite them, representing the northern nations, sat Loth, Tholarg and Uurad. The Damnonii and the Caledones were the two largest nations of the north, though neither was anywhere near the size of Brigantia. Uurad had bustled in with Tholarg before anyone could turn him away. He had stood with his arms crossed firmly across his chest, defying anyone to make him leave. His mismatched eyes were so fierce that no one had dared, so he took his seat with the others. At the final side of the table sat Carrick, Torwain and Umar.

Servants moved around them, setting out platters overflowing with fruit and nuts and ensuring everyone had their glasses filled with rich, amber-coloured mead. When they finally moved away, Lord Hightern cleared his throat and addressed the room.

'My friends, we gather here today to discuss these unfortunate, though not unexpected, events. I wish to thank you all for being here and to ask us all first to raise our glasses and drink a toast to Kariss, my confirmed heir.'

Everyone raised their glasses and drank to Kariss, who flushed and dipped her head in acknowledgement. As she did so, she noticed the cold, almost black, eyes of one of the unknown men glaring at her. His face was framed with long black curls and his skin had the weatherbeaten look of someone who spent the majority of his time outdoors in all weathers. She frowned, wondering what his problem could be, but the man refused to meet her gaze; turning instead to look at Lord Hightern, who was now announcing who was who. Kariss listened with interest as he introduced the man as Tarnn, Lord Hightern's leading horseman, and beside him Dainarr, the nation's current war leader.

Albion did not have armies in the same way the modern world did and this still came as a surprise to Kariss. A small contingent of permanent warriors were always close to the king and protecting strategic border areas but in times of trouble the mainstay of the armies would be called on from the general populous. They would be made up of various groups, organised amongst themselves by social class. The majority of warriors fought on foot, though horsemen and chariots were also used. All warriors ultimately answered to the war leader, including the leading horseman whose function was to direct those who were mounted or in chariots. Kariss supposed there must also be someone to head any sea-going vessels but if there was, he was not represented here.

Tarnn did not smile; instead, he seemed to bristle with ill-concealed hatred. Kariss felt heat creep up her cheeks; why was the man here if he was that annoyed at her presence? Dainarr could not have been more different. He was a few years younger, with dark blue eyes and a wide smile. He greeted everyone warmly, in sharp contrast to the gruff grunt from Tarnn.

Lord Hightern looked to Kariss to speak; she pushed her concern out of the way. Taking a deep breath, she introduced everyone on her side of the table, letting Tholarg, Uurad and Loth introduce themselves. Tarnn let out a snort as they did so and turned an angry face to Hightern.

'My Lord, is it not bad enough that we have to suffer these northerners in our woods, without having to suffer them around our table aswell? I see no reason for their being here.'

'You see no reason! No reason eh, lad?' Uurad was almost purple in the face, which made his eyes look even more alarming than usual. 'Let me tell you something.'

Tarnn's fist clenched on the table. He was in his thirtieth year and had not been called a 'lad' since he was about twelve. Uurad noticed but carried on regardless, 'If it were not for us "northerners"' he stressed the word sarcastically, mimicking Tarnn, 'then Kariss may not have made it down here at all. 'Twas a lass from my own nation that acted as her decoy, without care for her own safety.' Tarnn's face was getting redder. 'Not only that, but who do you think fought off the Romans today, eh? Was it your horsemen?' He did not wait for an answer. 'Was it hell.

It was us northerners. We were the ones in the woods watching out for ambush, first to retaliate and drive the Romans back. If it had not been for us, there would have been twice as many making it through to attack The Gathering.' He slammed his fist down on the table. 'That is why we are here!'

Kariss had never seen Uurad lose his temper before, though she had been warned that he could be volatile. She was glad he was not shouting at her. Tholarg and Loth were both grinning; though at least Loth made an attempt to keep his face straight. Beside her, she felt Anniel squirm; this was not the best way to start a meeting. Tarnn glared at Uurad, his face florid with rage, or embarrassment; it was hard to tell which. He had quailed slightly at the older man's anger but was determined to stand his ground.

'That is all very well,' he said, forcing his voice to remain calm and controlled. 'But this is a Brigante meeting, to talk about how we as a nation react to this blatant attack.' He looked directly at Lord Hightern. 'My Lord, are we to succumb to a northern rule now that she is here?' He flicked his eyes towards Kariss as he spoke.

At that, almost everyone around the table reacted, rising to their feet and shouting. Only Lord Hightern, Kariss and Bodvoc remained silent and seated. Bodvoc watched eagerly, his piercing blue eyes glinting in the afternoon light. He had seen Tarnn's anger boiling under the surface as soon as he had entered the room and wondered how long it would take before it showed itself. This was quicker than he had expected.

Of all the people there, Bodvoc was probably the least surprised at his outburst. He had heard the rumblings of discontent amongst the warriors, unhappy with the presence of the northern men. Whilst none of them wanted Martaani, they were wary of the northerners uniting against Brigantia once the Roman threat was defeated. The talk had started as whispers but Bodvoc knew only too well that whispers were apt to thread their way quietly amongst the people, tying them up in doubt and uncertainty. He understood the dangers in such new notions, Verbia had taught him well. The maiden goddess was bound with limitless possibilities, each one starting as a whisper.

Often, Bodvoc gave the impression that he was psychic. He would know things that were about to happen before anyone else did, all because he kept his ears open for whispers and the slightest sparks of ideas. He'd had time, therefore, to prepare a reasoned counter-argument to Tarnn's worries. He waved a hand to call Viroco over and spoke quietly in his ear. The guard nodded and moved to pass the message to Lord Hightern. Viroco banged his hand on the table and everyone looked up in surprise. Lord Hightern held up his hands for quiet.

'My friends, please.' His voice was quiet but it cut through the animosity in the room like a knife. 'These misgivings about the northern tribes have no place at my council table. The prophecy was clear. Kariss would unite the northern tribes to help us defeat the Roman threat once and for all. We do not go against the gods here, Tarnn.'

Tarnn looked murderous. 'They have done that, Kariss is declared. So why are they still here? If they unite against us…'

'Then you will have been the one to give them the idea.' Bodvoc spoke up. It had been a long time since anyone had heard him speak at a meeting and those who knew him were surprised at how strong his voice still was. 'The northerners are here because the Romans threaten their own lands. They have the sense to see that uniting now before the invaders have the chance to get a foothold in Albion is the wisest thing to do. The Romans are not yet defeated; they have not left our shores. I do not believe there is anyone who expects them to leave peacefully after their actions.' He smiled at the three northern men. 'I am quite sure that you have had to put aside your own petty arguments to be here; why is it that you cannot, Tarnn? Why do you persist in this needless scaremongering? Are you in the pay of Martaani, sent here to cause trouble from the inside?'

Tarnn's mouth fell open. He had been a stout and committed Brigante man all his life. Never had anyone been given reason to suggest otherwise. He looked around the table at the faces staring back at him, his mouth opening and closing like a fish gasping for oxygen.

Finally, Kariss got to her feet and signalled for everyone to be seated again. 'I am sure that Tarnn's actions mean no such thing. He has the right to be concerned about Brigantia's safety. If he did not, he would have no place heading up the cavalry.' She held up her hand to stop another outburst from Uurad, raised her eyebrows and continued, 'However, I can assure you that on this occasion your fears are unfounded. The north has already suffered far greater atrocities at the hands of Martaani and the Romans than Brigantians could possibly imagine. And whilst I am sure you intended no such offence, your accusations are insulting to every northman.' Her heart was thumping in her chest. 'As well as myself.'

Uurad sat back in his chair, appeased. At her side, Anniel was impressed. Apart from her speech at The Gathering, this was the first time she had really spoken as a leader. Tarnn opened his mouth to reply but Kariss talked over him, giving him no chance to continue his argument. 'Many people in the north have been killed or tortured in Martaani's quest to stop me. Their blood is on my hands; the guilt runs through my veins and will remain there as long as I draw breath. No matter that I was not the one holding the blade.' Her voice wobbled a little.

'My husband's family was all but wiped out by her; their blood will stain the cobbles of Dun da Lamh fort for ever more. The archdruid Dei, from the most important nemetons of the whole north, was murdered at her hand. Murdered because he kept secrets which safeguarded my whereabouts. People have been locked up in burning crannogs, children have been tortured in front of their parents, druids defiled and murdered. I am quite sure there is much more that we have not yet learnt about...'

A noise at one of the doorways made her stop. She looked up to see a man trying to push past the guards. He was staring straight at her. His intense dark eyes looked shocked. There was something familiar about him and it sent a jolt through her.

Hightern signalled the guards to let the man through. 'Taratus, I am sorry but this is a private meeting.'

Taratus dragged his eyes from Kariss and inclined his head to the king in respect. 'I understood it was to be a meeting to discuss the safety of Brigantia. Surely representatives from all the forts are included?' He looked around the table and seemed to realise for the first time that this was not the case. His face registered surprise and relief, though this was quickly hidden.

'There will be such a meeting. But it is not today. You will be notified when it is to happen. Now I am afraid I must ask you to leave us.'

Dismissed, Taratus nodded his head at the king, threw an unreadable look at Kariss, turned on his heel and marched from the hall. Kariss sat down; so that was her traitorous cousin? The man she had spent her childhood promising to marry. She shivered, unable to get the intensity of his stare out of her mind. Bodvoc leaned across Hightern towards her: 'A silly, angry man but of no consequence. Do not confuse his embarrassment at his mistake for more animosity. I am afraid he does not always understand how he is perceived.' She was saved from having to answer by Tarnn. He sat with his hands held up in a peaceful, apologetic gesture.

'I can see I spoke in haste. I had only Brigantia's safety in mind. We do not always share easy relations with the Votadini to the north east, nor the Novantae across from our north west shore. It is only natural to assume that other northern tribes are equally as confrontational.' He held his glass out to the northern leaders. 'I am sorry for your losses… Truly,' he added at the sight of their incredulous faces. 'When I am wrong, I say I am.'

The three men looked at each other. Loth shrugged his shoulders; he could see no sense in keeping the disagreement going. He reached for his glass and the other two followed.

'I hope that you will forgive me.' Tarnn took a drink. His face lost some of its hard lines as the three men followed suit. He turned to the rest of the table. 'When my actions bring my fealty to Brigantia into doubt, I can only beg forgiveness. I can assure you that my loyalty is as strong today as it has always been.' There were tears in his eyes as he spoke; it left no one in any doubt that his words were true. Clearly, Bodvoc's accusation had cut him to the core, as the druid had known it would. He held his own glass out to Tarnn before taking a sip. Everyone else did the same and the atmosphere around the table relaxed, along with the strain on the cavalryman's face.

Lord Hightern banged his goblet on the table, 'Now that we are all friends, I will proceed. I have only a short while left on this fine earth. Brigantia is calling me home, and I will not be able to resist her for much longer. I am under no illusions as to how little use I can be in this current situation. I therefore propose to pass much of the reins over to Kariss from this point forward, whilst I take on a more advisory role. If she will agree, that is.'

Kariss looked at him, stunned; the argument had shaken her more than she would like to admit. She had expected people to take some time to get to know her, to get used to her strange ways before they felt comfortable around her, but Tarnn's outburst indicated a level of mistrust that could not be his alone. Now, just as that realisation was sinking in, she was being asked to stand up and begin ruling straight away. Was she ready? She thought of Mailcon, how he had stepped up to ruling the Vacumagi people years before he had expected he would be needed, and wondered if anyone was ever truly ready for such a task. In the back of her mind, a fumbled saying about people having greatness thrust upon them tried, but failed, to become clear. What did become clear, though, was the image of the goddess Brigantia's face looking at her with so much hope and trust; of Cailleach's piercing green eyes smiling at her, and of Verbia, shining with all the possibilities of a new adventure. Kariss hid her trembling hands beneath the table and forced her voice not to betray her.

'I would be honoured,' she answered the king. Only Anniel beside her realised how much those simple words had taken. He laced his fingers between hers and held her hand tightly, hoping that some of his strength might pass into her.

Lord Hightern beamed as the rest of the table bowed their heads to Kariss. 'We have waited a long time for this day.'

'I do not come to you believing I have all the answers,' she said as all eyes turned to her. 'Nor do I expect you to have faith in me until I have proved myself worthy. You have already proved yourselves, otherwise you would not be here. I look forward to learning from each of you. I am going to need as many advisers as possible to...' She stopped short, throwing an uncomfortable glance in Lord Hightern's direction.

The king smiled, 'This is your time, Kariss. I am almost dead already, you will not offend me.' His voice was now little more than a croak.

Kariss flushed, still unsure. Cartivel came to her rescue. 'I understand that you have had much help from the crone, Cailleach, so you will understand the wisdom we old folk possess. We are proud to carry such knowledge, for we have lived long and hard to accumulate it. But what use would all this wisdom be if we refused to see when our light was fading? Only a fool would ignore what we have to offer but we do not delude ourselves, we are only a small part of what is needed now. Vitality, energy and action are the greater part and we cannot provide that. Age must ever give way to youth, this will never change. Just as Bodvoc moved aside for Corio and I moved aside for Dainarr, Lord Hightern is moving aside for you. Death will claim us three soon enough, it does no good to pretend otherwise. Speak freely, make your plans as if you were queen already. We will support you all we can and we will tell you should you err. Make use of us, make use of our wisdom, for soon enough we will be gone.'

'The wheel turns, Kariss,' Bodvoc added. 'Now is the time for the maiden, but she will not get far without the mother and the crone. All are needed to pass through the challenges we face. You are the one the prophecy talks of, you are the one to lead Brigantia through these troubled times and I can already see why.'

His words were met with much nodding of heads; even Dainarr and Tarnn were nodding. Anniel squeezed Kariss's hand again. She wanted to protest, to ask why they were now all so sure of her, but she noticed Tholarg pull his shoulders back, straightening his spine. He lifted his chin and gave an almost imperceptible nod of his head in her direction. She swallowed her words and her doubts; now was not the time. Straightening her own back, she tried her best to be the woman they needed her to be.

'It is good to know that such help is here and I thank you for your words of encouragement. We must all work together to rid Albion of Martaani and her

Romans. These are frightening times. The prophecy is clear, but the outcome is not. As far as I am aware, the prophecy was that I should obtain Lord Alpin's blessing in order to defeat the Roman challenge to the throne.' She looked at Corio.

'That is correct.'

'In many ways, I have already fulfilled that prophecy. I have defeated Martaani's challenge to the throne, but only for now. I do not doubt that she will be back. We cannot relax until the Romans are driven from Albion's shores once more.'

'We cannot relax until Martaani is dead,' Uurad interrupted. 'She is the female line, her children will always be waiting in the wings.'

'She does not have any children,' Umar told him.

'Yet.' Uurad stood and slammed a hand down on the table. 'We need to crush this line once and for all. It is the only way to end the threat.'

Kariss looked around the table. It was clear that everyone agreed with Uurad. She knew this was war and that war involved a lot of death. Already, there had been far too many, but at what time did a war death become murder? She pushed the thought away for now.

'I think it is clear that we need to know where this Trimontium that Martaani has fled to is. We need as much information about her as possible and I believe it would help if she knew nothing about us getting it. The less she knows of our knowledge and plans, the better.'

Everyone around the table voiced their assent. Kariss turned to Torwain and Carrick, 'Can I ask you two to do this?'

'I can give you guidance on some of their known camps,' Dainarr told them as they gave their assent. 'We have been keeping an eye on them with the help of Tarnn's men.'

Torwain smiled and for a while the talk concentrated around the whereabouts of the Romans and the belief Kydas had that he had been held somewhere in the Votadini lands. Kariss sat back in her seat and allowed herself a few deep breaths. 'You are doing well,' Anniel whispered in her ear. He had kept her hand in his under the table the whole time but the odd squeeze of her fingers could not adequately convey how proud he was of her performance.

He had wondered how he would feel, taking a back seat to his wife in the discussions, but when it came to it, he found that it was easy. He would find his place soon enough, for now he was content to be Kariss's support.

Umar twirled his empty glass between his fingers, sending it faster and faster until the base bumped off the table, threatening to break. He snatched it up before any harm came to it and looked at the staring faces around him. 'Maybe it is time to move on to the next point?'

Dainarr cleared his throat, looking to Kariss for permission to speak. She nodded. 'Our scouts have informed us that there is no sign of Romans gathering in any of our neighbouring nation's lands, even the Votadini. As we still need to keep our borders protected, I think that it is time to send out a war cry. We have no idea where an attack could be coming from; we do not want to be short of warriors.'

Again, everyone agreed. 'I was surprised at the number of Brigantian warriors,' Loth commented. 'I had expected there to be far more of them given the size of your nation.'

'We expected no trouble at The Gathering itself. We thought the Romans would harry our borders first, try to take out our numbers with small skirmishes, not strike at our heart in such a manner. The northern warriors are to our north east, so the Selgovae border was covered. I sent many of our men to protect the Votadini border, where I believed the greatest threat lay.'

Loth, Tholarg and Uurad nodded. 'Your reasoning makes sound sense,' Loth said. 'Might I suggest that we send small groups of our men to help keep watch over these borders, freeing up all your men to return here? Maybe one or two of your trusted warriors could lead each group?'

In that one sentence, Loth had made it clear that the northern warriors were here to support the Brigantes and not take over. He was not foolish enough to believe that Tarnn would be the only one to have had such concerns.

Cartivel smiled to himself. He had heard much of the Damnonii. In his younger days, they were a name that struck dread into a warrior's heart, even as far south as Brigantia. As the north quieted, the rumours lessened, but Cartivel had never forgotten the stories he had heard. He was pleased that their current leader was so diplomatic, though he had no doubts that the Damnonii warriors were still as fierce. 'Perhaps Tarnn would consent to sending a few of his men with you? They could get word back to us quickly, should the need arise.'

Loth frowned at this but then his face lit with a smile and he nodded thoughtfully. 'I was thinking of sending some of my own horsemen for just such a purpose, but it would indeed be wiser to have men who know the land.'

The suggestion pleased Tarnn; he may have rescinded his earlier hostility but his concerns had not fully left him. Sending some of his men to keep an eye on the northerners addressed those worries perfectly.

Lord Hightern held up his hand; his voice would not carry over the others. 'As soon as I sound the war cry, every able-bodied man and woman will be called to fight. Our numbers will swell tenfold; it will put much pressure on our supplies.'

Anniel spoke up at last, 'I think it is still a little early for that but maybe the people should be warned to be ready for the call.'

'News of the attack on The Gathering will spread very quickly,' Corio said. 'Martaani spoke well. Given time, she may have convinced many people to vote for her. Those who appreciated her words soon realised their mistake when Kariss began to speak. I saw the looks of shame on their faces. They will fear Martaani even more now and because of that, they will take warnings of her silken words and swift retribution far and wide. The people will be ready when the call comes, of that I have no doubt.'

'Still, it would not hurt to send word out,' Tarnn added. He wanted to make damn sure Brigantia was well accounted for when the fighting began. 'I will send riders to warn the people to be ready.'

'I think we have covered everything we can for now.' Corio stood and looked around the table, he was conscious of Lord Hightern's waning strength. It had been a long, hard day for the king and it had taken its toll. 'Has anyone anything further to add?'

'I have just one more point to make,' Kariss said. 'Martaani may be here for the throne but the Romans are here for the land. They plan to drive out our gods and replace them with their own. We know from the last time they were here that they will target the druids mercilessly and, from what we witnessed on the way here, that has already started. It may not be the usual preparations for war, but I want the druids protected.'

The air thickened around the table as each person considered the impossibility of her words. Umar was the first to voice his disapproval. 'The nemetons are sacred places buried deep in the land; the druids will not give up their locations so that they can be guarded. Neither will they put their own wellbeing before that of others. If the war cry goes out, the druids will fight along with everyone else.' He bristled as he spoke, his face almost as red as his robes.

The words were barely out of his mouth before Dainarr jumped in. 'We cannot spare the men to guard them. It is ludicrous to even think of such a thing.'

Tarnn snorted, he needed no words to make his opinion known. Everyone else was agreeing, only Torwain and Bodvoc remaining quiet. Torwain's capture was still fresh in his mind, as were Cernunous's words of warning. He closed his eyes and willed the memories to fade. Bodvoc, however, was watching Kariss thoughtfully. What she was proposing was new and unheard of and it piqued his interest. They were not facing an ordinary threat, maybe everyone else had forgotten that? This time, the threat was from gods as well as men, and the druids were caught in the middle.

So far, everything that had worked in their favour had been unlike anything that had been known before. Even three of the four druids around this table were unlike any that had been previously known; Umar was a warrior druid who had travelled and fought extensively, never had any druid been so battle-hardened; Torwain had retreated further into the wilderness than anyone would have believed possible, he was as much animal as he was human, with senses far superior to those of anyone else; even Bodvoc himself was extreme, for almost ten years he had played the part of a failing senile old man. It had given him the leeway to be able to do the strangest of things without comment or question, things such as planting the Straiph hiding place that had saved Kariss today. He wondered how many of his other actions would be needed before all was done.

He dragged his wandering mind back to the meeting and watched as everyone continued to grumble at Kariss's suggestion. She let the dissent rumble on for a few minutes before raising a hand for silence. 'I have no intention of suggesting that anyone guards the druids, nor will I ask them to stand by and watch others fight and die in front of them.' She took in a breath and looked around the table, 'I want them to leave Brigantia.'

Only Bodvoc smiled, everyone else was in uproar. Kariss caught the old druid's eye across the table, relieved to see the understanding in his face. She sat back and let the arguments run. Beside her, Anniel was shaking his head. There was no way the druids would agree to this.

Eventually, everyone seemed to realise that Kariss was not arguing back. Instead, she sat in a pool of calm, serenely watching them.

'There is no argument here,' she told them, when their voices trailed away. 'The druids leave, or the druids die.' She shrugged, 'It's that simple.'

Everyone turned as someone rapped on the table. Bodvoc put down his glass and looked around at them all. 'Tell me what ordinary measure has worked against these Romans so far?' He waved a hand at Kariss, 'Was dragging someone through time in order to keep her safe not extreme? Was having her travel all the way to the Vacumagi lands with only a boy as company, whilst the greatest danger to our nation turned the land upside down looking for her? Do any of you propose for one moment that any of that would have been agreed had there been a prior meeting about it?

'We are facing an extreme threat; our gods are facing an extreme threat.' He pointed at Tarnn and Dainarr, 'You think like warriors.' He pointed to Umar, Corio and Torwain, 'We think like druids. Kariss thinks for all that and everything in between. She has seen things, done things, experienced things most of us will never be able to understand. Always until now, we druids have been the ones with the ear of the gods, the only ones who could speak for the hidden ways. Now we have Kariss, and she is different to all who have gone before. Do not dismiss her so readily. Hear her reasons. I think you will be surprised.' With that, he sat back and folded his arms.

For too long, Bodvoc's words had been treated with a tolerant smile. People had forgotten what a force he had been in his day. They remembered now and felt suitably chastised. They squirmed in their seats as his words peppered them.

Kariss stood, her chin defiant but her voice soft. 'I am in no doubt as to how serious this matter is. If we fail, Brigantia will be lost. The Romans will come in ever-increasing numbers and the rest of Albion will fall. Our gods will be driven out, replaced by the Romans' own deities. Those that defy the Romans will be subdued, the worst offenders sacrificed to their gory entertainments. Maybe you have not heard of these? Let me tell you, they are not the wont of normal people. Crucifixions, death by wild animal, human torches, to name but a few.'

'I have seen this with my own eyes,' Umar interjected. 'I have witnessed things in their lands that no man should ever have to see, let alone endure. Some of the worst punishments are for people who follow a small religion called Christianity. I do not know why this particular one bothers them so much but it shows their aggression towards religions they do not approve of.'

'When I was in the future, the ancient Romans were known to have persecuted a number of religions. The time-lines may be different but the people are the same. I know the things they did; I know the effects of their presence in Albion. It is not something we can allow to happen again.' Kariss's voice cracked, she took a sip of mead. 'The druids are at far more risk than everyone else. The Romans need the people or they will have no one to rule, but the druids are their Achilles Heel.' She shook her head as their blank faces reminded her of the modern term. She tried again, 'The Romans rule by control and conformity, yet the druids encourage self-reliance. They cannot be broken;

they are strong and will not back down. The Romans fear that strength more than anything because they do not understand it.

'We do not know if we can beat them but if Brigantia falls, who will keep our gods alive? The people will try but they will have to conform if they are to survive and, before long, the gods will fade to nothing. We need the druids, the gods need them; it is vital that they should survive. Take the druids from Brigantia, keep them as far from the Romans as possible, and should we fail, our people and the gods will still stand a chance.' Kariss paused for a moment, taking another drink of mead to wet her dry throat before delivering her final point. 'Think of them as our last line of defence.'

There were no more arguments.

9

'Is Kariss alright?' Naraic toyed with the small black hag stone that hung around his neck, his eyes darkening to a midnight blue.

'Kariss is fine, I promise,' Garth assured him. 'I would not lie to you.'

Naraic had known something was wrong the moment he spied the men making their way up the hill to the stone circle. There was something about the way their eyes darted here and there, alert for any danger. He had bombarded Garth with questions as soon as he was within hearing distance. Cloud, sensing his anxiety, had immediately begun barking; only stopping when Naraic put a hand on his head.

'Everyone is safe and in a meeting, these guards are just a safety precaution. We think all the Romans have fled into Votadini lands but, just in case, Kariss wants you back in Stanwick as soon as possible. Both of you,' he added, smiling at Kydas.

'Do you know if my wife was there?' Kydas asked Garth as he struggled onto the litter.

The guard shook his head. 'I could not say, there was no time to find out before I left but we will be back before long. The journey will be uncomfortable for you so Torwain, another of our druids, made you this.' He held out a leather water pouch filled with a concoction of willow bark and valerian.

Kydas drank the sour potion and gritted his teeth; it would be too much to bear if he lost Faela now. He shut his mind to the possibility; fretting about it would only make things worse. His long confinement had taught him well. In the first few weeks he had made himself sick with worry. He had not believed Martaani when she had first threatened to hurt Faela. He had convinced himself that his wife was also a prisoner; driving himself almost mad imagining all the things that she was being put through. It was only after overhearing his captors speaking outside his cell that he had finally accepted that she was safe. After that he had sealed his love for her behind an iron door in his mind, never letting himself dwell on what had or what could be. He retreated into himself, leaving only a shell for the Romans to torment. He told himself that every blow and every burn he received kept those he loved a little safer. In this way, he kept hold of his sanity and even found his mental strength beginning to improve. Now his bruises helped him once more. As he rattled around on the litter, he focused on the pain. There was hardly a part of him that did not hurt. He tuned out Naraic and Garth's voices and let the pain engulf him as Torwain's concoction slowly got to work on his battered body.

He was barely aware of entering Stanwick, of being lifted from the litter, carried to a room and placed on a bed. It had been months since he had lain on a soft, warm sheepskin. His body sank into it, relaxing fully for the first time since his capture. He was asleep almost at once.

That night was the first one Kariss had ever spent in Stanwick. They had been allotted rooms within the fort itself which, though small, were infinitely better than anything they had slept in since leaving Dun da

Lamh. Despite her exhaustion, she struggled to sleep, constantly pulling at the torc around her neck.

'You will not always notice it,' Anniel had told her, fingering his own silver torc. 'You could just take it off to sleep, if it is bothering you too much.'

Kariss shook her head, she needed to get used to wearing it, alongside the fact that she really was the true heir to the Brigantian throne. Wearing the torc meant that she was not likely to forget very easily. There was so much she needed to remember now. Her head felt as if it would explode, it was so full. Even if Martaani decided to quit the shores of Albion without causing any trouble - not that anyone expected that to happen for a moment - Kariss's life was still about to change rapidly. There was no doubt that Lord Hightern was in the twilight of his life, they would not be sharing his workload for long. It was sad, she had liked him on sight. He had a wicked twinkle in his eye that spoke of mischief. It made her wonder what kind of a man he had been in his younger days.

Even with all the upset of the day and the worry about what would happen next, the king had never once made her feel as if he were unapproachable. It was so different from Lord Alpin who, although always friendly and kind towards her, had retained an authoritative and distant air, as if there was an invisible line drawn between him and everyone around him.

The thought of Lord Alpin brought a lump to her throat and she shifted uncomfortably on the bed. He had treated her so well, and died for her. She did not want the same end for Lord Hightern. Beside her, Anniel reached a hand out and clasped hers. 'What are you thinking?'

114

Kariss was not sure if she should be honest or not. She did not want to remind Anniel of his grief but she could feel a familiar panic rising again and knew she had to quell it before it got hold of her. 'I was thinking of your father and Lord Hightern.' She turned her head to look at him. 'How different they are.' She turned away. 'And how I don't want them to suffer the same end.'

'That cannot happen. Martaani has gone. She will not come back to Stanwick now and Hightern will not leave it. He at least is safe from her.'

They were silent for a while, each lost in their own thoughts.

All of a sudden, Anniel let out a long breath. His voice when he spoke was distant and thin. 'So that was the woman who killed my family. She looked so... beautiful; friendly, even. It was so hard to believe that she could be the one to have done it - until you stepped out of the crowd and started to speak. I was watching her face. She is not so pretty when she is angry.'

Kariss propped herself up on her elbow and looked down at him. Even in the dim candle light, his face looked drawn. She squeezed his hand but made no attempt to interrupt him.

'She tried to hide it but when the people began to cheer you, her face turned to stone. When she stood up, I thought she was going to try to kill you. I almost jumped up on the dais to stop her but she just left. She came so close to me and it was like I could feel the hatred coming off her in waves. I grabbed at my knife but one of her Romans pushed between us, and I lost my chance.' He rubbed his free hand over his face. 'I would have been no better than her.'

'You are no murderer, Anniel. You could have killed her then, if you had really wanted to. It was always going to be hard for you to see her today, sitting up there pretending to everyone that she was so good and pure. I could hardly believe that she was the right person myself at first. But you should have felt the tension around her. No one on the dais was comfortable. I have seen plenty of girls like that back in London, they look like butter wouldn't melt in their mouths but inside they are the meanest, most spiteful people. Martaani is an evil bitch, no one would have thought any less of you. Do not punish yourself.'

Anniel's face was damp and his eyes glistened with tears still waiting to fall. He had thought he was recovering from his families' deaths but coming face-to-face with their killer had shaken him more than he could have ever imagined. Not for the first time, he wished that he could speak with Nectan. His old druid would have known exactly what to say to him. His next choice would have been Torwain but he had left with Carrick to search out the Romans. Maybe he should try Bodvoc tomorrow? He was of an age with Nectan, Anniel should be able to talk to him easily enough.

Kariss could feel the tension in his body. Some of his words echoed in her mind… *so that was the woman who killed my family*. They sounded so desperate and sad, but he still had some family. Martaani had not killed them all. Gently, she reminded him. 'I am glad Mailcon decided to stay in the north with your sister. I was disappointed at first but Fayern should not be left alone.'

'Tharain, too. I know my brother really wanted to come with us but none of my family should ever have to see that woman again.' More tears fell and suddenly the dam wall that Anniel had built up around his emotions broke. It was the word 'brother' that did it. Inan, his youngest brother, had been so full of life and love. Martaani might not have been the one holding the blade that killed him but he held her responsible nonetheless. He remembered his little brother's crumpled body, lying in a pool of blood; how light it had felt as he carried it to the grave and placed him inside. He remembered his mother's last words to him, as Martaani's poison ate its way through her body; begging him to burn her body on a pyre so that she could rise up and finally see the resting places of both her son and her husband.

Kariss held Anniel tightly, tears pouring down her own face as she listened to his grief finally finding release. It had been a long time coming. The candle guttered and died, plunging them into darkness. Anniel did not notice, his eyes were closed trying to hold back the sorrow but the tears slipped out beneath his eyelids anyway. Inside, he felt a painful hollow. It was as if the cold lump he had carried around inside himself ever since he had found the devastation at Dun da Lamh had melted, turned into molten bronze and burned out his insides, right up into his throat. How could he ever feel whole again without them? How could anything be right in the world again? He felt Kariss's arms tighten around him and leaned into her, clinging on as if he were drowning.

In the darkness, Kariss needed the gods to give her husband some relief. She was not sure if Brigantia was the one to call. She was the mother goddess of the Brigantes, but Anniel was a Vacumagi. Did that matter?

It does not matter at all. Brigantia spoke in her mind. *He is here to protect you and so protect me, I shall always come to him when needed. But for now, it is not me he needs. He needs you, to keep doing what you are doing. To hold him, love him, to let him feel safe enough to let his emotions go. They will only weigh him down if he does not.*

It was strange conversing with someone who was not present. Kariss had no need to open her eyes to know that Brigantia was not in the room with them. The air had not changed and there was no light filtering through her eyelids. As if she could hear her thoughts, Brigantia explained.

My presence would only interrupt him now. I have no wish to encroach on his grief but I do want to speak with you, my child.

I cannot leave him now.

And nor should you. He will sleep soon, I will return then.

Kariss was left to tend to her husband. His sobbing was starting to subside. Kariss stroked his head, her own tears still falling. She had cried much more than Anniel had over the deaths of his family but this was the first time that her tears had not been swamped with guilt. She had seen Martaani now. Felt her malevolence. Finally, she understood what everyone had been telling her all this time. Her own guilt really was misguided. Martaani would have acted the same whomever her challenger was. Fate may have made Kariss that person but the blame for all the death and destruction was solely on Martaani's shoulders.

Beside her, Anniel's breathing had become soft and steady and she realised he had fallen asleep. Her own eyelids were feeling heavy and she struggled to keep awake.

Happy birthday.

Kariss gave a start. She had been so focused on The Gathering that she had forgotten all about her birthday. She thanked the goddess, stifling a yawn as she did so.

I will not keep you, my child; you need sleep just as much as Anniel does.

From deep within the ether above the bed, Brigantia looked down on them. It had been a hard evening for the pair but one that was sorely needed. They would both feel better now that they had cleared their energies of the weights they had been carrying. She knew that Kariss would always hold on to some guilt over the events of this year. It was in her nature to do so, Brigantia had no wish to change that. It was Kariss's concern for all around her, and her refusal to hold herself above everyone else, that was the very essence of what would make her a great leader. So long as she could keep the balance right.

I want to thank you for coming to Brigantia's aid. My nation needs you just as much as we gods do. Already my people have had to suffer much from Martaani's interference. She called on their goddess, Discordia, to cause disruption and chaos, hoping to unsettle the people. It has worked. More have died at the hand of Martaani's scheming than could ever be accounted for. I implore you, Kariss, when you are queen, do not forget the common people.

Kariss had spent the majority of her life living as a commoner. *There is no nation without them*, she told the goddess. *I will not forget.*

Light flared for a second in the room and Kariss felt a caress on her cheek. Something was pressed into her hand. She just had time to see that it was a small whittling knife before the light vanished and she was left alone with her sleeping husband. She rolled the knife over in her hand, wondering what its importance could possibly be.

The next morning, Anniel woke Kariss with a kiss. The sun was streaming in through the tiny window and, in the nests under the eaves, the young chicks were shouting for food.

'Thank you,' he said, stroking the hair from her face. His eyelids were puffy this morning but his eyes looked brighter than they had in weeks. 'I have sent Garth for some breakfast; I am going to speak with Bodvoc. I want to catch him early, I think he may be able to help me.' He gave her another kiss and was gone.

Kariss stretched out her body and pushed herself up from the bed. As she did so, her hand pressed down on something hard. She saw that it was the knife Brigantia had given her. She turned it over in her hand. It was not a knife she had ever seen before. It was small and had clearly been well used at some time in the past, though it didn't look like it had been well cared for lately. She hung it from her belt, intending to ask Umar about it later.

The fort was busy with people. Dignitaries from all over Brigantia were staying in the guest quarters, each anxious to find out the latest news. In the hall, food had been laid out on a large oak table: fruits, breads and meats, along with jugs of watered wine, goats' milk, and water. Kariss filled her plate, poured herself some milk and carried them over to where Naraic and Garth were sitting. She pulled out the little knife and started to cut her meat.

'Where did you get that?' Naraic asked, frowning.

'Brigantia gave it to me last night.'

He held his hand out. 'May I see it?' Something in his voice made Cloud sit up and whine, he put a paw on his knee and stared at him. Naraic ignored him as he ran his fingers over the knife, like he was caressing an old friend. He stopped at a nick in the pommel, rubbing his thumb over it again and again.

'This is my knife,' he told Kariss. 'At least, it was. My uncle gave it to me when I was first old enough to carry my own blade. He was always encouraging me to use it. It is the knife I gave to Brigantia as an offering when I was called to be your guide.' He looked up at Kariss, his blue eyes big and round.

She remembered Naraic telling her how he'd had a dream and then thrown the knife into a well for clear sight. It was just after he had killed his uncle... after his uncle had died, she corrected herself. Something jarred in her mind. She thought back over her conversation with Brigantia. She had been telling her of the disruption caused by the Roman goddess, Discordia, and about how many people had died because of it.

'Your uncle!' she cried, jumping in her excitement and sending her cup flying. Milk poured out over the table, dripping down through the slats. She could feel every eye on her as people wondered what was going on. Already she was the enigma everyone was hoping to get to know better.

Kariss ignored them, and the milk. Lowering her voice, she explained what Brigantia had told her when she had given her the knife. 'Don't you see, Naraic? You did not kill your uncle; it was Discordia causing trouble.' She shook her head. 'I don't know how she did it but it cannot have been you or Brigantia would not have given me back your knife.'

'May I?' Garth took the knife from Naraic and looked at it. 'It certainly shows signs of being in water for a while; you can see rust starting to come. Look, here and here.' He pointed out a couple of dark spots. 'You need to give this a really good clean, lad. It should be right as rain then.' He handed it back.

'May I join you?' They looked up and saw Corio hovering with his own food. Kariss hurried to clear away the spilt milk. When she returned with a fresh cup, Corio was looking at the knife and nodding his head.

'I think you are right,' he said, placing the blade on the table before them.

Someone called him from the doorway. He gave an apologetic shrug. 'It seems I am needed elsewhere.' Leaving his food untouched, he scurried away. Naraic watched him go without saying a word. He felt numb with shock. Could he really begin to let go of the knot of anguish that had settled deep within him all those months ago?

Kariss pushed the knife over to him. 'It is yours,' she said. 'Take it.' She smiled at him. 'And stop worrying, this is a good thing.'

Naraic took the knife. It settled in his hand as it always had. He itched to find a piece of wood to whittle but first, just as Garth had said, the knife needed a proper clean. His uncle had taught him to always look after his tools. They were expensive to come by and should be treated with care. He had carried his cleaning gear with him all the way to Dun da Lamh and back, regularly cleaning his other knife and Kariss's too. He still had the knife's sheath in his bag, tucked down at the bottom where it could not fall out. He stuffed the rest of his food in his mouth and took his leave. He would not be missed for a while. Garth was pleased to see the eagerness in his step. It had been a long time since the boy had something to be so pleased about.

The buzz of conversation in the hall had risen again. Here and there a word stood out from the rest. Kariss heard her own name numerous times and felt the hairs on the back of her neck prickle. Garth laughed when she told them. 'You will have to get used to it. You will be the talk of the nation for quite a while now. It will not all be nice, though; judging by the hard looks I have been getting, Tarnn is not the only one to dislike us northerners.'

10

Kydas did not wake until well after midday. At first he thought he was still a prisoner in the cramped box, his body was so stiff, but then he felt the sheepskin brush against his cheek. He opened his eyes. Above him, he could see a thatched roof. He noticed a new patch of heather and thought how apt it was that both he and his room should be in need of mending.

Gingerly, he moved his head so that he could look around. Pinpricks of light broke through the thatch here and there but the main light source was from where the leather door hanging had been pulled a little to one side. There was the usual hearth in the centre with its iron tripod, pots, trivets, tongs and pokers. A table stood on the far side of this with a couple of stools next to it. Two large trunks were pushed up against the wall and close to the doorway he could see a heap of discarded items. Kydas risked stretching out his limbs. At once, pain shot through him. He let out a groan and immediately heard movement. He craned his neck around to see. A woman had been sitting just out of sight; he heard something fall to the floor in her rush to stand and his heart leapt into his mouth as he realised it was his beautiful Faela.

Her hair was shorter than he remembered, her face lined with worry, but he did not care. He struggled to rise but the room swam and he grabbed onto her. There were tears in her bright eyes but he could not tell if they were tears of concern or tears of joy. His tongue felt glued in place. What words could possibly be right? Faela smiled at him; that smile he loved so much. It made her face shine and his insides melted even more. She raised a hand and gently cupped his face, using her thumb to caress his cheek. Then they were in each other's arms, holding on for dear life in case anything should try to part them again. Only when Kydas winced with pain did Faela pull back.

She hurried to the table and brought back a cup and plate. 'Torwain said you should drink this when you wake. It will help restore you and ease your pain.' She held the cup up so that he could drink, wiping away the dribble that escaped and trickled down into his beard.

Kydas pulled a face at the bitter taste. Why did tonics have to taste so foul? His stomach gurgled; it had been a long time since he had eaten. Faela handed him a piece of cold meat, watching whilst he ate it. She looked at him with wonder, as if she couldn't quite believe he was real. She continued passing him food until the plate was empty. Kydas sighed, replete. It was good to feel full again. He looked down at his gaunt body, suddenly ashamed at how he looked. What must Faela think of him now? Did she still live as a single woman? Had there been anyone else whilst he had been away? Would she still want him? Faela slipped her hand into his. She had always been able to read him, always known when something was wrong or when he was trying to hide anything. He had never been able to surprise her. She leaned forward and kissed away one of his concerns.

The gentle kiss grew in intensity until once again Kydas winced in pain. Faela moved to sit beside him on the bed, keeping his hand in hers. 'I searched for you for months,' she told him. 'Even when everyone kept telling me to give up, I never would. I was determined to find you fallen and injured somewhere.' She rested her free hand on her belly and when she spoke again her voice was quiet and strained. 'I lost our baby. I am so sorry.' A tear forced its way out of her eye and ran down her face. 'No one ever knew.'

Kydas felt his heart tear. He could hear the sorrow in his wife's voice and hated that she had been forced to endure this alone. One more thing to lay at Martaani's door.

'I lost it under the willow on the banks of Wendell; I buried it there in secret. I never even knew if it would have been a boy or a girl, it was too small to tell.'

Kydas reached an arm around his wife's shoulders. Ignoring the bruises on his ribs, he pulled her tightly against him and kissed her head. The smell of her hair was just as he remembered it. 'We will ask Kel to perform a blessing over it when we return. We have our lives ahead of us, we will have a second child.'

He was surprised when Faela shook her head; she pulled back slightly, so that she could look at him. 'Kel died, Kydas.'

The old druid had been a good man, always a little sad, and often distant when he thought no one was watching, but he had been a good man nonetheless. 'I have missed so much, how many more things have changed?'

'Shael is carrying a child again; she is getting big, it will not be long now. The children are excited and Taratus was pleased… for a while.' She trailed off, her one piece of good news turning sour in her mouth.

'I have heard some worrying things about your brother, I refused to believe them.'

Faela sighed. 'He is acting strangely; he is moody and always angry. I have heard talk that people think he is a Roman spy.'

'Tell me it is not true?'

'It is not.' Faela was adamant. 'I do not care what people say, it is not true. It cannot be.' She toyed with the silver bangle around her wrist. 'I know he is angry at Kariss. He feels that she should have come to see us first, that she should have at least sent word about our mother, but we have heard nothing from her. Still, he rallied our people to support her at The Gathering. He has strengthened all Wendell's defences and ensured there is plenty of food and weaponry ready in case Martaani brings war on us. I have not heard him say one single thing in support of that woman or her Romans.'

Her words were reassuring but then Kydas remembered all that he had been told and his relief dulled. 'He has been seen, with the Romans. He has been at Dumpender Law with them, and at Stanwick.'

Faela shook her head, 'He would not, he just would not.' Her brow pulled into a deep frown. Kydas would have given anything to be able to soothe that frown away but he would never lie to her.

'Kariss sent a spy into Stanwick, he brought back the news, and I know someone was passing information to Martaani from Wendell. She would ask me about things she had no other way of knowing about.'

His words were like rocks settling on her heart. Cold, hard and undeniable. Before she had time to answer him, the door curtain was pulled fully back, flooding the room with light. Garth ducked his head inside. Faela jumped, looking guilty.

127

'Should I come back later?'

'It is alright,' Kydas answered him. 'This is my wife, Faela. I was just telling her about her brother.'

'Ahh.' Garth stepped inside the room. He put down the bowl and the cloths he was carrying. 'I have brought some ointment for your bruises.' He smiled at Faela, 'But I imagine he would rather you apply it than me.'

'That I would,' Kydas laughed. 'Faela, this is Garth. He is Anniel's personal guard and someone we can trust.'

'We have met,' Garth told him, 'I have been sticking my head in here all morning waiting for you to wake and Faela has been sitting here since late last night.'

Kydas squeezed her hand. No wonder she had looked so worried.

Faela looked at Garth. 'Is it really true? Is my brother a traitor?'

Garth shifted his feet. He had no idea how to deal with an emotional woman. He tried to soften his words. 'He has been seen near to the Romans too many times for us not to question his loyalty but as yet we have no clear proof.' He shrugged. 'We do not know for sure, but it looks likely.'

To Garth's relief, Faela kept her composure. He quickly changed the subject. 'Kariss and Anniel would like to talk to you later, if you feel up to it?'

Kydas nodded. 'I would like some more time with my wife first, though.'

'But of course. You will be brought some hot food when it is ready. They will come after that; you have most of the afternoon until then.' Garth smiled. 'I will leave you alone for now.'

As soon as he had gone, Faela turned to Kydas. 'What bruises?'

He pulled up his tunic and she gasped. His stomach and ribs were a mass of deep reds, blues and purples. Here and there, cuts in various stages of healing crisscrossed his torso. 'I was not always this bad. They would leave me alone for weeks at a time but then they would get some news and beat me for more information. That is how I know someone was spying for them at Wendell.'

Faela was very careful applying the ointment. Even so, Kydas winced numerous times before she was finished. 'We will not be making any more babies for a while,' she told him firmly.

'I am sure we will find a way. Once we have more privacy.'

Faela laughed, her eyes glinting. It was a sight Kydas had thought he would never see again. He could face any number of injuries now that he had her at his side once more.

The afternoon passed far too quickly. There was so much to catch up on and so many hugs and kisses to enjoy. They cried and laughed and tried to explain just how much they had missed one another. Kydas had just finished telling the story of how he had escaped and found Kariss, only for them to have to escape again, when Garth called from outside.

'Can I come in? I have your food.'

As soon as they had eaten, Kariss and Anniel arrived. Faela had not seen her cousin yet and her stomach filled with fluttering nerves. She squeezed tight hold of Kydas's hand. Kariss had been equally nervous, wondering whether or not she would see her old best friend before her, or a stranger. She saw both.

There were flickers of the girl she used to play with all those years before. The defiant tilt of her head and those big brown eyes, but they had been cloaked by the intervening years. The cheeky, boisterous girl was now a strong, worry-worn woman.

'Faela, it is good to see you again.' Kariss opened her arms and Faela stepped into them. Kariss could feel her cousin's bones through her clothes. They had both been through tough times in the last few months. They pulled apart. After all their concerns, it was good to see each other again, it had been such a long time. 'I am so sorry it has taken me this long to come and see you. I should have come to Wendell, but there was never any chance. There was so much to do and at first I did not remember Albion at all.'

Faela looked at her in disbelief, 'You forgot Albion? How is that possible?'

'The goddess hid my memories to keep me safe. She hoped I would settle to my new life if I did not remember who I was and where I came from. They only came back to me after I started to return, but by then we were on our way north to find Lord Alpin.' She stopped when she saw Faela's baffled face, 'It is a long tale, too long for now. I promise I will explain better when I get the chance.'

'I am glad I did not have to forget you.' Faela smiled. 'I missed you so much.'

Kariss noticed the scar running along her cousin's jawline; she ran her finger along it. 'I remember this.'

They had been playing in a disused house not far from the fort. Their mothers had been collecting firewood nearby and the girls had sneaked off with Taratus to play. The inside of the house had bored them after a while. Outside, Taratus had dared them to climb up the conical roof, right to the top. Girls were far too scared to manage it, he had said. Kariss and Faela were not going to be bested by any boy. They hadn't notice the wicked gleam in Taratus's eye, or the fact that he never attempted to climb with them.

The roof had been easy to get onto; it overhung the walls until it reached almost to the floor. The girls had begun to race each other to the top. Just as they reached half way, there was a loud crack as one of the supporting timbers inside the roof split under the unaccustomed weight. Faela had fallen through the thatch, landing smack down on the central hearth inside, one of her arms at a funny angle and blood pouring from her cut face.

'We got into so much trouble that day.' Faela laughed. 'Taratus was so sorry. He never meant for either of us to get hurt. He told me later that he had just wanted to laugh at us when we realised how high up we were. Then he would have had to come and rescue us and we would have thought him so brave, but it had all gone wrong.' Concern flashed across her face for a moment, 'He missed you, too.'

The atmosphere in the room changed at the mention of Taratus. Faela's eyes grew watery, 'I cannot believe he has betrayed you, Kariss, he loved you so much. He was hurt that you did not come to us when you first returned. And he was angry. But to betray you? I just do not believe it.'

Kariss dropped her arm and shook her head, 'I don't want to believe it either but I cannot trust him now. He has caused too much suspicion.'

Faela took a step backwards, alarmed. She knew the punishment for treason. 'What are you going to do?'

Kariss pulled her face into a weak smile, letting it drop as soon as it appeared. 'I don't know. He was watched at The Gathering. He voted for me, as did all the Wendell people. He showed no signs of supporting Martaani and when the Romans attacked he helped to get all his people to safety. He even fought one of the legionnaires.' She shrugged, 'I do not know what to think.'

Kydas spoke up, 'Taratus is my good friend. I see how bad his actions look but he has always been the most loyal of men. I cannot believe that he has turned traitor. If he has been seen talking to the Romans then I can only think that it is to spy on them. He was so eager for you to return, he mentioned it often. I am hoping he will come and see me soon.'

'He has already left Stanwick,' Anniel answered him. 'He went at first light.'

'What? He cannot have, he would not have gone without telling me.' Faela looked at each of them in turn. 'He knew you had been found, Kydas, I was with him when I got word. He should have been here, he should have at least come to see that you were alright before running back home like a scared hind.' She dropped back to her seat. Kydas took hold of her hand.

'That is not like him,' he said. 'Something is not right.' The emotions of the day were starting to take their toll. Kariss noticed the slight tremor of his hands.

'You need to rest, we will speak again soon.' She bent and hugged Faela. 'It's wonderful to see you. I am so very sorry about your mother. She was a wonderful woman, I was looking forward to seeing her again. I hope her passing was a kind one?'

'Thank you, it was painful but swift. The illness was only on her for half a moon before we lost her. Father was sick with grief. He could not bear to stay at Wendell with all its memories so Lord Hightern gave him command of Mona. He will be pleased to hear that you are home again.'

'And what of Dimmi, I guess he is not so little anymore?'

At this, Faela and Kydas laughed. 'Indeed he is not,' Faela said. 'My little brother now towers over me. He left Wendell only a few years after you did. He went to train with the druids, we still see him often.'

'Even Taratus does not speak back to him now,' Kydas said. He tried to stifle a yawn but did not quite manage it.

'We must go,' Kariss said again. 'Rest is coming for you, Kydas. It is not fair that I keep you from it. We can catch up later, Faela.'

Faela helped Kydas back into bed then she too left, promising to return as it grew dark. The anticipation of sleeping beside him again filled her body with a tingling longing. Just to lie in his arms and know that she was loved - it was all she had wanted for so long. She almost skipped as she made her way through the town.

Umar was speaking with Dainarr in a small guard room by the entrance to the fort. He threw his arms wide and roared his welcome as she waved to him. Dainarr jumped back, eyeing the druid warily. Umar clapped him on the back and laughed. 'You have nothing to fear from me, my friend.'

Dainarr made his excuses and left the guard room, rolling his eyes at Faela as he passed. She couldn't blame him. Umar took some getting used to. She stepped inside, taking one of the small stools. 'Thank you for helping Kydas.'

Umar laughed again and sat down. 'I told you. The gods are never wrong.' The mention of the gods made his face darken. Nantosuelta's cruelty at the time of his father's death had not been forgotten.

Faela held out a wooden box. 'I think this is for you.'

Umar took the box like a small child, eyes wide with surprise and anticipation. He lifted the lid and dropped it with a cry when he saw what lay inside. Carefully, he picked up the small lock of hair, turning it over and over in his hand. He looked up at Faela, speechless.

'Kel was your father?' she asked him.

Umar nodded. It was the first time that anyone had made the connection.

'After you had gone, I went to his house and found him, he looked so peaceful. This was by his bed. Everything was so strange that day: the things you had said, the way you were acting and how upset you were. Then I found this and suddenly it all made sense.' She leaned forward and touched his arm. 'No one else knows, I took the box before anyone had a chance to see it. I will keep your secret for as long as you want.'

Faela was a blurr before him. He nodded his thanks and the movement cleared his vision for a moment. He saw Faela's concerned face looking back at him. Still he could not find any words to speak. He looked back at the box.

Faela reached inside and picked up a piece of willow. 'I think this must have been your teething stick. Shael had one for each of her babies, I recognise the marks on it; see where your little teeth scraped the wood?' She pointed to the marks where small milk teeth had chewed at the stick.

Umar touched the marks in wonder, blinking until his vision cleared enough to see them properly. He tried to remember but he had been far too young to lay down lasting memories.

'This must have been what they wrapped you in,' Faela pointed to a kidskin. 'And maybe these were your mother's?'

Umar lifted out a quartz point and a small stone carving in turn. He dropped the carving as soon as he turned it over and saw Nantosuelta's likeness looking up at him. He knew immediately that this would have been his father's icon, placed in the box to keep everything else safe. He wanted to smash it, to throw it across the room or grind it beneath his feet, but this box was all that he had of his father's: Kel's most precious possessions. Who was he to decide which ones were no longer precious? The icon would stay safe in the box with everything else and maybe one day Umar would be able to forgive her. He replaced the lid, patting it carefully in place. 'Thank you,' he said finally, grasping Faela's hand in a firm grip. 'Can you leave this with me for tonight?'

'It is yours now.'

Umar shook his head. 'I cannot keep it safe here. I am a long way from home and have much work to do. Can you keep it for me; take it back to Wendell with you, until all is done? There is no one else I can trust with this, you are the only one who knows.' At her agreement he added, 'I promise to tell you the whole story when I come to collect it. I will owe you that much at least.'

'You will owe me nothing.'

Faela watched him go, the box tucked under his robes but held tightly against his body, almost as if he could feel the warmth of his father from it. She returned to Kydas, bringing a few of her belongings from her small room in the fort. They had put Kydas in one of the guest houses close by. These had been left empty by the departed Romans and offered a little more space and privacy. She found her husband awake and waiting for her. His face lit up as she entered. She hurried over to kiss him, tripping over something on the way. Her toe was throbbing as if it would burst and she swore loudly, glaring back at the rock she had kicked.

She had noticed it there earlier and wondered why anyone would put such a thing on the floor. Not wanting to trip over it again, she picked it up to throw outside only to find that the stone was covering a shallow pit filled with the remains of something undeterminable. Now that the covering was removed, an awful smell was released. It made her gag, as did the sight of the maggots crawling all over what was there. She looked to Kydas in horror. Carefully, he raised himself onto his elbows to look.

'Fetch a druid.'

11

Lord Hightern rubbed a shaking hand over his face and made an exasperated sound. 'I do not know what to think. If it were any body else, I would have had him dragged before me.'

'The man is a liability and we cannot afford liabilities at the moment. Do not be too soft on him, just because you respect his family.' Cartivel had never had any time for doubts.

Kariss was about to speak when Bodvoc arrived, patiently helped along by Corio. He might not be the senile old man he had pretended to be for the last few years but he was still well past the age of being sprightly. He shuffled along, one foot barely making it half a length past the other at each step. Kariss waited until he flopped into his seat and took a number of heavy breaths before continuing. 'I have just spoken to Faela and Kydas, both are adamant that he is loyal. Kydas goes as far as to say that if he really has been seen consorting with the Romans then he must be spying on them.'

Bodvoc cleared his throat, holding up his hand to interrupt. 'You would do well to leave Taratus alone; he will do us no harm.'

'How can you say that?' Cartivel rounded on him. 'You know nothing, old man. While you have been pretending to be losing your mind, that traitor has been telling goodness knows what to our enemies.'

Everyone glared at Cartivel. 'Too harsh,' Corio reprimanded, his face set in stone. Now that Brigantia had lifted the block the Romans had placed on him, he could not only feel his own gods but also the taint left behind by the Roman ones. It clung to the air, especially by the guest houses. The whole area was going to need a thorough cleansing. He could only imagine how hard it must have been for Bodvoc. He would have been subjected to the full force of their presence, yet he had shown no sign of any discomfiture. Corio's respect for him had grown immensely.

Bodvoc only looked at Cartivel with sadness. 'Taratus has been close to this all his life. Being Kariss's cousin and growing up at Wendell, how could he not be? It is not unreasonable for him to want to learn everything he can about the Romans, to see what Kariss is up against. He could not learn it from her, after all.'

Cartivel snorted and turned away, pointedly disregarding Bodvoc.

Lord Hightern had been watching the druid carefully; he saw the sense in his words and was relieved. He had always liked Taratus, and had no wish to accept his possible perfidy. 'It is not traitorous for a man to form his own opinions. Taratus may have been misguided in how he went about it but I cannot see that he has actually done anything wrong. He voted for Kariss, as did everyone from Wendell. No vital information has been passed to Martaani...'

'That we know of.'

'No vital information has been passed to Martaani,' Hightern repeated, 'that caused her to win the vote at The Gathering. Neither was she able to get to Kariss and harm her. So what treason is he guilty of?'

'He actually fought some of the legionnaires when they attacked us,' Corio added, 'he was injured in doing so.'

'A good cover story,' Cartivel barked, his temper not abating in the slightest. 'I am sorry but there is no way I can believe that this man is innocent; and you would be a fool to do so, both of you.' He glowered at Hightern and Kariss. 'I did not become war leader by ignoring danger signs. Druids may read a man's soul but I read his actions.' He slammed his hands down on the table and then folded his arms in front of him. End of subject.

'I think the best way forward is to make sure that Taratus is watched,' Anniel said. 'Leave him free to go about his business but make sure that none of it is unseen. We need to know exactly what he is up to.'

'I am sending Kydas and Faela back to Wendell as soon as Kydas is strong enough to make the journey,' Kariss said. 'He has been through enough at the hands of the Romans. He will not let his friendship with Taratus blur his responsibilities to the nation. I think we can trust him to report anything suspicious.'

Everyone was in agreement, though Cartivel had one last comment. 'Send a couple of men posing as guards for Kydas, it will not seem unreasonable. They can act as messengers. That way, Kydas does not have to include anyone else at the fort.'

They had just moved on to talk about other things when Faela's voice distracted them. She was arguing with Volisios at the doorway, clearly out of breath and anxious to be admitted. Lord Hightern nodded his head and Kariss called out to let her in. She burst into the room, almost falling in her haste.

As soon as they neared the guest quarters, Corio could feel the cloying of the foreign gods growing thicker in the air. He shuddered, muttering cleansing words under his breath. He could feel waves of power emanating from the house, where Kydas sat still staring at the remains in the shallow pit in the floor. Corio was not familiar with the Roman religion but he recognised an offering when he saw one. He turned to Umar, 'Do you know what this is?'

It was Bodvoc who had insisted on Umar's presence. Without breaking her promise to keep his secret, Faela could offer no suitable reason why he should be left in peace. Umar took one look at the stone and let out a curse. He had seen these often when he was overseas and recognised it immediately. He turned and rushed out of the door. The rest of the guest houses were empty, left that way when the Romans had vacated the day before. Umar thundered into each one, turning over tables and beds in his search. There were no other stones. Umar cursed again. He rushed back to where a baffled Corio, Kydas and Faela waited.

'This is a Terminus stone,' Umar explained. 'It is Martaani's claim on this land. Terminus is their god of boundaries, invoked in perimeter rites across the Roman world. Such boundaries define a person's land, they protect the area within. The fact that this is a solitary stone means that Martaani is considering no boundaries to the land that she is claiming. This spot is to be the stronghold of her empire here, just as there is such a shrine in Rome.

'It was built long before memories began, on a hill where other shrines also stood. Then a young king decided that instead of the many there should be just one great temple dedicated to their king of gods, Jupiter. All the lesser gods agreed and left their shrines but Terminus refused. Not even to Jupiter would he yield an inch. So his shrine remains intact within Jupiter's temple and a hole is kept in the roof so that Terminus may always see the stars.' They all looked up to see the tell-tale area of new thatch.

'There is much power here. I could feel it seeping out of the house as I came.' Corio shivered, the power was like an icy breeze on his skin, setting his body hair on end, even under his clothing. 'I do not think we can call on Brigantia to cleanse this. If what you say is true then this god will not shift for another.'

Umar paced the room; there must be something they could do. He stared at the mess on the floor; nasty, rotting and crawling with maggots. They had not disturbed it, leaving it intact in the bottom of the hollow; even the stone lay where it had come to rest when Faela had dropped it. The smell was still as bad as it had been when they first arrived. Umar glanced at the roof again, idly. He thought how nice it would be to always see the stars, he could understand why Terminus would demand it.

'Bahaaah!' he cried out suddenly, making the others jump. Umar grinned at them, his eyes wide with mischief. 'This stone and this offering were made by Martaani and her priests, to lock Terminus to this place and ensure that it was always theirs. But the offering is still here, still being absorbed by the land. The clever person who mended the roof blinded Terminus to the happenings outside, shutting him off from the rest of the world. He is trapped in this room but he is not yet fixed here.' Umar grabbed one of the sheepskins from the bed. Taking care not to get any on his skin, he scooped the offering out of the hollow along with plenty of the surrounding earth. He added the stone and wrapped it all up, tying the bundle tightly. 'We are going to send him back.'

Corio felt the air lighten considerably. 'This room needs blessing, I will call on Nantosuelta. She would be the best one for such a task.' He turned to Kydas and Faela. 'You did well to find this and tell me. Brigantia will be smiling on you now.'

'I must take this away,' Umar said, rushing from the house before he could be stopped. The sharp eyes of the goddess still tormented him in his sleep; he had no intention of ever seeing her again. She may well have been the shining light in his father's life but she had cut him deeply with her words. Not even cauterising those wounds would cause them to heal. Luckily, there were a number of druids in Stanwick just now for The Gathering. It should not be too hard to find one willing to take this bundle over the water to Roman lands.

12

The raven's beak opened once more. She could see right down into its gullet as the bird stretched forward, forcing the cry out. The sound of it was like gravel scraping down stone, yet it was eerie and almost human at the same time. The hairs on the back of her neck stood on end and a thousand more electrified her body. It felt as if she would disappear down that gaping throat, into oblivion. Then the beak snapped closed again. The resounding clack, defiant and final. She jerked her face back just in time, only to find herself staring at the bird's beady eyes. The intensity of their stare was unnerving and she could see her own shocked face reflected in them. As she looked, the dark green eyne showed her features twisting and cracking, before bursting into a thousand pieces. She watched them scatter into dust. Glancing at her hand, she saw the veins rise to the surface and turn black, forming cracks the same way her face had. Her fingers began to warp out of shape but before her hand could shatter, the raven's vicious beak opened again and it crorked even louder than before, echoing inside her head over and over.

Martaani woke with a start, her breath coming in ragged gasps. It took a few long moments before her awareness fully returned; bringing with it the anger that had been her constant companion since The Gathering. She threw back her covers and walked, naked, over to the small table, pouring herself a drink of wine from the ornate glass pitcher. The cool night air soon chilled her damp skin but for once she did not reach for something to warm her. The cold made her feel alive and whole. She took another gulp of wine. It could have been vinegar instead of the fine vintage shipped specially from Rome, for all she tasted it.

The dreams were getting worse. No longer were they content to just plague her sleeping hours, now they followed her into waking; confusing her mind for longer and longer each time. She found herself feeling her face, checking for injuries. Finding none, she inspected the backs of her hands. The dream had been so real. It was hard to believe there were no marks. There was just enough pre-dawn light in the room to see that her skin was the same as it had been when she had gone to bed only a few hours before.

A sound came from the doorway. She jumped as the covering was eased aside and Proculus slipped into the room. His face broke into a smile as he saw her standing there like a jet-haired goddess but his smile faltered and slid away as he realised she was shaking.

'More dreams?' In two strides he had covered the space between them and gathered her into his arms, spilling some of the wine as he did so. 'They are playing with you,' he whispered into her hair. 'But you are stronger than they, and you have never been one for games. They cannot defeat you this way.'

Martaani kept quiet. Not even to Proculus would she admit the truth. It served her to let him think that her nightmares were sent by the Albion gods. She closed her eyes for a moment:

Is it hurting yet? Her grandmother's voice crashed into her mind, throwing her back into her childhood. Cloda held her wrist in a vice-like grip, forcing her

144

open hand to remain above the candle. She could feel the heat on her palm. Palms were her grandmother's favourite place for this lesson. Martaani could feel tears pricking behind her young eyes. She held them back as long as she could. It did not matter when they fell - they would be mocked. If she cried early, Cloda would say that she was weak. If she cried late, she would tell her that she was a fool to ignore what was clearly hurting her.

'The flame is the goddess, Brigantia,' her grandmother told her. 'When you get to Albion, she will be there waiting for you. You cannot escape her. The longer you are there, the more you will be able to feel her. Is it hurting yet? Do not mistake her initial warmth for comfort, it will soon start to burn into you; destroying you.' Martaani's palm was already burning but Cloda did not let go. Martaani was crying openly now, sobbing as the heat swallowed her whole hand in a furnace of pain. At last, Cloda released her and she fell to her knees, clutching her hand to her chest.

'There are many gods in Albion, child, imagine if I had used a candle for each of them. If you do not learn your lessons, I may well do that next time.' She glared down at Martaani, not a trace of compassion on her hard features. 'Now tell me, who are the most dangerous men in Albion?'

'The druids.'

'And what must you do to protect yourself from them?'

'Take a Pontiff with me.'

Cloda smirked, 'Was it really so hard, girl?

Martaani looked warily up at her. She was not about to answer and get herself into even more trouble. If she had kept her thoughts about how stupid people's obsession with religion was to herself, rather than making an idle comment about it to her grandmother, she would not have incurred this recent bout of the woman's wrath. Cloda ignored her silence and carried on as if the question had never even been asked.

'I do not care if you hate the priests. I do not care if you are ignorant towards religion. None of that changes the facts. For seven generations, we have kept ourselves ready, learnt what we needed to learn, remembered what must not be forgotten. Every one of us has kept faith with Cartimandua's vision; every one of us has been ready and prepared to cross to that infernal isle and take back the throne that was stolen from her. It should have been your mother's privilege. It should have been her name in the prophecy.' For a moment, Cloda's mask slipped and her eyes lightened at the thought of her beloved Atia. Martaani was able to glimpse the beauty that her grandmother had once been famed for, before bitterness had eaten away at her. Then Cloda's features closed once more and the resentful old woman was back. 'But Libitina had other ideas.'

Martaani felt the usual stab of irritation. For years she had been trying to live up to the impossible faultlessness of her late mother… and failing. Nothing she ever did even came close as far as Cloda was concerned. Martaani remembered her mother as a warm, loving woman, full of laughter and light. Then the goddess, Libitina, had come for her and she had gone willingly, leaving Martaani bereft. She had cried for days, begging first Venus and then every other god she could think of to send her mother home and to

146

punish Libitina for having taken her when she was still needed so much. But the gods had ignored her cries and over time the young Martaani's grief had hardened into anger. Her mother did not deserve the honour of avenging the wrong done to Cartimandua. She did not deserve the idol status that Cloda had laid upon her, and she certainly did not deserve the love and respect of the daughter she had turned her back on.

For once, Cloda did not dwell on Atia's perfection. 'Now you,' she spat, 'the eighth generation, threaten to ruin all our efforts with your refusal to understand the importance of all that you are up against. I only pray that I can live long enough to drive that insolence out of you. Because if I do not, you will surely fail.'

Martaani's hand gripped the stem of her goblet so hard that it snapped. Drops of blood appeared. She could still hear Cloda's words echoing in her mind: *fail, fail...* She bent to pick up the glass but Proculus took her hand. He kissed away the blood and pulled her over to the bed.

'There is still time to get an hour or two of sleep. The dreams are gone now.'

She lay in his arms, listening to the sound of his breathing. Her grandmother's ghost was still with her, shaming her for her failure. Martaani knew that the dreams had not left. The fear Cloda had instilled in her of the Albion gods was as real now as it had been when she was a child. The skin on her palms had toughened the more her grandmother had forced her to endure the candle lesson. Each time it had taken a little longer for her to feel the pain but the result was always the same. She shuddered and wondered what other damage she had not felt the Albion gods inflicting.

For the first time in her life she found herself admiring her grandmother. Her teachings were cruel, harsh, but they were remembered. Eventually, Martaani had learnt that the best way to avoid them was to become smart enough not to warrant such punishments. Or, when she couldn't manage that, to cause enough of a distraction to allow herself to slip through the net. This was her own lesson, and she had learnt it well.

The Albion gods' punishments might also be harsh but Martaani had no intention of suffering through another one. She was not going to be her mother and disappear quietly before she could be called upon. Nor was she going to be Cartimandua and leave Trimontium by sea, shamed and defeated. Martaani was going to march right back into Brigantia and take the nation for her own. What she needed was a distraction, to keep all eyes away from her whilst she gathered her army and prepared to attack. Now, thanks to that memory, she knew just what distraction she was going to use. She rubbed her palm absently as a smile wound its way around her face, and finally she slid into sleep.

13

In the dead of night, the first flames licked their way up the roof. Silent at first, until the moisture inside the thatch began to hiss as it evaporated in the heat. Insects scuttled to safety but unless they had wings there was nowhere safe for them now. The sounds of the fire increased but the wind carried the sound away and no one heard.

Another roof flared, then another, and finally the torch was thrown on a fourth building and the culprit crept away before the pandemonium could begin. In the first house, the wooden roof supports began to expand and crack as the fire intensified. The noise finally woke the inhabitants just as the timbers fell onto their beds, trapping them where they lay. The woollen blankets and sheepskins were slow to burn but the heather-stuffed mattresses caught immediately. They began to scream.

'Fire! Fire!'

In a town consisting of wooden round houses, packed tightly together to make the most of the limited space inside the palisade walls, fire was the one thing that everyone dreaded. Those closest to the house raced to help but the shouts had cut off almost as soon as they had begun. There was barely anything left that was not already engulfed in flames. The inhabitants had never stood a chance.

The other three houses were by now also well ablaze. Only one person had managed to escape, running from his home with his hair aflame. Someone threw a blanket over him, smothering the flames, but there was no time for sympathy. The wind was whipping the fires into a frenzy and sparks were ripped up into the air to fall as glowing rain onto the nearby roofs.

People rushed towards the burning buildings, bringing with them anything that could carry water. They formed chains of people radiating out from the well. Smoke billowed thick and heavy, clogging the air and stinging eyes. The fire was noisy now as it consumed the buildings. Each time a spark ignited another roof it roared anew.

At the opposite end of the town stood the fort. Though mainly built of stone, it was not insusceptible to flames. Lord Hightern was already awake by the time Volisios came with two guards to rouse him. He had struggled into his tunic and sat gasping for breath on his bed, trying to gather enough energy to put on his trousers. He waved Volisios away, ordering him to send most of the men to help the townsfolk.

'But Sire, the fort?'

'The fort is not in danger yet, the houses are.' His eyes were steel in the dim torchlight. Volisios knew better than to argue. His Lord had always put the people first. He turned to leave and Hightern called him back. 'Go yourself, check on that woman of yours. Viroco can manage here until you return.'

Volisios nodded and fled, for once happy to put his personal life before duty. He ran out of the fort with the other men, peeling off to head towards the house that Callimai shared with her father. As he ran, his concern grew. Their house was on the edge of the town with its back to the palisade. They made the tallow candles for the fort; it was how Volisios had first met her. They had a small workroom tacked on to the side of the house with a separate doorway to keep the smell from permeating through to the living quarters. A number of barrels of animal fat in various stages of rendering were stored there. If any of these were to catch alight, they would never get the flames out.

The air was thick with black smoke, hampering his vision, and for a while he could not tell where the fires were. Then, to his left, a great whoosh of flames flared in the darkness and Callimai's house was lit up in the glow. Already, there were a number of people in front of the workroom, pulling out the heavy, sealed barrels. The flames were dangerously close. Volisios rushed forward to help someone struggling to tip one onto its side. They rolled the barrels along the side of the palisade wall and out of the nearby eastern entrance. The ground here was uneven and rocky so there were no tents to hinder their movements.

He was relieved to see Callimai. She was busy organising the placement of the barrels well away from the wooden fencing, where they could pose no danger. Her face lit up to see Volisios, then darkened again with worry.

'Is the fort alright?'

'It is far from the flames. Lord Hightern has sent the men out to help. He ordered me to come and check on you. Thank the gods you are safe.' Volisios hugged her tightly to him, her hair smelled of smoke and animal fat. 'What about your father?' He felt her head move up and down against his chest. Her voice was muffled as she answered.

'He left to help free the horses in the stables. It was their screaming that woke us. The fire had reached them and they were trapped.'

He released his smothering grip and looked around him. Everyone else had returned inside the palisade and they were alone. He threw caution to the wind, lifted her face up to his and kissed her, only breaking away at the sound of clattering hooves. A group of terrified horses galloped through the gateway, their eyes showing white with fear. One of them slipped as it rounded the corner, its hind legs going out at an angle. Volisios cringed, thinking the animal would break a leg, but it gathered itself together and ploughed on. No sign of a limp to heed its progress.

Everyone in the fort was now awake and gathering anxiously in the large hall. Lord Hightern made his way slowly there with the help of Viroco.

'The wind seems to be keeping the fire from spreading further into the town,' Cartivel told him as he took his seat. 'There will be nothing left of the north east quarter, though.'

'Do we know how it started?' Hightern asked him.

His friend shook his head, 'No one seems to know. Maybe we will find out in the morning.' He glanced over to the three druids sitting facing each other in the centre of the room. 'They are imploring Bodach to send rain or at the very least keep the wind from turning.'

Corio, Bodvoc and Umar sat with their hands on each other's shoulders. Their eyes were closed, their expressions calm. Even old Bodvoc sat with his back ramrod-straight, his legs crossed in front of him like the others. The low murmuring of their constant chanting was oddly reassuring.

Kariss wished she could join them. Her nerves felt frayed. She really wanted to be outside, helping. She was not used to this life of privilege but she had been forbidden from leaving the safety of the fort. The people of Brigantia needed her to remain safe, it was her duty, no matter how much it frustrated her. Anniel had gone with Carrick and Garth to check on the visitor camps outside the palisade and Naraic had gone to help rescue the horses from the stables. All around her, she could hear people voicing their concerns. She paced the hall, chewing anxiously at her nails.

Someone handed her a glass. She took it, more for something to do with her hands than for thirst. The fruity red wine slipped easily down her throat. She took another sip then realised what she was doing and thrust the glass down onto a table. There were people fighting fires, others maybe dying in them, and here she was drinking wine, like a princess in her ivory tower. She turned to see Lord Hightern shuffling off with Viroco. Cartivel came over to her, smiling. He nodded towards the king.

'Alas, nature calls all too frequently when you are old and too weak to trot off easily to the pot room.'

Kariss smiled back at him. She still felt a little shy around Cartivel. He was a battle-hardened war leader, experienced in tactics and strategies. Though Brigantia had been at peace with its neighbours for many years, there had been a time when that was not the case. To the south of Brigantia lay the Cornovii and Coritani. The Coritani to the east were a peaceful nation on the whole, but the Cornovii had to contend with the Ordovicii on their eastern border. The two nations

153

had a rocky relationship. Both consisted mainly of hardy hill folk, who refused to let their differences lie.

Caratacus, or Caradoc as his warriors had called him, had made his last stand against the Romans on one of the Ordovicii hills. After the battle was lost and his wife and daughter captured, he had fled to Cartimandua for help. She of course had handed him straight over to the Romans, who marched him and his family to Rome to be paraded through the streets. Before his death sentence was carried out, Caratacus had been allowed to plead his case to the Roman Senate. His words had convinced them that clemency would be a better way for the emperor to prove his greatness. Never again were they allowed to leave Rome but at least their lives were spared.

The rest of the Ordovicii had not fared so well. The Romans had swooped over their lands, killing everyone on sight before turning their attention on the neighbouring, and still troublesome, Silures. In the aftermath of the Roman eviction, the Cornovii had taken advantage, helping themselves to the empty forts, the livestock roaming wild and untended, the crops withering in the fields. The Ordovicii, however, had not been completely eradicated. Slowly they re-grouped, biding their time; they gathered their strength and with the help of their old allies, the Silures, they took back their stolen lands.

Animosity holds down the generations and the Ordovicii had more reasons than most to hold a grudge. Not only did they blame the Cornovii for the historic theft of their lands and property; they also resented Brigantia because of Cartimandua's betrayal. Over the years, they repeatedly demanded that Brigantia's southern lands be split off from the rest, bringing its size more in line with the other nations and thereby reducing its overall power. Naturally, Brigantia always refused. The Ordovicii grew even more belligerent and eventually, over a hundred years after the Romans had been expelled from Albion, they invaded both nations with a ferocity to ignite legends.

Cartivel had been in the thick of the fighting. Not one to lead from the rear, he had been instrumental in driving out the rebels and securing both the Brigantian and the Cornovian borders. The Ordovicii were not subdued, they came at both nations time and again. It had taken five years to finally quell the troubles. The Setantii people, who inhabited the west coast, came into the disagreement as arbiters. They were a quiet nation, overlooked by the Ordovicii because of their strong ties to Eriu across the sea. Now the Setantii brought together the leaders of the three fighting nations and sat them down to talk over their differences. For almost the turn of a moon, the Ordovicii thrashed their grievances out, refusing to listen to any reason.

Finally, it was Cartivel himself who had stood up, slammed his fist down on the table and said his piece. The Brigantian people had been wroth at the handing over of Caratacus, Caradoc, or whatever name they wished to give the man. They had jumped at the chance to support Venutius in his campaign to drive both Cartimandua and the Romans, not just from the north but from the whole of Albion. It was only down to the nation's size that they had been able to mount the initial campaign and garner enough support from the northern nations to be successful. As for the Cornovii, could they really still be blamed a century and a half later, for the actions of their forebears? The

Ordovicii had suffered greatly in the past but the gods had clearly been with them, helping them to crawl their way back and become what? From a nation strong and brave enough to stand up to the might of the Roman army and protect Albion's gods to one that now resembled a petulant child, throwing stones at the people who had annoyed it. Was this really the way to show their gratitude? The gods deserved better from their people.

In the silence that had followed his words, Cartivel had slowly stood and raised his glass. 'The wrongs done to you have been noted and avenged,' he had told the Ordovicii king and his military leader. 'I salute your bravery, your nation and your people. Let us honour your return to strength by drinking a toast, drawing a line under the past and moving forward. If not as friends then at least as peaceful neighbours.' Lord Hightern rose to his feet beside him and also raised his glass. After a moment's pause, the young Cornovii king and his war leader did the same.

The Ordovicii king looked to his military leader and raised an eyebrow. Maybe it was time to put the past behind them? He had been angry and shamed at being likened to a petulant child. What bothered him more, however, was the depth of truth in Cartivel's words. He had been boiling towards an angry retort when Cartivel had stood and offered his salute. It was the recognition that the Ordovicii had been craving. The king's anger had fizzled to nothing as, one by one, the other leaders had also raised their glasses. His military leader studied the standing men, his mind ticking over their possible responses. There was only one which made any sense. He had nodded his head to the king and together they had risen and lifted their glasses in acquiescence.

Kariss had been told the story by Cartivel himself. Not that he had been bragging, he was not the sort to go in for self-congratulation. He had merely been filling her in on the past actions of the Brigantian army. Letting her know the depth of his experiences so that she could better understand the ways in which he could aid her. Cartivel had not been the nation's military leader for a number of years now but he still carried a lot of weight. His age had not diminished him; rather, it had blanketed him with an aura of eminence. He was a man Kariss needed to have on her council. But still, he made her nervous.

Her disquiet was not invisible to him. Whilst he could not deny that his ego was somewhat massaged by her obvious awe, he was more than a little discomforted at his inability to put her at her ease. He had not been sure what to expect of the young heir. Ordinarily, she would have grown up around the court. Be known to the nation and so understand their ways. Kariss, however, was an enigma. She had not been seen in Brigantia for almost ten years and was unrecognisable from the flame-haired child he remembered meeting in Wendell.

It was obvious that someone had taken the time to school her in matters of leadership, though she was still very green in practice. He had watched her carefully at the war council after The Gathering. Despite her earlier ordeal, she was calm and composed. She did not rush in, like a headstrong novice, she took the time to listen to everyone's opinion and think before speaking. Her input had been reasoned and practical and it was clear that she was used to taking advice from those she trusted. He hoped that he would soon become one of those people. If some of the tales he had heard about her journey were anything to go by, he could see great things ahead for her.

Just now, she looked frustrated. He could sense that she would sooner be outside helping than cooped up in here. He reached around her for the glass of wine she had just discarded. 'The brain cannot function without sustenance, my dear.' He smiled again and held out the glass. 'It has been well watered.'

Kariss accepted it and took a sip. Her throat was feeling dry. Although the messengers had reported that the wind was blowing the fire away from them, there was a definite tang of smoke in the air now. She took another sip and wondered how long Anniel would be before he returned. She stifled a yawn. Before she was finished, Cartivel was yawning too. 'Sorry,' she said, 'I never understood why yawning was so contagious. It seems so silly. Either you are tired or you are not. It shouldn't make a difference what anyone else is doing.'

Cartivel grinned. 'Whenever I find myself having to suffer a boring situation, I often make a point of yawning... So I can watch everyone else following suit,' he added when he saw her bemused face. 'It is amazing how much it can relieve the boredom.'

Kariss laughed, relaxing a little. 'I will have to watch out for that in the future, then.'

Cartivel pulled an exaggerated face. 'Aghhh, I have dropped myself in it now.' He coughed and took a drink. 'Is it me, or is it getting smoky in here all of a sudden?'

Kariss could smell the smoke now, as well as taste it. Behind her, she heard a shout of alarm and swung around. The doorway through which Lord Hightern had left was full of thick black smoke; it was beginning to curl into the hall. On its heels was the unmistakable glow of fire. Corio and Umar dragged Bodvoc to his feet.

'Quickly,' someone shouted, 'The fort is alight. Run!'

The sound of crackling grew louder as the corridor outside was engulfed in flames. Screams filtered through the smoke. Umar and the guards ran to the doorway but before they could reach it there was an almighty crash and the corridor roof collapsed, sending a shower of sparks and flying cinders into the hall. Kariss looked back at Cartivel in horror, 'Lord Hightern was through there, what do we do?'

Cartivel's face was a picture of sorrow; he shook his head, words failing him for a moment. Then he pulled himself together. 'Viroco will look after him,' he said briskly. 'We must get out of here.' He led the way towards the other door, his limp barely showing in his determination. Mercifully, the flames had not yet reached this side of the building and they were able to make their escape easily. Outside in the yard, they watched as the fort burned. No one else came out.

Volisios watched the horses disappear then turned back to Callimai, 'I must get back to the fort, I do not like to leave him when he is so frail.'

She looked at his worried face; there were new lines there since The Gathering. She was not surprised. They had all expected trouble from Martaani when she failed to secure the succession but no one had expected her retribution to come so swiftly. This fire was the last thing everyone needed but fate was not apt to take notice of suitable timings. Callimai stroked Volisios's cheek. Even though she had barely seen him in the last few weeks, she did not try to argue. The king must come first, she had always accepted that.

'I will try and see you later,' Volisios told her. 'Stay safe and if you have any problems come to the fort.' He kissed her quickly and turned back to the entrance. Already he had been gone too long.

Callimai watched him go and sighed. She had no idea when she would see him again, despite his hopes. These were troubling times, nothing could be guaranteed. The happenings at The Gathering had been all anyone had spoken about for the last two days. As yet there had been no official news. The people of Brigantia were on tenterhooks, waiting to see what would happen next. Many of the visitors had left to spread the news in their own villages. By now, the whole of Brigantia would know that Kariss had been chosen as heir and Martaani had fled in a violent rage.

There had been some repercussions with the people who had backed Martaani. Numerous fights had broken out and Lord Hightern was said to be considering reprisals for anyone caught conspiring with the Romans. Traitors could expect no quarter in Stanwick now and the Roman sympathisers had slipped quietly away that first night.

Callimai would not be surprised if the tension in the town had somehow sparked the fire. She rolled her eyes at the thought; maybe she had inhaled too much smoke? Moods might cause fights but they did not cause fires.

A scraping noise, high up on the palisade, made her jump. She squinted through the smoke. The figure of a man had appeared, silhouetted by the orange glow of the fires within. She watched as he climbed over the top, disappearing from view as the blackness enveloped him. She held her breath as she heard him descending. He must be using a rope, she thought, or he would have surely fallen. Coward. Whilst everyone else stayed and helped fight the flames, this man was deserting the burning town. Curiosity got the better of her; she wanted to know who it was. Silently, she crouched down beside one of the barrels. Her kneecap clipped a rock and she suppressed a cry of pain. She made to move the stone out of the way but thought better of it and kept hold of it instead.

The man had reached the bottom now. She could see his dark shape as he moved towards her. He was furtively looking over his shoulder every few steps, to check that he was not being followed. Callimai hunched down even further. With a bit of luck she would be able to see who it was as he passed. When he was just about level with her, he looked back once more. As he did so, he collided with one of the barrels and fell. He cursed. Callimai was horrified to hear his thick Roman accent. This was not a coward escaping from the burning town; this was one of the enemy.

Before he had the chance to pick himself up, she launched herself at him and hit him hard over the head with the rock. He thumped to the ground, unconscious. With shaking hands, she felt the man over for any sign of a weapon. She found a knife hanging from his belt and took it. Quickly, she ran over to the palisade and found the rope still hanging there. She cut as long a section as she could reach and ran back to tie his hands and feet. He began to groan, just as she was finishing. She panicked and hit him with the rock again. Satisfied that he could not get away if he woke whilst she was gone, she hurried into the town to find a guard.

Volisios had not gone far when he realised that there were flames in front of him as well as behind. Dread spurred him on. When he arrived at the area that separated the fort from the town houses, he saw a pitiful number of people standing watching the inferno, in varying stages of distress. No one was trying to put out the flames. The majority of the guard were still fighting the fires in the north of the town. The few people left here could do nothing against the intensity of the fire. He saw Cartivel standing with Kariss and rushed over. Cartivel looked at him with tears in his eyes that were nothing to do with the smoke.

'Lord Hightern? Viroco?'

Cartivel shook his head. There was nothing he could say to make the news any more bearable.

The wind was still blowing towards the north east but now, instead of carrying the sparks safely away from the town, it was blowing the ones from the fort right into the centre. Suddenly, someone realised the danger and everyone raced to gather whatever bucket, pot or bag they could find.

'We need more men,' Volisios shouted.

'Get the northern warriors,' Kariss yelled to him. 'Hurry!'

14

In the cold dawn light, the ruins of the town could be seen clearly for the first time. Exhausted townsfolk slumped in groups wherever they could find the space. The arrival of the northern warriors had finally enabled them to bring the blaze under control. Still, they had been at it most of the night. Only six houses remained unscathed. Six houses in a town of forty or more.

Ash fluttered in the breeze like summer snowflakes, carrying the tears of the gods to mingle with those of the townsfolk. Burnt-out skeletons of houses stood in pools of mud. Every so often, hot ashes would spark into flames but they were quickly noticed and beaten out. The smell was awful.

Miraculously, only eighteen people had died in the town and five in the fort, including Lord Hightern and Viroco. As news of the king's demise spread, people began to gather in front of the burnt-out shell of the stronghold. The fire here had burned so ferociously that no one had been able to get inside. Even now, the stone walls were still radiating heat.

They had thought the fire was under control, that the town had been saved; but then, whilst everyone's attention was focused on the north, the south side had begun to burn as well. With hardly anyone left to fight the flames, this area had quickly got out of control. The wind that had appeared to be so kind to them initially now proved to be the town's downfall as it carried the sparks from the fort's burning roof onto the nearby houses. There was nothing they could do but stand by and watch everything burn until re-enforcements arrived to help.

As soon as it was deemed safe enough, Volisios scoured the gutted fort. The floor was thick with ash and cinders and the rooms were strangely light now that the roof had gone. It seemed to him as if the building was in shock; still settling to the new state it found itself in. In many places, he had to drag pieces of charred debris out of the way, stamping on the odd hot spot his actions uncovered. When he managed to get into the hall, he stood and looked around at the devastation. He tried to picture the banners that had hung on the now blackened walls. He knew that the inhabitants had gathered here to wait out the news of the fire. He was glad they had left when they had; they would never have survived otherwise. Both doorways had been blocked by falling timbers.

He crossed the room and forced his way out of the other doorway. The corridor outside was gone completely. The wall had collapsed along with the roof. He scrambled over stonework and remnants of beams, making his way to a small room that had stood at the end of the passageway.

It was here that he found the bodies. At first he hadn't even realised what he was looking at. The corpses were as black and charred as the wood surrounding them but as he got closer, he noticed something glinting. It was the hilt of Viroco's dagger catching the morning light. He was laid across the body of the king. A closer look made it clear that the second body could be none other than Lord Hightern; his golden torc was still around his neck. Volisios closed his eyes and gulped but the image of his friend attempting to shield their lord from the falling roof flooded his mind. He hoped their end had been quick.

His vision was blurred as he turned away, unable to look at them any longer. The sadness of them ending their days in such a way was almost unbearable. It struck him that if Lord Hightern had not sent him away to check on Callimai, it could very well have been him lying there masquerading as charcoal.

He heard someone else coming up behind him but did not turn to look. Corio placed a hand on his shoulder. He said nothing for a long while, letting Volisios vent his grief in silence.

Finally, he moved over to the bodies and removed the dagger from Virico's corpse. He handed it to Volisios, who shook his head and pushed it back to him. 'It should be buried with him.'

'His sword, spear and shield will be buried with him. You were his closest friend, take it and honour his memory.'

Volisios lifted the dagger, turning it over in his hands to admire the delicate scroll-work etched into the handle. He tucked it into his belt; it would be safe enough until he could get a protective sheath made. Corio returned to the corpses. Standing over them, he called out to Brigantia, imploring her to take the dead men's spirits into her care. He would say more at the funeral but for now that would suffice.

More guards arrived. Corio's voice must have alerted them. They peered into the small room with shocked faces. 'Bring something to carry them on,' Corio instructed. 'They cannot be lifted, otherwise; their bodies will not take it.'

The guards returned with two cloaks, acquired from one of the remaining intact houses. Carefully, they separated the bodies and carried them out. Corio and Volisios followed solemnly behind.

Outside, all the bodies were laid on the grass close to where the western gate had stood only the day before. Lord Hightern was placed a little way from the others, with Viroco by his feet. Guards formed a protective ring around them and the townsfolk filed past to pay their respects. The macabre sight finally broke through the stunned hush that had prevailed all morning and at last the sound of wailing began.

People cried for the king, for their dead friends and their lost homes. They cried for their past memories and their future uncertainties. It was clear that the town was no longer a viable home for them. Their houses, tools, livelihoods and food all wiped out in a single night.

The northern warriors proved to be their saviours. Whilst the people of Brigantia mourned their losses, the warriors rounded up most of the livestock and made temporary corrals to keep them from wandering. Even the horses were brought back, though the smell of smoke and char was clearly upsetting them. At the edge of the wood the warriors set to building simple shelters. There would not be enough to house everyone but the eldest and youngest would at least have some protection. Everyone else would have to make do with the trees for cover.

Loth had arranged the slaughter and butchering of the injured animals and those that could not be kept in the corrals. The smell of roasting meat was a welcome relief to the hungry townsfolk. They gathered around the fires, grateful that the warriors were there to help them. Everywhere Kariss went, she was thanked for bringing them. Townsfolk dropped to their knees to beg her forgiveness in resenting the northerners' initial appearance. Even Tarnn sought her out, shame-faced and clearly uncomfortable. He had even made his peace with Uurad. It had taken the depths of disaster for the two men to realise their many similarities. Of course it helped that the Epidii warriors had such a knack with horses. Already, Uurad's men had the cavalry steeds beginning to settle.

Whispers about a captured Roman soon became open talk. No one was sure where he was being held, or indeed if he was being held at all. Rumours grew like buds sprouting on bindweed. Many wanted the man paraded in front of them. They wanted to hurl abuse at him, to throw things at him and make him suffer.

In a rough-looking shelter, hurriedly thrown together with sticks and holly branches, in the heart of the Caledone camp, the man heard their talk but had no idea what was being said. Martaani had been clever in her choice of arsonist. She had made certain to pick someone from the lower ranks, who could only speak his native Greek. Even if he gave in under torture, he would be unable to divulge anything the Brigantes could understand. Trussed so tightly that he could barely move, the man waited. He could not understand why they were leaving him alone. He was given water, scraps of food, and a pot to relieve himself in but other than the occasional kick he was left alone. His anxiety grew the more that time passed. He knew there was no chance of rescue; his only hope was to escape. He forced himself to stay alert, watching for any chink in his captors' defences.

15

It was a somber sky that lightened over Stanwick five days after the fire; the clouds were grey and heavy with the threat of rain. Men had been digging day and night to prepare a huge pit. Now they lined up with ropes and logs, ready to manouvre four massive boulders into each corner for support.

Most of the dead had already been interred. Their fresh graves scarring the ground; silent reminders of the people who had been lost. Only two bodies remained, protected from the elements by a simple make-shift shelter.

Volisios was busy scouring the blackened ruins of the fort, looking for a number of items that he knew had been important to his dead king. In Lord Hightern's sleeping chamber, he broke down and cried amidst the rubble. The room had been as familiar to him as his own and it was a shock to find it relatively unscathed compared with the rest of the building. The only damage had been caused by remains of the already burned-out roof and a little of the wall collapsing in.

Lord Hightern's bed stood defiant and unscathed in the centre. At its foot was the trunk Volisios had hoped to find. One of the roof beams had landed on it, breaking open one corner so that some of the contents had spilled out onto the dirty floor. It was this sight - the empty bed on which Lord Hightern may possibly have survived, and the escaping royal trinkets, that had broken through Volisios's firm resolve and reduced him, once again, to tears. He didn't even need to close his eyes to see Lord Hightern laid on the bed, covered with the dark-haired goat skins he so favoured.

The king would never have been able to sleep in such a bright room, Volisios thought as the tears soaked his tunic. The chamber had always been dimly lit by only a small window and a few torches. Behind him, he heard a noise and turned, seeing a large bird, russet-brown in colour, with a grey head and hooked beak.

For a moment he had expected to see Viroco but his old friend was dead, gone with the king to attend him in the afterlife. The red kite spread its wings wide for balance as it continued to hop amongst the debris. Angrily, Volisios picked up a stone ready to hurl at the bird but at the last moment he caught himself and let it fall harmlessly from his hand. What was he doing? Kites were his favourite bird; they were majestic and graceful, with just the right blend of tenacity and aggression. His tears dried on his skin and he turned away, leaving the bird to its scavenging.

He spread out a length of material on the ground and began to extract the contents of the trunk, laying each piece carefully in the centre of the cloth. Gold, silver and electrum jewellery, inlaid with precious jewels; wide leather belts adorned with cast-bronze buckles and belt plates; daggers with gold and enamel hilts; figurines of gods and goddesses. Carefully, he rolled the edges of the material over the hoard and tied the ends to form a sling which he wore across his body and over one shoulder. He took a number of the cleanest goat skins and made his way back to the makeshift camp. He returned a number of times, until he had managed to retrieve all of Lord Hightern's personal effects. He would allow no one else to help. This was his last duty as the king's personal guard; he would not shirk his responsibilities.

In the early evening, when everything was ready, Lord Hightern's body was carried to the pit on the back of a ceremonial chariot. The way was lined with townsfolk and warriors. Many of the northerners were also present, standing well back to watch as the Brigantians paid their final respects to their beloved leader. The air was filled with the sounds of grief and many of the guards found their vision blurred as they followed behind, carrying the remainder of the funerary items. Last of all came the body of Viroco, laid on a wooden board and carried aloft by four guards. Corio led the procession, with Volisios flanking the king's body, guarding him until the last. At the pit, the elderly and infirm waited with heads bowed, Bodvoc and Cartivel to the fore.

The horses were removed from the traces and led away. Then the guards carefully pushed the chariot down the ramped end of the pit until it settled in the bottom, well below the level of the surrounding land. Lord Hightern lay covered in his goat skins with only his head and arms showing. Those who had not already seen him cried out in horror when they saw what remained of him. His hair and beard had been burned away; his skin was so blacked and charred that without the thick golden torc showing proudly around his neck there would have been no possible way to identify him. Several of his fingers were missing, leaving only burnt stubs on the lumps that had once been his hands.

Someone had placed his enamel-crusted dagger by his right side. His sword was by his left hip and his shield lay across his knees. Between his feet sat his ornate helmet. Made of iron, overlaid with gold and decorated with silver patterning and enamel inlay, it was a dazzling piece of craftsmanship. The cheek pieces boasted depictions of boars' heads with fierce tusks, surrounded by intricate foliage. It had been one of Lord Hightern's most treasured possessions.

Once the chariot was in place, the guards filed down to add the many other items to the pit: a long, curved ceremonial trumpet; gold torcs and armlets; goblets; weapons; jars of food and flasks of wine. Finally, Corio placed a small statuette of Brigantia next to Lord Hightern's head. He spoke to the king in hushed tones, offering his own private blessings for his passage to the afterlife.

When everyone was settled, Corio stood at the head of the pit and threw his arms wide. 'Deae Nymphae Brigantiae. Bless our king, guard his passing and ease his transition to the afterlife.'

'Deae Nymphae Brigantiae,' the people chanted.

Corio stood to the side. There was still a little space at the far end of the pit and into this now walked Volisios, leading the four guards carrying the body of Viroco. Volisios was dry-eyed and calm; the tears he had shed earlier had cleansed him of the worst of his grief.

Viroco's corpse had borne the brunt of the fire and was barely even recognisable as a body. It was beyond dressing and only the most careful of handling could prevent it from breaking apart and crumbling to ash.

171

The guards placed him on the end of the chariot, at the feet of the king, setting his weapons and shield alongside him. Volisios added a silver armlet, sitting it reverently on his friend's chest. Viroco had died protecting his king; it was only fitting that he be buried with him, so that he could continue to protect Lord Hightern in the afterlife. It was a far greater honour than any guard or warrior could ever expect to receive, and one which Volisios fervently approved of.

Corio called out to Maponus, asking him to take Viroco into his care, to guide him onward and help him in his duty to watch over the king forever more. Then, the pit was slowly filled with soil, each shovelful of earth sending waves of sadness through the watching townsfolk. When at last the ground was level, Corio called out to the gods once more: blessing the grave, blessing the grieving, and asking for strength for the times ahead. He kept the eulogy short, still wary of invoking Albion's gods for too long lest there be any Roman deviants nearby who could call down their own gods to cause them harm.

Finally, more boulders were rolled into place, sealing the grave below. These were covered with yet more earth, until there was a fair-sized mound created - a lasting monument to the bodies beneath.

Feasting followed the funeral. Again, the northern warriors had taken control and, whilst the Brigantians were saying their farewells to the king, they had been busy roasting boar, deer and goat over huge fires. The rich smell filled the air and though there was no wine or ale for most people, they celebrated nonetheless.

'Are you alright?' Callimai whispered in the darkness. Volisios had disappeared for a long while after Lord Hightern's funeral. Not returning until the dead of night, where his swollen eyes could not be seen. Deep within the woods, the birds were the only ones to bear witness to his anguish. It tore from him in ragged, heaving gasps, so different from the silent tears of the morning. It was the unreasoned remorse of survivors when everyone around them had been lost and it bore no resemblance to the truth of that black night when Stanwick had burned. It left him feeling raw, his insides a hollow wound.

He hacked at a sapling oak with his dagger, over and over again until the young tree snapped and fell. Eight years of growth fallen to nothing. The reckless loss jolted through Volisios, stopping him in his tracks. He closed his eyes and muttered a rapid, heartfelt prayer to Cernunous, begging his forgiveness. The god breathed an idea into his mind in return. Without questioning the urge, Volisios cut a section of the wood and began to carve. His hurried snatching of the blade on the bark soon bit back and he sucked at the blood welling from a slice in his thumb. Gradually, his breathing calmed as he concentrated more and more on what he was doing. His mind stopped racing through the cacophony of black thoughts that had overwhelmed him and settled on the sure, confident strokes of his knife. He had perfect control of the tool now, shaving piece after piece of wood so they fell like pale scales to scatter amongst the leaf litter.

He had no real idea of what he was carving; he was just letting the wood speak to him as he went. He could not have said at what point he finally realised that his presence in the fort during the fire would not have saved the king. Hightern did not need two people to help him to the pot room. Maybe it was not guilt that he was feeling after all; maybe it was just the horror of what he had found? That and the knowledge that the great king had been killed in so basic a task as emptying his bladder. Volisios did not want to leave this world yet, the very thought of perishing in that fire sent shudders of terror through him. Yet how did he reconcile himself with the fact that Lord Hightern and Viroco were no longer here, but he was?

The knife was dulling slightly, he could feel the wood offering more resistance with each cut. He pulled a strip of leather from his pouch and stropped the blade, taking his time to hone the sharpness properly. As he did so, he thought of Viroco. There had been nothing in his life apart from his work; no woman to warm his bed at night, not even any casual encounters to lighten his days and give him something to look forward to. He had no family and few friends, his dour demeanour too off-putting for most. No one else would be crying for Viroco tonight. Volisios thought of Callimai and his heart seemed to miss a beat or two at the thought of what she would be going through had it been him in that grave instead. He shook the thought away and began to carve again.

The slow, dedicated strokes of the blade on the wood was calming, almost hypnotic. The green wood came away easily and he breathed in the smell of it, thinking of nothing else for a while. The rough shape was really showing through now and he began to neaten it up, smoothing away the cut marks and adding in the detail.

He paused as a cloud drifted across the moon, plunging the land into darkness. His mind drifted again, coming to rest on Lord Hightern. It would have weighed heavy on the king if Callimai had been injured or killed in the fire whilst Volisios remained by his side. It was not the first time he had sent guards to check on their families. The king had always had a soft heart under his firm command of the nation and he had been loved dearly for it.

Now, as Volisios lay in Callimai's arms, he answered her honestly. 'I will be,' he said. 'I am a lucky man, in many ways. Lucky to have been the guard of one such as Hightern, lucky to have counted Viroco as my friend, and lucky that I was not in the fort when it burned.' He turned and kissed her upturned nose. 'Most of all, I am lucky to have you.'

Callimai pulled him close. 'What will you do now?'

'I do not know. I was guard to the king and the king is no more. I presume I will go back to being a guard of the royal household.'

'Will you not be Kariss's personal guard?'

Volisios shook his head. 'I cannot.' He kissed her again; this time there was the hint of passion in his lips and Callimai felt familiar flutterings growing inside her. 'It would not be right to be so close to another woman,' Volisios admitted. 'You are the only one whose bed chamber I want access to.'

Callimai laughed, 'It is not her bed chamber that I would have a problem with, it is her bed and her heart, but it is clear those are already taken. She needs good people around her and you are one of the best.'

Again, Volisios shook his head. 'It would not be right.'

Callimai pushed him away gently and raised herself up on her elbows to look at him. 'She needs you, love. I am not a jealous woman; I know I have your heart. I am proud of your work, I would be proud of you being her guard.'

175

'I will grow to love her… as my queen.'

'As we all will.'

'It is not the same. I would be putting another woman before you.'

Callimai frowned at him. 'I knew from the first moment I met you that you would always put people before me. You have to do that, you are a warrior and a guard. That does not mean that you love them before me. This is why we cannot marry, so I cannot put a claim on you. I have always known that, and accepted it. I am a strong woman, Volisios; I do not need you here for me every moment. Go, be the queen's guard with my blessing. Keep her safe. She could have no one better.'

Volisios thought of the owl he had carved and left sitting on the dark earth of the burial mound. It would protect Viroco's spirit as it settled to its new duty of guarding Lord Hightern in the afterworld. He still could not agree with Callimai. He could not put a woman he did not know over her. He would rather return to being a general guard. He silenced Callimai with another kiss and this time he did not stop to speak again. He needed to sate himself in her body and she was more than willing to let him.

16

Torwain and Carrick had seen enough to be very worried. They had left Stanwick immediately after the crisis meeting, heading north. They travelled quickly, using tracks and byways that were unknown to the Romans. It had not been long before they caught up with the rear of the retreating legionnaires. It was clear that they were very disciplined and well organised. Each small group was formed of eight fighting men supported by two others who looked after their pack pony and supplies. Torwain and Carrick passed two of these groups on their first day.

The second day, they passed two more in the morning and another one before nightfall. It was hard to believe that so many legionnaires could have been in Brigantia without anyone raising the alarm.

'It is these small groups,' Carrick said. 'They can just melt into the trees.'

He had never seen a fighting force organised quite like it and it sent a chill up his spine. Unlike the Albion warriors, these men did not appear to be passionate fighters, driven by their emotions and love for their individual nations. The legionnaires were cold, calculated men, here for one purpose - to conquer. If Carrick had any doubts about his observations, they were dispelled as soon as they crossed over into Votadini lands. Here, the small groups gathered together, setting up their makeshift camps with quiet efficiency. Torwain and Carrick watched from the cover of an ancient oak and tried to work out their next step. They decided to split up, Carrick staying to watch the army and gather as much tactical information as possible, whilst Torwain tried to find exactly where the Trimontium fort lay.

Torwain's journey was both helped and hindered by numerous further groups of legionnaires, this time heading south to join the camp he had just left. Presumably, they were coming from Trimontium, therefore he only had to follow their tracks and they would lead him directly where he wanted to go. The only thing slowing him down was having to take to the treetops as each new group marched below.

Some were a little more ragged, with only half of the men looking like time-served soldiers. Most of the groups travelled in silence but here and there he heard snatches of conversation. He was not very good with Latin but sometimes he heard his native language and realised that some of the men were in fact Votadini. Anger fizzled in his gut. That men of Albion could fight amongst themselves was one thing but to join forces with the Romans, essentially turning their backs on the gods who had watched over them since time began, was enough to make his blood boil.

It got the better of him once, when a group consisting of seven Votadini and only three Romans passed beneath him. He could hear the men talking excitedly about the Mysteries of Mithras.

'My knees are still hurting,' one of the men complained. 'It is hard to kneel when you are blindfolded and your hands are tied behind your back. I went down hard.'

'These initiations are to weed out those not capable. I am surprised they let you through.'

'They say there are seven. Each one is getting harder; imagine what we will need to go through on the last one.'

Torwain had heard enough. The tree he was hiding in was hollow and contained a hornets' nest. Already, the creatures were angered at his presence. He remembered the Pontiff and his bag of hornets and it gave him an idea. Torwain sent out a silent prayer to Cernunous for protection, grabbed hold of the nest and lobbed it at the men. He ducked back into the hollow and held his breath. The men were no longer laughing. Curses could be heard in both languages as they broke ranks and fled. Torwain hoped they had been stung numerous times each. Amazingly, he himself had only been stung once. He dropped to the ground as soon as it was clear and found a fast-running stream. The water was cold and clear, soothing his hand. It would sting for a day or two but it was worth it.

Torwain already knew something of the Mysteries of Mythras. It was a cult many legionnaires belonged to and one that only men could join. Their secretive worship was done in underground chambers because the god Mythras had been born out of rock. Due to its nature, Torwain had no idea what went on at these meetings, but without doubt the slaying of a bull was one of the cult's key aspects. Animals were sacrificed every day, it had been so throughout time, but what abhorred Torwain was that Mythras had absolutely no respect for the bull.

Torwain had been told that the underground temples dotted throughout the Roman Empire contained carved reliefs of the story of Mythras. These carvings told of how the god had harassed a white bull to the point of exhaustion, chasing it and riding it before completely overpowering it and dragging the terrified animal into the underground chamber where he had knelt on it and, holding it by the nostrils, killed it with a sword thrust to the shoulder. It was the ultimate imagery of the god's dominance over animals and completely at odds with everything Cernunous represented and held dear.

The Romans were known for their cruel practices and so-called entertainments. Stories of men pitted against beasts were legendary so it was no real surprise that the Mysteries of Mithras had flourished. Torwain could well imagine the cult's followers looking at the images of the god and seeing themselves in his place. Not equal to animals but better, superior, and - most of all - dominant. Torwain had no idea if those following the cult exacted the killing of their sacrificial bulls in quite the same manner but he was in no doubt that, however it was done, the animals suffered needlessly.

A blackbird flew scolding through the trees. Torwain pulled his hand from the stream, sending water droplets flying as he shook it dry. He looked around for a suitable tree, making sure to steer well clear of the hollow one. He had no wish to face the angry returning hornets.

This time, the group of legionnaires was more orderly, the men older and better disciplined. They passed by, unaccosted by the hidden druid, oblivious to his presence. As soon as it was safe, Torwain dropped to the ground and headed in the direction they had come from.

Back at the camp, Carrick watched as more and more men arrived. At first the majority were dressed the same. These were the men they had seen travelling from Brigantia. The new groups arriving from the other direction had as many as six men who did not conform with the rest. These were not as disciplined, earning themselves frequent punishments from their respective group leaders. Carrick watched them with interest - these men must be new Votadini recruits. They would make much less daunting opponents. As the numbers in the camp swelled he was angry, but somewhat relieved, to see that there were almost as many Votadini as there were Romans.

The camp was not an idle place. The two auxiliaries from each group erected the leather tent that would house all ten men together then stored away their supplies, tended to their pack pony, built fires and prepared food. Line upon line of neatly ordered tents soon filled the clearing.

The majority of the legionnaires gathered together to drill and train. For the new recruits, emphasis was on increasing their stamina and fitness levels, marching for hours at a time at both normal and quick paces. When they were not marching, they were practising their weapons skills. For this, a number of posts had been driven into the ground for the men to aim at with either pilia or heavy wooden training swords. Carrick watched with a critical eye. The new recruits may be green but they were eager.

Far more interesting, and worrying, was the one-on-one sparring that the seasoned legionnaires undertook. From his vantage point in the trees, Carrick noted how well the men's bodies were protected by their large, rectangular shields; how they wielded their short, thrusting swords. This was all information that their own warriors would need to know.

Those not training were busy with other jobs necessary to a travelling army. Wheelwrights were replacing broken spokes and re-attaching any loose metal rims; blacksmiths set about repairing weapons; fletchers made arrows. A small group of men broke away from the camp, intent on hunting. They passed directly beneath the gnarled oak that Carrick was still using as his vantage point. The camp was not a silent beast and the sounds of hammering and sparring would carry a long way through the trees, driving the bigger prey far away. The hunters would likely be gone for quite a while.

Faela and Kydas were making ready to return to Wendell. Kariss had refused to accept their offers of help and support. 'You have already suffered more than anyone should have,' she had told them. 'You have played your part. Now go home and be safe. This tent is needed for someone else. Far too many people are having to sleep in crude attempts at shelters, and many are still out in the open. Besides, I need someone to watch over Taratus - someone I trust.'

With resignation, they had finally agreed. The following morning, they were bundling their belongings onto their cart when the rich robes of Umar caught Faela's eye.

'Give me a moment,' she told Kydas.

Face-to-face with the druid, she found that she did not know how to begin, how to tell him what had happened. Tongue-tied, she tried more than once to get her words out but failed. Umar read her distress perfectly; he caught hold of her arms and bid her to stop.

'The box is gone?'

Faela nodded, ashamed. 'I am sorry. You trusted me with such a treasure, and I left it to burn in the fire. I have been so tied up with everything that I did not even remember about it until now...' Her voice trailed off.

Umar's shoulders drooped but he pulled his head up. 'I saw it once,' he said, 'I had that at least, and I have you to thank for it.'

'But you trusted me and I let you down. I did not even remember the box until now.'

In typical Umar fashion, he flapped his arms about his head and looked at her sternly. 'Everything was in turmoil. You had a good man to protect, it is right that he was your priority. This should be the least of your concerns. Go now and think no more of it. Take your man home and be safe. You have given me far more than you can ever realise. I will not forget. When all is done, I will tell you the story of how Kel came to have his secret child.'

The war council met each day just outside the blackened town. A ring of warriors surrounded them, ensuring no one who was not eligible could get near. Tarnn's men were not present - they had at last been sent out to deliver the news of Lord Hightern's death and the long-awaited war cry. Kariss had ordered it the morning after the fire. Brigantia's voice had been clear in her mind and with it had come yet another warning. The druids, who had complained ceaselessly at being evacuated from Brigantia, would no doubt try to return to pay their respects. Should they return, there would be no time to harry them away again.

With a heavy heart, Kariss had made her first law. Anyone aiding, hiding or even ignoring a druid would be severely punished. They were not, under any circumstances, to be allowed back into Brigantia until she gave the word. Only Corio, Bodvoc, Torwain and Umar were exempt. Not everyone would understand her actions but it was a risk she had to take to keep the druids safe.

Tarnn assured her that his men would make her reasoning clear and that the people would know that the druids' safety was at stake. The horseman still made her uneasy. Outwardly, he was deferential and polite, but he carried with him an air of arrogance, as if he knew something he was not letting on. After meetings with him, Kariss would find her jaw aching where she had clenched her teeth too tight. It had been a relief to see him ride out with his men.

As the message spread, the camp began to swell in size and numbers. Those arriving brought with them all the vital supplies they could carry; clothing, food, cooking equipment and tools. Their offerings were accepted gratefully but soon they were struggling to find room. People cramped together on the open ground grew fractious and impatient with each other. The looming facade of the burnt-out palisade walls and the blackened remains of the town and fort within did nothing to help relieve the tension.

The royal party moved into the northern warrior camp, freeing up precious space. The returning cavalry, along with those who had not gone to guard the Votadini border, moved to a new camp across the nearby river. It was close enough to be within hearing distance but far enough to relieve the pressure. Best of all, Kariss found that these makeshift homes were much better quality, made when wood and time were not as scarce as now. They were sturdy and covered with mosses and leaves, all the better for keeping out any rain.

Anniel set men to work at the edges of the forest, clearing shrub and preparing more ground for people to sleep on. They felled some of the smaller trees and dragged larger branches from further afield. Before long, there were many more shelters and far fewer people had to sleep out in the open. Not all were wind- and water-tight but it was the middle of summer and so far Bodach was managing to keep the weather favourable.

Blacksmiths had set up makeshift workshops and were busy making weapons. These were then honed to perfection by a number of willing volunteers. The rhythmic sounds of stone on metal made the air sing. Bowyers scoured the surrounding woodland for the best branches to make their bows. There was no time to jealously guard the choicest limbs until they were considered perfect. Every suitable branch was felled and more than one bowyer had a tear in his eye when he saw wood that he had been coveting for years cut early. Fletchers made piles of arrows, laboriously attaching the flight feathers and arrow heads with glue and sinew threads.

Tanners worked on every fresh animal skin they could get their hands on, the smell of their trade relegating them to the outskirts of the camp. Children ran around searching the ground for small round stones that could be used in slingshots. They rounded up stray livestock and foraged with some of the women in the surrounding woodland. New looms were built and women sat, hastily preparing the few scraps of fleece they had available. Everywhere, people were busy, preparing for the coming confrontations and just trying to survive in the aftermath of the fire.

There had been no further word on Martaani's whereabouts although riders came in daily, bringing news from the patrols. The Romans seemed to have disappeared from Brigantia completely; even the borders were free from spies and scouts. The lack of news was making everyone edgy, even as it gave them more time to prepare. The war council longed for Torwain and Carrick to return.

In the woods to the north west, Kariss had found a small stream and followed it a short distance through the trees to a small pool. The surface was dark and smooth; only when you got right up to it could you hear the faint sounds of water lapping at the gravel bank. She visited the pond every day. It was her little oasis of peace in the bustling chaos of the camp.

The sounds of birdsong filled the air, interrupted every so often by the harsh clacking of the jackdaws that nested high up in the branches of the nearby elms. On the far side of the pool, a number of large rocks sat like old men, hunched and gossiping. The sight always made Kariss smile. She would make her way over and sit amongst them, chatting away as if they were old friends. They listened eagerly to her concerns, letting her vent her worries without fear of ridicule.

The sun was sending down shafts of light amongst the branches. She closed her eyes and rested her head against the largest of the old men. A breath of air fluttered against her face and she opened her eyes to see the raven perched atop the stone opposite. A moment later, it had transformed into Cailleach. She nestled down amongst the rocks and took Kariss's hands in hers.

'My child, what a sight you are to these old eyes.' It was hard to determine whether or not there were any more wrinkles in her ancient face but her hands betrayed her concern with a slight tremble that had not been present before.

Kariss felt her heart contract. 'What is it? What's wrong?'

The light in the goddess's eyes dimmed for a second but then their brightness returned and she smiled. 'Everything and nothing, my child,' she answered. 'I have no news to tell you, other than to say how proud I am of all your achievements. You have accomplished so much in your short time here.'

'But I have done nothing. It is the men, the war leaders, who are doing all the work. I am just the figurehead. I cannot claim the glory.'

Cailleach smiled. It was so typical of Kariss not to see her own worth. 'You are the one everyone has gathered behind. You inspire them, you ease their worries, and your very presence compels them to their own greatness. Do not underestimate your power here. Everything could so easily have fallen apart after Stanwick was burned. You have given the people a focus for their grief and anger.'

Is that true? Kariss thought to herself, forgetting for the moment how easily Cailleach could still hear her.

Cailleach squeezed her hands, 'Yes, it is true.'

Overhead, the jackdaws clattered and complained, rising into the air and landing again in a chorus of indignation.

'Oh, hush!' Cailleach snapped at them. Immediately, the birds fell silent and the goddess rolled her eyes. 'There are always some who fail to understand just how annoying they can be. I am sure you are finding the same?'

Kariss thought of Tarnn, then almost as quickly she thought of Taratus. He had arrived back in camp only four days after leaving and had tried a number of times to join the war council meetings but his attempts were always politely rebuffed. A number of others also came to mind, most especially the leader of the Cerones, Gartnet.

Cailleach sat back and let Kariss's mind wander whilst she ran a critical eye over her. She noted how Kariss had changed over the months she had been in Albion. No longer was she pale-skinned and slight. Her body was hard and strong, muscular, possessing a confident posture, and her weathered skin had developed a healthy glow. It was a far cry from the nervous young woman she had found in London. A fish jumped in the pool, startling them both. Cailleach laughed and looked around her.

'This is a fine place; you did well to find it. This pool has been used for scrying by many over the years. I wonder, would you like to see what the future holds?'

Kariss glanced at the dark water. Did she really want to know? Once before, she had received a vision she had not understood and it had affected her badly. Then again, the earlier image she had been given of herself wearing the gold torc of Brigantia and leading her warriors into battle had given her courage and strength many times. She thought of the time they had almost been caught at the Carvetii village. The gods had known what was about to happen, they had guided Darnus to his sacrifice. Would it have helped Kariss to know that the rest of them would be safe?

No. She knew for certain that she would never have been able to face Darnus if she had known what was about to happen. Yet the conversations she had had with him had been so important. She shook her head.

'I already know the future. We are to face Martaani and her legionnaires in battle. We have many allies, warriors have come from all over the north, some are even arriving from the southern regions. I have sent the druids away to safety and I have a strong council of advisers. No good can come from knowing any more.'

Cailleach trailed her fingers in the edge of the pool and let the ripples fan out across the surface. Watching them, she paused, before turning back to Kariss. 'Only those with true strength and wisdom can give such an answer.' The ripples softened and the water was once more like darkened glass, mirroring the branches of the trees overhead.

'When the Romans return, you may struggle to hear us again. Never forget that the future timeline you were hidden in was not chosen by chance. You did not always have a connection with us there but you succeeded, regardless. The knowledge you gained about the Romans will be invaluable soon enough.' She reached forward and placed a kiss on Kariss's forehead. 'To look forwards - you must look back.' She winked, raised her arms, and the raven took to the air. It hovered for a moment then dipped down and skimmed the top of the pond. One claw dropped and caught the water, rings circling out from its touch, catching Kariss's eye.

Before she could turn away, she saw a barn owl flying just below the surface. Taratus's face looked up from the depths, his bloodied arm reaching out to another. The ripples rode across the image, distorting the view. As it cleared again, the arms clasped and Kariss realised that the face had been replaced by that of Bodvoc. The old druid held on tightly, whispering words of reassurance to the man no longer in view. The barn owl cut across the scene once more, leaving only darkness in her wake.

Kariss stared at the water long after the images had faded from sight. *To look forwards - you must look back.* She heard Cailleach's words echo in her mind; but to where, and how far? Taratus and the owl were a memory already hovering at the edge of her mind. She had thought of it often since the morning at Barmrr Craggs, when she had recalled Taratus's youthful proposal. The barn owl was also a favoured guise of the Maiden, and the one she had used when Kariss had first come back to Albion.

What had her message been then? Kariss struggled to think. So much had happened since that cold dawn in the woods outside Naraic's village. Overhead, the branches rustled in the breeze and the jackdaws began to complain again, reminding her of that first lesson when Verbia, the maiden goddess, had told her to learn to listen and she would hear the answers she needed. Not all messages were audible ones, however, and Kariss had soon realised that the goddess's meaning of 'listening' was not quite the same as simply using her ears.

Her mind became a whirl of confused thoughts. Bodvoc was the Maiden's druid and he was the one who had stood up for Taratus when everyone else advised against it. What on earth was their connection?

Kariss could easily find links with various aspects of the Maiden in her relationships with each of them. Taratus, in the early years of her life, could easily link with the Maiden's youth and impetuousness; Bodvoc at the start of her reign could be the Maiden's innocence and naivety. None of these things seemed relevant to the war that was almost upon them, though. She was missing something.

In her frustration, she scooped up a handful of the water and splashed it over her face. The water was shockingly cold and she gasped. That was it! The maiden was also symbolic of discovery. Was Taratus acting as Bodvoc's spy, trying to find out as much as he could about the Romans by pretending to be their ally? It would certainly explain his actions over the last few months. Overhead, she heard the harsh croak of a raven. She blinked her eyes slowly, thanking the spirits of the pool for their insight.

She could not do anything with this knowledge just yet. The information was secret and if she had understood the message correctly, Taratus's life would be in danger if he was found out. Yet Cailleach had given it to her for a reason, despite her saying that she did not want to see what the future held. Kariss sat back on her heels, for once wishing that the old stone men could offer her some advice. For the goddess, just showing herself at this time was dangerous enough - especially so close to the camps - so this news must be vitally important.

Over on the far side of the water, invisible to all, the Maiden watched. Just as she always watched whenever Kariss appeared at her pool. Brigantia materialised beside her. 'It is time to go, daughter, we have lingered long enough.'

Verbia took one last look at Kariss. *You must learn to listen.*

She blended back into the ether. Brigantia looked over to where Kariss sat, lifted her hands to her lips, and blew a kiss across the water. *You will understand when the time is right.*

Hours passed and still the hunters did not return. Carrick had long since lost the feeling in his legs. It was not a good situation; he would never be able to make a quick get away should one be needed. Every so often, he would tense his muscles in short pulses. It was easy on his thighs and buttocks but isolating his calves was almost impossible. He knew that if he was to drop from the tree his legs would never hold him. Just when he thought he could not bear it any longer, he noticed a commotion at the far side of the camp. It was the hunters returning, a large boar strung beneath a long branch and carried over their shoulders. He breathed a sigh of relief and slowly began to unfurl his cramped body.

A curlew called close by. Moments later, Torwain appeared beneath him. Carrick forced his legs to work, trying not to stumble as the stiffness gradually released its hold. They were a long way from the camp before either of them spoke.

'I found Trimontium,' Torwain said as they paused for a drink at a fast-running stream. 'Cernunous stopped me from getting too close. I saw enough legionnaires and their tracks to believe that this is where they must have been gathering all this time. It is no wonder that we got no reports of them. The complex is huge, with plenty of space for men to hide. The access is guarded by a number of small villages. It is not a place one would pass without reason.'

Carrick rubbed at his chin, 'They have been recruiting the Votadini to their ranks. I saw many being trained. They are not strong enough to be of much concern to our fighters but their numbers swell the Roman forces to almost double.'

It was approaching dawn when they found themselves nearing Stanwick. The horses they had borrowed from the border patrols shook their heads and stamped, uneasy at the heavy charcoal smell still emanating from the remains. Even with the patrol's prior warning, the sight of the town was a shock. It seemed fitting to be viewed in the cold pre-dawn light. The horror and the panic of that flame-filled night still hung in the air, lending itself to the oppression of the ruins. They passed in silence.

'So, they have cobbled together an army of new recruits and a few legionnaires?' Uurad curled his lip. 'Do they not think we are worth anything better?'

Tholarg frowned, 'I find it hard to believe that the Romans would front such a weak fighting force.'

'With respect, you misunderstand me,' Carrick interrupted. 'I did not say this was a weak force; far from it. It is still much larger than anything we were

193

expecting and the legionnaires are cold and determined. They have skilled craftsmen amongst their numbers and will be fielding a formidable opposition. A good part of their number are raw recruits but just as many, if not more, are seasoned fighters. I have never seen an army with so much discipline.'

Loth considered his words, 'We must not get ahead of ourselves, these new recruits are an unknown entity - we do not know how they will act when we come to blows. From what Carrick tells us they are training constantly but they do not have the time to perfect their skills. Have no doubt, friends, when we face this enemy, we are facing many unknowns.'

'We know a fair bit about the Roman ways of fighting from our friend Umar here,' Loth continued, 'so we have been planning our strategies according to his advice. However, these new recruits are something else. Carrick is of the opinion that most have never had any sort of training before so with the limited time they have we cannot be sure how they will react when faced with battle. After the things Torwain overheard from them, there is a good chance that their egos will be so inflated they forget themselves, break ranks and charge forward. We must be prepared for all eventualities.'

Umar looked agitated. In all the months he had spent overseas learning about Roman warfare, he could not remember ever having observed how the Romans handled raw recruits on the battlefield. Whichever way they were used, they would be an unknown entity and one they had not thought to prepare for on such a scale. That, however, was not the greatest problem he could see.

The foreigners' tactics differed greatly to those of the Albion warriors. The legionnaires excelled at fixed battles, whereas the Albion warriors favoured smaller surprise attacks, catching their enemies unaware and unprepared. Umar and the war leaders had been concentrating their plans on just such tactics. They did not want to wait until battle lines were drawn and they were committed to a set battle. Now, though, with the confirmation of all the Votadini aid that the Romans were receiving, there was the probability that the traitors and possibly even higher members of Votadini society would have told their new Roman friends all about Albion's fighting skills and strategies. Not only that but some of these men may well know the local area, enabling the Romans to not only anticipate where their enemies would strike at them but also to attempt their own surprise attacks. In short, there was every possibility that Brigantia and her allies had now lost every advantage they had expected to have.

Umar let out a string of curses and pulled at his hair in frustration. Silence followed his explanation as each leader contemplated the realisation that all their preparations might have been for nothing.

Kariss had spent a lot of time thinking about Cailleach's warning, dredging her way back through everything she had learnt about the Romans whilst she was still travelling between Albion and the future. Much of her time in London had faded to obscurity but she did remember many of the things she had researched, especially about Caratacus. His defeat and subsequent betrayal by Cartimandua were common knowledge; not so well remembered were the details of his successes and failures. All this information had been later documented, supposedly by the Roman,

Tacitus, as part of his Annals. She spoke now, surprising everyone with what she had to say.

'I don't know why I didn't think of this before but the Romans kept detailed records of all their defeats and achievements. This knowledge was stored and eventually, in the future, everyone will have the chance to learn about it. I know the timeline that Cailleach sent me to was not the same as this one now but up until the battles between Cartimandua and Venutius, they are identical. This means that the Romans already know about the tactics Caratacus used against them the last time they were here. They know about his swift hit-and-run attacks before disappearing back into the cover of the trees, which do not sound so different from the things you have been planning.' She paused and looked around at the faces of the men. 'They will also know that his downfall always came in fixed battles, where the Romans proved the better. This is what they will be concentrating on.' She shrugged. 'But so can we. Umar's knowledge and experience is invaluable. We now know far more about their battle set-up than they will be expecting. We need not fear their formations in quite the same way Caratacus would have.

'We now have contingencies to use against their shield walls and surge attacks. We know to expect their silent waiting troops and noisy intimidating charges, and can prepare plans to implement when the battle is joined.

'It may be that they have got these Votadini to help them with our surprise attacks but that should not matter too much. It is the cunning and unpredictability of them that makes them so successful, and that has not changed. We just need to make sure that we don't use the more obvious ambush sites and that we choose our attacks with more precision. In short, my friends, the Romans may know more about our tactics than we would like them to, but thanks to Umar and the things I was able to learn when in hiding, we know far more about theirs.'

17

Martaani stood on the hill that rose not far away from Trimontium and watched as the Pontiff spoke furtively with the centurion. The two men were easy to distinguish, even at this distance - the centurion was wearing his crested helm, the Pontiff his distinctive priest's robes. At her side, Proculus was busy strapping his belt back over his tunic. He reached over and plucked a leaf from her hair. 'It would not do for people to know what we have been doing.'

She pulled her eyes away from the scene below and smiled at him. With one last check of her own clothing, she turned and began to walk, heading once more for the summit of the triple Eildon hills.

'One of the local men warned me that the little people are rife up here,' Proculus said as he caught up with her. 'These hills are supposed to be named after them. Maybe we could blame them for leading us astray?' His face lit up in a boyish grin.

Martaani snorted and rolled her eyes. 'This land is full of such nonsense.'

Proculus feigned a shocked expression. 'You are not afraid of them?'

'They might have chased away the people who once lived up here but they did not stop the Romans when they built their tower, nor will they drive me away.'

'You are indeed a courageous leader, my lady.' Proculus held his arms wide and dropped his head in a low bow. Martaani gave him a sidelong glance; she could always count on Proculus to lift her spirits. She might have razed Stanwick to the ground but nothing was going to soothe her temper fully until she had annihilated every threat to her reign. The palm of her hand itched. *Yes, Cloda, I am going to crush them under my foot.*

By the time they reached the northern summit and clambered over the ramparts and ditches into the centre of the once-enclosed area, the wind was chasing the clouds across the skies and whipping Martaani's hair around her face Everywhere they looked they saw scooped-out hollows that had once formed the bases of houses. There were hundreds of them. Towards the west end of the summit was a circular area, surrounded by a ditch. Proculus led the way over the causeway and together they stood on the stone floor of what had once been a Roman tower. The majority of the building had not stood the test of time but the floor stones were still scattered with fragments of pottery and old roofing tiles. Martaani gathered her hair together, pushed it into the neck of her tunic and laughed. This was more like it. This was what she would do to Stanwick. She would grind the remains of their burned-out town into dust and build a tower over the top of it. No matter that Stanwick was not on a hill. No matter that it was surrounded by thick forest and the tower would be obsolete. It would be enough just to show those peasants how irrelevant their life had been before she arrived.

She should have insisted that the Pontiff make the trek up the hill with them. He would have understood the significance of all these ruins; the man was as cunning as a bear. He knew full well that the only way to survive was to stay on top. He had been doing so himself for years. The atmosphere in Rome was still tense after the murder of Emperor Geta. Thousands had been killed in the ensuing turmoil. Caracalla wanted his brother's memory eradicated. Anyone known to have associated with Geta was assassinated. It was only through his sheer cunning that the Pontiff had so far escaped the net.

Martaani was not fool enough to think that the Pontiff had any loyalty to her. She knew that he was thinking to outwit her. She suspected the centurion was in on his plans, too. For now, though, it suited her to use them both. Centurions were often victims in battle. It was their job to lead their men into skirmish. It would be easy enough to ensure that he did not survive the coming conflict. As for the Pontiff, as soon as she had secured the Brigante throne, Martaani would send her own secret message. Julia Domna would love to hear of the tergiversator priest. He would not be so arrogant then. Whilst her son, Caracalla, was away fighting in Raetia, Julia Domna had taken over his administrative duties in Rome. Not afraid of her own controversies, she was not a woman to cross.

Down in Trimontium, the Pontiff had noticed the increase in the wind. He looked up and frowned at the sight of the coming storm; the weather on this isle really was intolerable. He found the Augur in the far corner of the complex, watching the birds as they wheeled about overhead.

'Do you see anything to worry about?'

The Augur's eye never left the birds as he waited for the right time to throw his bolas. Then, with a quick flick of the wrist, they were sailing through the air. At that moment, a sudden gust of wind lifted the birds higher and the bolas clattered to the floor, empty. The Augur turned and for a heartbeat the Pontiff bristled, waiting for an ill-conceived rebuke.

'Is Martaani inside the fort?' The Augur's usually dispassionate features were tinged with a frown.

'She went up the hill to view the old tower. She should return before long, there is a storm coming.'

The Augur raised an eyebrow at the mention of the weather - as if it were not his job to read all the signs of nature. The Pontiff felt a flush creep up his cheeks. He turned away quickly before the other man could see, scanning the side of the hill for any sign of Martaani and the praefectus. He could just make out a narrow pathway leading up to the saddle area between two of the peaks. There was no sign of any walkers. The sky was looking angry now and it would not be long before the rain began in earnest. They were going to get wet. The thought was amusing; he turned back to the Augur. 'Skin comes to no harm in a little water, she will cope.'

The Augur's return smile did not reach his eyes. 'That may be so, but there is something hidden here, something I cannot read. It may spell danger.'

The words doused the Pontiff's amusement and he looked again at the hill. This time he noticed movement - two figures were hurrying down the hillside. He barked an order to one of the legionnaires and immediately men were rushing from the fort.

Martaani thundered into the room, bedraggled and furious. The exhilaration of racing the storm down the hill had been suffocated by the arrival of a band of legionnaires to see her 'safely' home. 'How dare you send men to escort me home? Do you think I am some silly woman who is quailed by a little rain?'

The centurion's arrival was timely. He looked towards the Pontiff. 'I have secured the outer gates. No one will be entering or leaving without my knowledge from now on.'

Martaani swung around to him. 'On whose orders?'

'Mine,' the Pontiff said, taking a step forward. 'There is reason to believe there may be trouble.'

'What reason?'

'I have been unable to read the signs, everything is hidden.' The Augur waved a dismissive hand. 'Why would anyone go to the trouble of hiding nothing?'

'Have you ever been to the top of Eildons? You can see far into the distance. If there was an army out there we would have seen it.' Martaani glared at him. 'Did you ever consider that, just maybe, you could not find anything because there is nothing to find?'

The Augur did not flinch, he looked her straight in the eye, and with a quiet voice said, 'And would you be able to see a single spy?' He had still neither forgotten nor forgiven her refusal to accept his warnings once before.

The silence in the room was palpable. Martaani rolled the words around in her head as she thought back to her time on the hill. She and Proculus had lain together in the blanketing ling under a hawthorn tree, knowing full well that the mass of plants would hide them from view. If they could be so active, secure in the knowledge that they could not be seen, then clearly someone lying still and making no noise would be easily overlooked. The thought made her skin crawl. Subconsciously, she raised her chin; what went on between two people in private was not wrong, she would not let the thought of a voyeur make her feel shamed.

The three men were looking at her, waiting for her response. The Augur's face was defiant, almost challenging. She was growing tired of his ire. Still, she had ignored his warnings once before and paid the price, she would not be such a fool a second time. 'Have men sent out to search the area, immediately. If there is anyone out there, I want him found. Whatever he has seen must not get back to Brigantia.'

The centurion nodded. Hunching his shoulders against the rain, he hurried outside. The courtyard was only partially paved. Already, puddles were beginning to form where the rain had run from the flagstones and pooled on the dry mud. It oozed over the soles of his boots, through the open leatherwork of the upper, and soaked his socks. The legionnaires would not be happy at being sent out in this weather. He rounded up four groups, ignored their complaints, and sent them on their separate ways. One over to Eildons, another across the river, and two to cover the remaining expanse of flat ground.

Martaani paced the room as the men argued. They had been going around in circles for hours and her head was beginning to throb. Even the Augur was showing signs of frustration. The centurion was adamant, 'If we move now, we use the weather as cover and the element of surprise will be ours.'

'To do so would mean losing our best advantage,' the Pontiff argued. The plan had been made, as far as he was concerned. Unless they heard anything further, they should stick with it.

The centurion threw his hands up in the air. 'You are not a military man, you do not understand the intricacies of war. The advantage is lost if the Brigantians get wind of our plans.'

His sergeant, the Tesserarius, was quick to support the centurion. 'If we press on now, we have the knowledge of what is following. A back-up plan, if you like. How can we fail? It is like putting both plans into action at once.'

Both men had been dismayed at how the original plans had developed over the last few weeks. They wanted the glory of conquest for themselves; they did not believe the new plans were necessary. Neither of them had seen the amassing northern army and so were basing their knowledge on the Votadini recruits. If they had seen it, they would not be so quick in urging haste. After all, diluted glory was better than failure, any day.

The Pontiff slammed his hands down on the table. 'The gods have spoken.' He could feel his nerves starting to fray. It had begun with the loss of Torwain. That filthy druid had got under his skin, destroyed his resolve and thrown bare his vulnerability. The cold, calculating eyes of the Augur bored into him whenever they got the chance. Did he somehow know what had happened? The Pontiff hid his doubts in anger. Brigantia must be theirs; he could not be on the losing side again.

For the Pontiff, Albion was a safe haven from his precarious position in Rome. His connection with Geta made him vulnerable. Only by securing his favour with Caracalla would he finally feel safe again. The Pontiff's swift change of allegiance had saved him for the last few years but for long-lasting security he really needed to ingratiate himself into Caracalla's good books. The Emperor's hatred of Albion was well known. He would love nothing more than to conquer the island and swallow it into the vast Roman Empire. He would look favourably on anyone who helped him achieve this goal.

The Pontiff prided himself on his own knowledge, accumulated over the years through ingenious and frequently dubious methods. He courted those in positions of privilege wherever he could and made it his business to learn as much as possible about such people and their plans. He guarded his secrets carefully; after all, knowledge was power. Martaani may think that she would be in control of Brigantia and the subsequent take-over of Albion when she defeated Kariss but the Pontiff knew full well that once he was finished conquering the troublesome Alamanni, Emperor Caracalla would be straight across the sea and no matter what her plans might be Martaani would be reduced to nothing more than an ineffectual client queen.

Martaani stopped her pacing as the Pontiff's voice rose; she was torn. Did they wait for their requested extra troops, knowing full well that the Brigantians were building a substantial army against them, or did they take the swift and hopefully decisive route? The gods wanted them to wait; the promotion-hungry centurion wanted to move now; and she... she just wanted to kill them all. She looked at the Augur. 'You have been quiet ever since you gave us your vague warning. You have caused these problems by blinkering our plans, what do you suggest we do?'

A smile played around the edges of his mouth. 'The men are not yet back from their searching. We do not know what they will find. To move now would be folly. We would be walking into blackness with only half our strength. The gods have better eyes than we have, we should wait... but!' He rushed on as the centurion and tesserarius made to interrupt. 'We should be preparing to move at a moment's notice.'

'Might I interrupt?' Proculus had been leaning against the wall at the back of the room but now he stepped forward. 'If we cannot see the way ahead as it was planned - why not change the plan to our advantage? Send two runners to the coast then, when the ships come into view, one of the runners sails out to intercept them and direct them to land down the coast at the estuary east of Stanwick. The other runner races back here to give us word, and we march. Our enemy will have their eyes to the north; they will not expect attack from the east as well. If there has been a spy watching us, it will have done them no good at all. He will be taking the wrong information back with him.'

Martaani threw back her head and laughed. The centurion, though annoyed that his plans had been thwarted, could not deny the ingeniousness of the scheme. Not sure whether he wanted to praise him or punch him, he nodded his respect to Proculus. Smugly, Martaani turned to the priests. 'Does that satisfy you?'

The Augur looked sidelong at the Pontiff before speaking. 'We must still tread carefully. Until the threat becomes clear, we do not know what the warning entails.'

Martaani's impatience had cost them dearly before; they could not afford for it to do so again. She rolled her eyes at their caution. 'I warn you, once we take

Brigantia, I will not tolerate such pessimism. You will need to learn my ways quickly if you want to keep your places at my side.'

18

The boards were slippery and narrow. Kariss trod carefully. Where the boards ended, she stopped and opened her pouch. Inside were three small staves. She thought back to the trees they had come from. The yew stick had been a gift from Fiantann. When she had been travelling north with Naraic they had visited the tree for guidance before entering the secret tunnel beneath Schiehallion, Cailleach's sacred mountain. Fiantann had given them both a stave to act as their protection in the dark, a reminder that help was still there even when they could not see it.

The hazel had come from Coll, under whose branches she had once been hidden to keep safe. The stave had been placed in her hand by the druid Nectan and had helped to draw her spirit back to her body when Martaani's priests had blocked her from returning to Albion. She closed her eyes and hoped that someone had done the same for her parents.

The last one was a rowan. She had rested against Luis on their journey south. He had given her the stick, along with a warning vision. She had worried about that vision so much. Lifting it out of the pouch, she was about to throw it into the bog when something stayed her hand. This stave was associated with a time that was painful to remember - the time she had misinterpreted a message from the gods and Naraic had been captured. It was no sacrifice to let it go. She returned it to the pouch. Closing her eyes, she breathed in deeply, holding the air inside her for a long time. As she finally exhaled, she remembered the image Coll had given her. She was seated astride a horse with Anniel at her side. Around her neck was the golden torc that signified her status as Queen of the Brigantes. She was leading a war band and they were going to battle. She held the memory for a moment, feeling all the weight of responsibility that her new role carried pressing down on her. Her hand tightened on the hazel stave as if, for those last few seconds, she could leach from it all the protection it had to offer. Feeling a deep pang of loss, she threw it far into the bog.

Making her way back along the wooden walkway to firmer ground, she felt a tear roll down her cheek. She could not deny the fear she felt. Anniel touched her lightly on the shoulder before making his own way out to the offering site. He already knew what his sacrifice would be. He pulled the gold cuff from his arm, kissed it, and hurled it far into the mire. It had been his father's last gift to him.

One by one, people made their way forward to give their offerings. Kariss watched them, knowing that this was yet another thing that people in the future would misinterpret. They believed such votive offerings were always valuable items. They were, of course, but the value that counted was sentimental, not financial. A lock of hair from a loved one, a good luck stone or even the hazel twig would be overlooked or else rot into the bog, never to be seen again. Yet these were treasures too - just as important, if not more so - than trinkets and weapons.

The light was beginning to fail by the time everyone had taken their turn. Corio stepped forward once more. 'Deae Nymphae Brigantia, have no doubt that our love for you is true. We sacrifice our most treasured possessions so that our nation may be protected and in order that you, our mother, may be safe. Your land and your people are under threat but we will stand firm in the face of the tyrant Martaani. We will abnigate the viper's claim on this nation whilst ever we still have breath in our bodies. We will not be part of the Roman Empire; the Romans will not grind us under their feet. We give so that we may all be saved, so that in their turn every one of Albion's gods may be saved.'

He moved away from the boardwalk and the crowd followed him to a nearby stand of hawthorn trees. Here, held tightly - one guard on each of his arms - was the man who had started Stanwick's fire. His defiance had left him days ago and his remaining anger had evaporated the moment he saw the huge group of people he was being led towards. Now only fear remained. It showed in his eyes, which flicked from the tall druid to the crowds behind. He tried to back away, choosing the armed guards over the strange religion. If he was to die, he wanted it to be by something he understood, but he had forfeited that right the moment he touched flames to the roofs of their houses.

The townspeople formed an arc behind Corio, with the northern warriors at their rear. Even the kings and warleaders took their places at the back. Rank held no bearing here - this part of proceedings was the Brigantes' right. Their justice, their redress. Tomorrow, some of the northerners would be quietly heading out to make a start on their plans. Until then, they were happy to stand back and let the Brigantians have their retribution.

'Uath awake! Hear us now. See us standing here.' Corio began to walk around the hawthorns, touching them here and there, making sure to connect to every one. The thorns caught at his hand but he made no attempt to avoid them. Standing in front of the trees once more, he bowed his head in greeting and everyone else followed suit.

'We have been vulnerable,' he called out. 'Our energies blocked. We ask that you release us from our bindings so that we may let go of our fears and trust in ourselves again.' He turned and signalled to Callimai. She stepped forward, her head held high. Volisios squeezed her hand and let her go; she deserved this honour. It had taken courage to tackle the man, alone as she was in the dark. Beside him, Callimai's father watched with pride. He had always known that his daughter was a strong woman, it pleased him that everyone else saw it now.

She had been reticent at first when Corio had given her the chance to take part in the ritual. Her father had talked with her long into the night, convincing her that she should accept. The people needed to see an ordinary person recognised for their bravery and she owed it to herself to look into the face of the man she had already bested. Let him see just who it was who had stopped him.

She walked towards the prisoner, looking him straight in the eyes. A step or two away she stopped, waiting. He was puzzled; this woman was not frightening, she was no druid or warrior. Then, from behind her back, she produced a rock. Corio started to speak again but the prisoner had no idea what he was saying. He struggled against his captors, keeping his wide eyes on Callimai and the rock. Surely she was not going to be the one who killed him?

'We do not ask this of you without payment. We do not seek to take and not to give.' Corio moved to stand beside Callimai. 'This man stole into our town, fired our homes and killed our kin. Without Callimai, he would have been free to return to his own folk a hero. This coward attacked us in the dark with our eyes turned away. But we will not be victims! We will not let the taint of his actions lay over us.

'Here, as the dark falls once more, we let go of the fear this man made us suffer. We cast back the weakness he sought to instil in us. We give you his spirit so that ours can be freed. His life was used to aid our downfall; his death will give us back our strength.' From inside his robes, Corio produced a knife and held it aloft. Trickles of blood danced across his hand from the cuts made by the tree's thorns. He squeezed the bone handle tightly to help it flow. This was the payment the trees had wanted - or else they would not have harmed him when he touched them. He gave it gladly.

The guards tightened their grip on the prisoner's arms; he was struggling even more now. One of them grabbed the man's hair and forced his head back. The man did not need to speak their tongue to understand what was to happen. The knife flashed in the last of the sunlight as Corio brought it swiftly down and across the man's throat. Blood spurted from the wound, splattering the front of Callimai's dress as she stepped forward and brought the rock down hard on his head, one final time. The guards let the body drop. It crumpled in a heap at their feet and the crowd cheered. Corio said a few quiet words of thanks to the trees and then turned to face everyone.

'We are not victims,' he declared. 'Each and every one of us has a role to play.' He took hold of Callimai's hand and raised it into the air. 'We do not all need to be warriors to be heroes.' Letting go of her hand, he kissed her forehead. 'Brigantia blesses you, my child.'

Kariss felt a little sick but she hardened her heart to it. She had only to think of Lord Hightern, suffering such an unthinkable end. Once again, Martaani had swept in and taken out a king that had meant so much to her. The viper might not have used her own hand this time but there was no doubt that this man had been working in her stead. He had chosen his path, he deserved such an end. He would not be the last Roman to die at their hands and if his death could inspire the townsfolk to strengthen their resolve and stand united with the warriors, this sacrifice would not have been in vain.

She watched Callimai carefully, feeling more than a little similarity in their respective lives. Callimai had been living her quiet life, making candles with her father, until she had found herself in the position of having to face her fears or run away. Choosing courage, she had found herself thrown into the limelight and her life would never be the same again. Kariss knew exactly how that felt. When the town was re-built, Kariss intended that Callimai and her father would be given a bigger house. She was even toying with the idea of giving her a position in the fort, so that she could be nearer to Volisios. Her father would have to be compensated for the loss of his daughter in the family trade but the bigger premises and provision of a couple of apprentices should suffice. For now, Kariss had ensured that they were given one of the better shelters.

Corio felt his skin prickle again. It had been happening ever since the offerings the previous day. This time, the butterflies in his stomach were even more pronounced. There was no doubting it - someone was calling him. He thought of Ioho or the scrying pool in the woods but something told him that they were too close. He had no time to make the trip to How Tallon but there was a sacred spring to the north west, by the far bank of the river Tees. If he rode, he could easily make it there and back before nightfall.

Grateful for the rest, the horse blew out a sigh and stamped a foot, showering the ground with water droplets from his wet fetlock, then contented himself by ripping mouthfuls of grass out by the roots. The dapples in his grey coat blended well with the surrounding woodland. Corio loosened the girth strap and threw the reins over a branch. He would not be long and the horse would be safe enough here.

The rushing sound of water over a stony bed could be heard close by. Here, the river formed a double snake, where the water wove back and forth. It did not take long to locate the spring in the larger of the two loops. The sweet, clear water bubbled from the ground in a pulsing flow. Corio perched on a large stone, crossing his legs and concentrating on his deep, even breaths. Verbia appeared almost at once.

You have no need to call; I have been waiting for you.

Corio opened his eyes. The maiden stood before him with her feet in the water, the hem of her flowing gown turning translucent in the wet. She plucked a hazel leaf from an overhead branch and waved it in the air.

'It is not Brigantia who has been calling you,' she told him. 'It is I. Events are moving swiftly, too swiftly for much intrigue and planning. You must be fluid and ready to change course at a moment's notice - a little like my water here.'

Annoyance prickled at Corio; the maiden was not averse to playing her youthful games. 'Why would you distract me from Brigantia? She will need me at Kariss's side.'

Verbia's eyes flashed dangerously. The meek and mild child-like goddess was gone. 'Brigantia does not need you to speak to Kariss for her. Do not mistake my youth for foolishness, Corio,' she snapped. 'If Albion is to triumph then you must listen to me.'

'Albion? What about Brigantia?'

The goddess's eyes twinkled again, her mouth hinting at a smile. 'Well done,' she told him. 'You must remain this attuned. For in order to stand any chance of defeating the Roman threat, it is the little things that will give you the best advantage. This is a new time, Corio, a new beginning. Whilst the others are distracted with their own roles, you must watch for that which has not been expected.'

Corio looked at her with distrust. Were the goddesses playing with him? He had spent years developing his connection with Brigantia and serving her nation. Now he was being told that in the coming battle, he had no part. That Kariss and Brigantia had no need of him. Was this more of the Roman priests' doing, did they think to emasculate him?

Verbia held out her arms, reaching towards him. He faltered for a moment or two before answering with his own outstretched hands. As she took hold of them, he felt her warmth flow through his fingers and along his arms, filling his whole body with love and light. 'There is no slight here, Corio. Of course Brigantia values you. She values you so highly that she trusts you and you alone to watch for the new danger that we believe is coming.'

'What danger?'

Verbia released his hands and folded her arms across her body, her light dimming a little as she did so. 'We do not know. The Roman gods are blocking our senses but there is something in the air that we cannot explain. I fear that we will not see it until it is too late. I implore you, Corio, no matter how obvious the battle ahead appears, you must be wary, for when the mist of battle descends, you will not hear our calls.'

Corio could feel the concern coming from the goddess. Panic blossomed in the pit of his stomach as he listened.

'The Roman priests are strong but it weakened them when the Terminus stone was found and taken away. Once it had left our shores, we were able to feel the presence of something cloaked coming closer.' She shook her head in frustration, 'If you could find a way to break the priests, then...'

She caressed his face, smoothing the lines of worry from his brow. 'Be vigilant, Corio. Let the others fight whilst you watch for our signs.'

The druid stayed at the spring long after the goddess had left him. Thoughts tumbled around in his mind, each one discarded, as useless to him as the one which came before. He had been unable to fight the priests when they resided at Stanwick. How on earth was he going to defeat them now that they were elsewhere? He could not leave Kariss's side. Even with her skills at communicating with the gods, he was still needed. He picked up the hazel leaf that Verbia had dropped. This task had been given by the goddess of youth and new beginnings; he needed a new way of looking at it. He twisted the leaf idly between his fingers.

Plants and the goddess, he thought. The image of Bodvoc appeared in his mind. Suddenly, he remembered the gorse hideaway behind Ioho. Bodvoc had planted a number of such places in preparation for the coming troubles. Could they be used somehow? His horse whickered in the distance, it was getting impatient. Corio watched the leaf; hazel was renowned for wisdom, the essence of knowing and deep listening. He tucked the leaf inside his robes, next to his heart. By the time he reached Stanwick he knew what must be done.

19

The air was full of sound: birds singing, insects buzzing, and from far away an axe chopping wood. Kariss could hear the call of the wren, louder than all the others, leading her on. She had dreamed of the bird first. Actually, she had been dreaming about riding horses with Anniel but the wren had found her. It had flown onto her horse's head and started singing its demanding song. Then it had flown straight at her face with its sharp, stubby bill. She had woken with a start, unharmed, only to see the wren on the floor of her makeshift home, still singing. Kariss looked over to Anniel. He was fast asleep, his mouth curved into a smile. The wren grew more insistent, hopping from place to place with a burr of fluttering wings, its voice never letting up for a moment.

Kariss got the message. She slipped out of the bed, pulling her dress over her head and tying her belt around her waist. Her knife and pouch were already hanging from the belt but she grabbed her smallest blade as well, just in case she needed extra protection. The blade was only the size of her little finger and pushed up into a tight leather sheath, which hung around her neck. She tucked it down the front of her dress and, shoeless, she ducked outside.

The wren was waiting for her. She followed as it led the way down towards the ceremonial area. The sky was only just beginning to lighten and the dawn chorus was already in full swing. Even so, the wren's voice stood out above all the others.

It was clear from the sounds of chopping wood that Kariss was not the only one up and about but she saw no one else. The world in front of her was as fresh as it could be.

From time to time, she felt a light brush on her face as she walked through invisible strands of cobwebs. She could even make out the tracks of a fox in the dew-soaked grass. Her own feet were wet now and she rather liked the feeling.

It was no real surprise when the wren flew into the branches of Ioho. By the time Kariss had picked her way amongst the heavy branches, Brigantia was already waiting for her. The goddess's face was drawn, concern clouding her features, making her look stern. Kariss felt her insides flip as she bowed her head in greeting. They sat amongst the fallen yew needles on the compacted soil between two of the large branches that had returned to the ground. Here they were hidden from view, should anyone pass their way. Brigantia reached for Kariss's hands, just as Cailleach always did when she had news to impart. Beside her, Verbia appeared, looking just as worried. Kariss's heart sank a little more, plummeting still further when Cailleach herself arrived.

'What is wrong? What has happened?'

'We have... grave news, it is something we did not foresee and had not planned for.'

'What?' Kariss almost shouted.

Brigantia stalled again. Her daughter and mother moved closer in silent support. Kariss wanted to scream at them. She looked from one goddess to another. They had never appeared in unison to give her news before. Her immediate thought was Anniel but she knew that he was safe. She ran through everyone she was close to; when she got to her parents she felt Brigantia's hands tighten around hers.

'Your father has been taken by the Romans.'

Kariss felt her skin go clammy - hot and cold all at the same time. The blood drained from her face. 'What of my mother? Is she taken? Is she safe?' She fired the questions one after the other, giving the goddesses no time to answer.

'Your mother escaped but she is trapped.'

Images and thoughts flashed through Kariss's mind: her father's voice as he hugged her in the forest; the sight of her mother's face; the memory of her own terrifying escape from the future. 'She can leave any time she wants,' Kariss told the goddesses, 'Doesn't she know that, she just has to...' Even though she knew that her mother would be safe enough, she could not bring herself to say the words.

Brigantia smiled, though it never quite reached her eyes, but it was Cailleach who answered her. 'Your mother will not leave your father. I have already given her that option. Right now, the Romans cannot bring your father back. He is protected by my magic and unless they can find a way to break its hold, they are all stuck there for now. Your mother has the means to bring herself home to Albion but she knows that it is a final act. That doing so will mean she will be unable to return to where she is now - to where your father is being held.'

'Your mother has the heart of a lioness,' Brigantia told Kariss. 'She has a plan. She will get them both home if it is at all possible. For now, you will have to put your faith in her, just as everyone in Albion has put their faith in you.'

Kariss pulled her hands from Brigantia's and rubbed them over her face. 'Aggghhhhh, this is such a mess. I can't believe this is happening. How is my mother supposed to bring them both back if Father is a prisoner?'

Cailleach tutted and shook her head. 'You know the answer to that, my child.'

'Your mother insists that she is strong enough and we must believe her,' Brigantia said.

Verbia moved forward and stroked Kariss's hair. 'This is a time for new strength. If ever you begin to doubt your mother, think about what you would do in her place. You have already had to find the courage to bring yourself home. Could you send Anniel back first and then follow him?'

Kariss thought of her own return. She had been so scared and so desperate. Life in London had become intolerable. If her plan had failed, at least she had known that oblivion was better than staying put. It was one thing to take such a chance with her own life but to take it with the life of someone she loved..? Then again, Cailleach had already told her mother that this was their only way. Kariss's shoulders went back and her chin lifted. Yes, she thought, if I knew for sure that it was our only way home, I would be able to kill Anniel.

'Your mother loves your father just as much as you love Anniel. She will be able to do this. She has managed every challenge put to her; she will not fail this one.' Verbia moved back beside Brigantia, and Cailleach moved forward.

'Know that Martaani will try to use this information to weaken you. She will not know that we have spoken - that we already know. The Roman gods have no power in that future world,' she wrinkled her nose in disgust. 'Their names are no more than stories. They do not cross the divide as I do. Martaani relies on messengers; she will assume that it is the same for us. The Romans know where your mother is, though they cannot get to her. They will know that no messenger has been sent. My child, the way forward is harder now than we had ever envisioned. Put your faith in your mother, as you once put your faith in us, as we are putting our faith in you.' She leaned forward and placed a kiss on Kariss's brow.

Kariss felt a warmth flood through her, filling her with courage. She hoped that the goddess had done the same to her mother. She knew Lizzelle was a strong woman; she had to be, or she would not have been able to manage the things she had already done to keep her daughter safe. Not once had Lizzelle refused, not once had she lost her faith in Kariss. She realised now just how proud she was of her mother, how honoured she was to be her daughter. She could not remember Margeof, her grandmother, but she wondered if she had been a strong woman too. Was it a family trait?

'It is the royal blood in your veins, child.' Brigantia answered her unvoiced question. 'Your father always told you right, it is rare blood indeed.'

Kariss felt a lump forming in her throat. The thought of her father as prisoner to the Romans was unbearable. She closed her eyes and pushed away the images that were forcing their way into her mind. She would not think of it. Kydas had survived all those months of captivity, her father would survive too.

When she opened her eyes again, Verbia and Cailleach had gone. There was just Brigantia left in

222

front of her. 'You must stay strong, Kariss. Remember, everyone close to you has suffered because of Martaani and her priests. I think only Carrick has evaded them but then, he has suffered enough already.' She waved her hand to dismiss the comment and Kariss wondered again just what had happened to that man in the past. 'You have all come this far because of your strength; do not let this news weaken you. Your mother is proud of her fight for my nation; she would not want you to quail now.'

Kariss took a deep breath, filling her lungs with the fresh morning air. She held it for a few counts before releasing it slowly. In her mind, she heard the words her father had said to her when they had been forced to leave her in London: *One day we will be together again, one day we will see what a fine, strong girl you truly are. I will live for that day.* She smiled at Brigantia.

'Martaani has made a big mistake,' she told her, 'if she thinks that holding my father will stay my hand. She is very wrong. The only way to get him back is to fight. The only way any of us have got through our challenges has been to remember our gods, and to fight: Naraic fought his terror to get out of The Cauldron; Kydas fought his weakness to escape his captors and get himself to me; Anniel fought his grief; Torwain fought the Pontiff. Not everyone has won their fights.' She thought of Darnus and of Dei, of Lord Alpin, Annyetta and Inan. 'But fighting gave them their only chance and each time, it saved others; it saved me. I will not let them die in vain. Nor will I let Martaani use my father to break my spirit. He would never forgive me if I gave up because of him. He is waiting for the day I prove how strong I can be. That day is coming and I am ready for it.'

Her journey back to the fort was not as peaceful as her walk to Ioho. Voices could be heard in the surrounding woods; people were running, their shouts echoing through the trees. Volisios came hurrying down the path from the town with two guards behind him. He stopped dead when he saw her and bowed his head. 'My Lady, we thought you had been taken.'

Kariss was still not used to being called 'my Lady', it made her a little uncomfortable but she knew better than to complain. It was a mark of respect and one that she hoped she could do justice to. At least royalty did not have such formal roles as they would have in times to come. She would never have been able to cope with all that.

Even the titles of King and Queen, Lord or Lady, were not universally used; each ruler seemed to be different. She thought of Loth, Uurad and Galan; each of them kings of their respective nations but none of them using the title. Kariss liked this way of ruling. It was as if 'leader' were just another role, like a blacksmith or a farmer. A farmer would not tell a blacksmith how to work his magic with metal any more than he would tell a king or queen how to rule. Likewise, a ruler should not tell a farmer how to work his land, or the blacksmith how to produce a sword. Later centuries could keep their self-inflated importance; Kariss was quite content to keep all that to a minimum.

She could see the worry in Volisios's face; it was mirrored in those of the accompanying men. She held up her hands in a peaceful gesture. 'I am fine, really. I am sorry I caused such worry. The gods called, I had to answer them.' She saw his face relax a little but with it came a frown.

'You must leave word next time; the warriors are all out searching, Anniel is beside himself with worry.' As he spoke, he flicked a hand out and the two men raced off to spread the word that she was safe.

Conflicted, Volisios turned, ready to accompany Kariss back up to the fort. Part of him was impressed by this strange woman. Her pull to the gods must be very strong to make her walk out of the camp alone and unafraid whilst her enemies gathered ready for battle. Yet her naivety was concerning. She did not seem to realise the great danger she was in. She needed a guard of her own; someone who could be trusted to watch over her and keep her safe. He thought of his conversation with Callimai and before he realised what he was doing, he had dropped to one knee. 'My Lady, you need a personal guard, someone who is there for you and you alone. If it is not too presumptuous, I would be happy to fill that role.'

Overhead, Kariss heard the cry of an eagle; she looked up to see the bird circling, leisurely riding the thermals. She signalled for Volisios to rise and moved to sit on a fallen tree. 'I am very different to Lord Hightern. I have protection that people cannot see. I was in no danger this morning.'

Volisios raised an eyebrow.

'You do not believe me, but in order to be my personal guard you would need to trust me with such things. You would not be able to accompany me everywhere I go.'

'As your personal guard, it would be my duty to see you safe always.'

Kariss sighed, she had expected as much. 'It is for that reason that I cannot accept your offer. I have no doubt in your abilities and that you are a good man, but I need someone who will recognise who I am and work with me.'

Volisios looked puzzled. 'You are our leader, our queen. I would do as you ask.'

'But you would not let me leave the camp alone or wander in the woods by myself? You would question if I did something you felt was unsafe?'

'That is what a personal guard does, my Lady.'

'That is what a personal guard does for other people. I am not the same.'

'Every leader is different, I agree, but keeping you safe is the same. In that I have all the experience needed, there is no person here better able to protect you than me.'

Kariss shuffled sideways, making room for Volisios to sit. He shook his head and stayed standing. Kariss sighed again. She liked him and she liked the fact that he hadn't taken her refusal and walked away. She knew that she would be safe with him as her guard, but she needed flexibility. 'To be my personal guard you would have to throw out all that you are used to, tear up your rule book and start again.'

'Rule book?'

'See,' she said, flushing, 'I don't even speak the same words as you. I have been places, lived places, that you could never imagine. Places where the people speak very differently to here, so you need to allow me some mistakes.'

Volisios nodded. Her speech was a little different. She clipped words and joined others as he had never heard done before. He saw her cheeks colour and wanted even more to protect her. She was very young for such an important role; it would make a refreshing change from guarding an old man.

In the woods, the sounds of the searchers were fading as word got around that Kariss was safe. Volisios was still wary, though; he did not want anyone creeping up on them unawares. He suggested that they move back to the camp.

'We are quite safe, I assure you,' Kariss said, ignoring his concerns. It was important that he understood. 'I came down here to Ioho because Brigantia came for me. She woke me from my sleep and guided me to the tree. There was never any doubt as to my safety. Brigantia wouldn't lead me into danger. The gods see far more than we can, they don't appear unless it is safe. Even now, Bodach is watching us.'

Volisios looked around him nervously. He was a devout man, never doubting his faith in the gods, but he had never heard them speak, let alone seen one watching him. Kariss pointed up to the eagle. 'The gods have guided me ever since I returned to Albion. I am only here now because I put my faith in them. They come to me in bird form, and they come to me as themselves. If they cannot come, they send word some other way.'

As if to prove her point, the eagle let out a sudden, angry screech. Kariss looked up to see the bird plummeting downwards. 'We must leave.'

They ran together up the hill towards the camp, Volisios keeping two steps behind to protect Kariss from whoever may be following. Kariss tried to ignore the pain in her bare feet; it seemed as if every sharp object possible was in her path. She stumbled a number of times but luckily did not twist an ankle. They made it safely to the camp and found that everyone was already mustering.

Anniel stood with Loth and Tholarg; he saw Kariss and Volisios approaching and hurried to meet them. In his hand he held a small wooden boat, still dripping with water. 'Torwain's message has arrived.'

'Send Uurad's warriors,' Kariss ordered as she ran to grab her things. 'Where is Tarnn? Are his men ready?'

Voices called back to her, confirming that Uurad was already preparing to leave. Tarnn himself appeared shortly after, half his cavalry close behind. They exchanged a few words and then the horses were gone, charging north to intercept the Roman forerunners. In the main camp, word was quickly spreading. There was not really any panic, only the strained actions of people who knew their roles and had been anxiously waiting for the dreaded time to arrive.

Kariss caught sight of Taratus, organising his men and preparing to leave with the main army. He appeared calm but concerned for his men. No different from anyone else, really. In the time that he had been at the camp he had never once tried to talk with her. He would be distant but always polite if they came across one another, though that had rarely happened. He was keeping himself well to himself, tucked firmly amongst the Wendell contingent and causing no trouble.

The war council had finally opened up their meetings to the representatives of each of Brigantia's forts. For all that he had been eager to find out what was being planned, Taratus had not taken a prominent position, choosing instead to sit at the back, far away from the stern eyes of the war council. He seemed happy to go along with whatever was asked of him. That pleased Kariss. Whilst she had relaxed her concerns about him since her meeting with Cailleach, she preferred to keep him close at hand so that she could be aware of anything out of the ordinary. She had not mentioned anything about that meeting to anyone, let alone Bodvoc or Taratus; they must have reasons for keeping their own counsel and she knew better than to interfere.

They were ready to leave by the time the sun hit its zenith. Gathered together, the force was huge. Kariss and Anniel rode in the front, just as Coll had predicted. The majority of the warriors were on foot and marched behind the leaders and remainder of the cavalry. At the rear came the support waggons and army followers. Only the old, the young with their mothers, and the infirm would remain behind, with a small number of men to protect them. The children ran after them for a short way, cheering and laughing with excitement until their anxious mothers called them back. Kariss did not envy them staying behind. It was frightening heading out to battle but better to be busy than waiting around with no idea who would be coming back.

Corio took a moment to say farewell to Bodvoc. The old druid was too infirm to take to the road with them and would remain at the camp. He was not so sorry to be missing the action; he had played his part over the years to get the area ready. There was only one thing remaining that he still had a part in but it was not yet for Corio's ears. Bodvoc let him go with a sigh and stepped back amongst the waiting women. Only Taratus caught his wink as he passed. He responded with the slightest nod of his head.

20

The air was calm, the early morning mist still rising. It was going to be a hot day. They had been waiting since long before dawn, hunkered down in the shrub layer. Through the trees they could just see the hidden valley which Loth's scouts assured them the first wave of legionnaires were heading towards.

A horse stamped a foot and shook the damp from its mane. Tarnn shot a warning look in its direction. The last thing they needed was to have their location given away by restless horses. One of the cavalrymen slipped silently through the trees and led the mount further away before it could set the others off.

Time seemed to slow and every noise sounded louder to the waiting warriors than it should. Bodies stiffened and joints ached as they tried to keep their thoughts under control. It was the same before any conflict. Men would find their minds wandering over their lives, their accomplishments, things they were proud of; although more often it was things that they regretted or would miss that came to the fore. If they were not careful, their thoughts would turn maudlin as the waiting time robbed them of their eagerness.

Suddenly, every ear pricked up. The noise came again - unmistakable this time. Tarnn raised a hand and every man made ready. Through the trees, they began to catch sight of movement. Troops making their way along the valley floor. They marched in silence but there was no way to cover the sounds of their rattling mail and their footsteps hitting the ground in unison. The scouts had told them this was just a small group and they were right. When all the legionnaires were in sight, Tarnn dropped his arm, rose to his feet, and let out a roar.

All around him, the forest came to life as warriors charged from their hiding places and ran in full voice down towards the legionnaires, their war cries ricocheting off the trees. Behind them, a carnyx sounded long and loud, the noise resonating deeply.

The legionnaires were slow to react. By the time they had unsheathed their swords the men were upon them. The rout was over quickly. Nineteen legionnaires and two Brigantes lay dead on the ground. Only one Roman still drew breath - but not for long.

'Tell me your plans,' Tarnn demanded.

The legionnaire looked blank, his blue eyes wide and defiant. Tarnn pushed his blade against the man's throat.

'Tell me your plans,' he repeated, in Latin this time.

A trace of fear flashed across the legionary's face; he had not expected these barbarians to speak his language. Then again, he had not expected to be ambushed so far from Stanwick. From the corner of his eye he could see the bodies of his small force being dragged away. Only their blood would remain, painting the greenery with bright strokes of red.

The legionary gulped, feeling the tip of the blade pressing into his adam's apple. Would his death be quick? Would they torture him for information? Or just offer him as a sacrifice to their blood-thirsty gods? It was well known how the druids loved to honour their gods with blood and fear. Better to die a soldier's death than a goat's. With a scream, he plunged himself forwards, catching those holding him unawares. He felt a moment of pain as the blade pierced his skin and then the world went mercifully blank.

Undeterred, Tarnn ordered the men to clear the area. The bodies were hauled from the valley and dumped in a heap where bushy ground cover would hide them from prying eyes. Satisfied, Tarnn gathered his men and they rode away with two bodies slung over the backs of the spare horses. They did not leave their own men behind to rot with the Romans.

Torwain watched as the blackbird flew scolding through the dense holly and bramble. The warning was clear. He turned and made his way towards the fast-running stream. The Spenny Beck began life a little further north, trickling sedately through dense ground cover until it broke free of the peaty ground. Here, the beck hurried over a stony bed before sending its white water crashing over the cliff. In his hand, Torwain carried a piece of birch, a handspan in length and carved to resemble a little boat. He dropped it into the water and watched as his second signal was carried away.

Further downstream, Uurad waited, watching the water for the sign. The cliff towered over the surrounding land, offering unrivalled views for many miles. Anyone coming down the winding cliff path would be reassured that a waiting army would be easily spotted, but the area was deceiving. A hidden hollow provided plenty of room for Uurad and Galan's warriors to hide unseen.

The remainder of Galan's men had arrived late. They had been delayed by swollen rivers, bad weather and sodden ground over the Spine of Albion. Their apologies had been waved away. There was barely enough room or food to cope with the numbers that had congregated outside Stanwick. Already, the land had been stripped almost bare. The men's delay had done everyone a favour - surely yet another sign that the gods were still watching over them.

Spenny Beck narrowed as it carved its way southwards. It was an easy matter to step into the flow and retrieve the little boat. Uurad took out his small eating knife and scored a deep cross in its hull before dropping it back into the water to continue on its journey. Someone would be watching for it further on. Uurad wasted no time; he hurried back into the hollow and signalled the waiting warriors to hush.

At the top of the cliff, Proculus scanned the land beneath him. The ground cover was minimal here, with too many rocks for woodland to take hold. He smiled; at least they would be able to relax for a while now. They had made a point of travelling south in three groups. The two smaller ones, made up mainly of new recruits, were taking the more dangerous paths, where ambush would be most likely. The Albion scouts would hopefully be distracted by these whilst the main army, following half a day behind, would take the safer route.

Proculus watched for a long time. Finally, he was satisfied. He raised a hand to the others and nudged his horse forward. They took the path down the cliff slowly, relaxed in the knowledge that there was no possible chance of attack.

Uurad accepted a skin of wine from Galan; they would be here for a long time, so might as well make the most of it. The Selgovae, still not recovered from their long, disastrous journey south - followed almost immediately afterwards by the quick march to the hollow - took the chance to sleep. Uurad's men, meanwhile, gathered in groups and whiled away the time challenging each other with quiet games of skill. Sticks and pebbles were put to good use and the small *chink, chink* sound of the pebbles hitting each other was quiet enough to go unheard by the passing Romans.

Further south, Kariss waited with the army. They had chosen an area of moorland that suited their skills perfectly. Dense trees lined the lower slopes of the western hills, behind which the edge of the great Spine of Albion could just been seen. A group of warriors had secreted themselves amongst these trees. It would do the Brigantes no good to declare the full extent of their number straight away.

Not that all their warriors were here. The morning after the sacrifice of the Roman arsonist, Loth had taken the mounted part of his substantial war band and worked his way around to the northern borders, gathering up the warriors who had been dispatched there and scouting the whole area for as much information on their enemies' whereabouts as possible.

He had sent word back regularly and his information had proved invaluable. Torwain had left with Loth and was now once again doing what he did best, using his exceptional relationship with Cernunous to work his way ahead of Martaani, unseen yet fully observant. Using the Spenny, he was able to send pre-arranged messages alerting them to the Romans' progress.

A day and a half's march north, Uurad and Galan waited patiently; they would join up with Loth and his men once Martaani's main force had passed. This large group would then follow on behind, effectively trapping the Roman army between the waiting Brigantians and themselves. To throw the scent, Tholarg and Gartnet had remained with the Brigantes so that a lack of northern warriors did not alert the Romans to their plan.

Volisios had stayed with Kariss. He found himself awed at her belief and a little part of him had begun to understand what she had been trying to say to him before the alarm was called. The moment danger was apparent, she had changed, instantly on the alert and ready to listen to those around her. She had taken no chances with her safety and had not left the protection of the war band at any time since. She had accepted Volisios's presence without comment, simply nodding when he had returned from his brief farewell with Callimai, who had remained behind at the Stanwick camp. He stood to Kariss's side now as she scanned the area in front of her, listening as Umar and Dainarr made plans for their defences.

They ordered trees to be felled and stripped back into staves, ranging in size from as large as a man to only knee-height. These were dug into the ground at the base of the rise close to the main camp, where Kariss and the war leaders would be stationed. It would offer limited protection should the fighting get too close. They had considered whether or not to dig pits to stop the Romans' horses. Umar assured them that the Romans did not rely heavily on cavalry. What they had brought would no doubt be positioned out on the wings. Still, he reasoned, it would do no harm to dig the pits. At the very least, it would stop any mounted archers getting near enough to shoot at them.

Spenny Beck ran to the right of the open ground. Any horses attempting to come at them from the east would have to jump the water so Dainarr ordered large rocks to be rolled into the stream. This had the effect of slowing the flow, causing the water to back up and burst over the banks. Men then rode up and down these wet areas, churning the sodden ground to mud before more stakes were buried. The stream was now a much more formidable barrier. The other side of the open ground was flanked by woodland. There was nothing much they could do with this, apart from lay a few barrier branches between the trees. They needed to keep the area open for their own warriors.

The area to the side of the small rise, and directly in front of the main camp, was where the Brigantian forces would congregate. Umar had warned them countless times how the majority of deaths came as retreating forces were cut down as they fled. To protect themselves, more pits were dug in the woodland at their rear; bramble briars were dragged across the obvious pathways, leaving only a few narrow routes through the hazards. It would hopefully slow down any chasing legionnaires, if everything went wrong and they were forced to break and flee.

He had done this before, Naraic told himself, and he could do it again. To stop the trembling from starting in his limbs, he forced himself to think of everyone he held dear. They would be safer, if he did this right. He ran through the names in his head, picturing each person in turn: his mother, his father, his aunt and her small baby - did it have a name yet? He supposed it must by now. They had set their heart on a little girl. They had lost one before. She had only lived for half a moon. So when the boy arrived, they'd had no name ready for him.

Concentrate.

The faces swam in and out of his mind but the one that kept pushing itself forward was his father's - and he was frowning. Naraic repeatedly pushed the image away, he could not let himself be distracted now. His father would be proud of him after all this, he told himself, over and over, like a mantra. Garth and Carrick had assured him as much and now was not a time for doubts.

Naraic knelt amongst the scrubby gorse bushes, his pile of arrows in a neat heap in front of him, feathers closest, ready to be quickly lifted and fitted to the bow string. Through the thorny branches, he could see only a tiny area in front of him, a narrowing of the pathway that the Romans would soon be using in order to reach the battlefield.

Torwain was with him, perched precariously in the thin branches of a rowan tree. Naraic would be relying on the druid to time his shots. Their task, set by Corio, was simple. Using the numerous gorse dens planted years ago by Bodvoc, they were to try and take out the Pontiff or the Augur on their way past. Even better if they could kill both of them and get Martaani as well.

Torwain had been recalled from monitoring the whereabouts of Martaani's army to lead Naraic safely to these hideaways and be his eyes, guiding him as to exactly the right time to take his shots. Naraic would only get the chance to loose one or two arrows at each place before the Romans would lock on to their position and send men to find them.

Naraic pushed his father's disapproving face away again, along with the attached memory of the uncle he had accidentally killed. He thought instead of Kariss. Sliding a hand into his pouch, he felt the long red hair he kept there, remembering the day that Kariss had taken the knife to her locks so that she would not be as easily recognised. She probably could not remember him taking a handful of it but he had kept it ever since, tied up in a thin strip of nettle cord. Martaani's men had not bothered to take it from him when they had captured him. What good was hair to them? He imagined Martaani dragging her poison ring down Kariss's face and his resolve hardened once more. *I have killed a man to save Kariss,* he thought. *I can kill Martaani too.*

A twig landed beside him and he looked up. He could barely make out Torwain squatting amidst the greenery. He lifted his first arrow and placed it on the string. A few minutes more and Torwain let out a gentle coo, which was quickly echoed by a wood pigeon in a nearby tree.

Concentrate.

Naraic slowly began to draw back the arrow, stopping halfway, waiting. A second call came from the druid. At the third, Naraic pulled the string right back until his thumb was anchored in its usual place on his jawbone. Nerves made him tense. Realising his mistake, he unlocked his left elbow and twisted it away to ensure that the string did not whip down his forearm when he let loose. He waited, keeping his breathing steady and both eyes fixed ahead. The next call would determine his target.

The jarring clatter of a magpie's call sounded from Torwain. The target was one of the priests. There had been no point having a different sound for each of them, Naraic did not know one of them from the other. He only needed to know to aim for a man in priest's robes. A heartbeat later, Torwain's signal called again. Naraic loosed the arrow straight through the narrow gap in the branches, grabbing a second straight away and setting it to his string. He caught a brief sight of the robed man on horseback but his second arrow had barely left the string when the man toppled from his bay mare. A heartbeat later, Torwain crawled into the gorse. He whispered a few words and the branches appeared to close behind him. They sat in complete silence but the look on Torwain's face left Naraic in no doubt that the shot had been a good one. He knew how frighteningly powerful Martaani's priests were. Corio had been insistent that they were to be the main target but Naraic could not help feeling a twinge of disappointment that it was not the woman herself who had been hit.

It was hard to make out what was happening outside. They heard a few shouts, and many horses riding away at speed, but they heard no sound of anyone coming in their direction. Torwain raised a hand in warning, holding a finger to his lips. The snap of a twig a short while later confirmed his suspicions. The ragged breath of a legionary could be heard close by. That was followed by a stifled curse as the gorse caught on his bare leg. It seemed an age before Torwain finally relaxed and they were able to uncurl themselves from the bushes.

There was no sign of the priest in the defile but there was no doubt that the shot would prove fatal.

Even if he had managed to re-mount his horse, the poison on the tip of the arrow would soon do its job. Torwain had prepared it specially, using a blend of monkshood - also known as Queen of Poisons - and hemlock. The latter was not really needed but it gave the druid a sense of justice to add it.

Taking great care, Torwain retrieved the rest of the lethally-coated arrows from the den and tucked them safely into a leather sack. Naraic shouldered his quiver of normal arrows and together they set off for their next hideaway.

21

Carrick watched as the legionnaires dug their trench, heaping the soil alongside it to add to their defences. Inside, the rest of the army set up their tents in ordered rows. In the distance he could hear the sounds of axes on wood as, one by one, young trees were felled. Darkness was falling by the time the fresh staves were driven into the top of the earthen banking to form a basic palisade. It enclosed the whole camp, apart from a single entryway, and severely restricted Carrick's view of what was happening inside.

He had already seen enough. This was no makeshift army, cobbled together from a handful of Romans and the dregs of the Votadini. It was a determined fighting force, guided by all the experience of the Holy Roman Empire.

Beside him, Cloud lay with his ears flat to his head. The rope around his neck was not tight but Carrick could not risk letting him free. The moment his attention drifted, the dog would be away, searching for his master. Carrick rubbed the top of Cloud's head. 'Come on, boy,' he whispered. 'I have seen enough.' Keeping to the cover of the trees, they made their way back to the hidden camp amongst the heavily wooded slopes to the western edge of the battlefield. Roughly a third of the Brigante army were stationed there, ready to back up the main force whenever they were needed.

More men arrived just before dawn and Carrick was soon commandeered to help. They had to work quietly; they were not far enough from the Romans to be sure that noise would not carry. Men spoke in whispers and directed each other using gesticulations and pictures scratched into the ground. It was slow, tiring work and Carrick soon found himself longing for a cooling shower of rain.

He passed Taratus, helping some of the new Carvetii arrivals to find suitable room amongst the trees. Carrick paused for a moment, eyeing him suspiciously. They had never managed to identify the spy from the Carvetii village. Indeed, they had forgotten all about it in the last week or so. Could it be that they were actually working together?

One of the Carvetii saw Carrick watching and raised a hand in greeting. Carrick recognised him as one of the scouts they had used, and waved back. There was no sign of their leader, Kinithu. No one was sure if the reports of his ill health had just been for the Romans' benefit, or if he really was suffering. Maybe he was already at the main camp? Carrick made his excuses and hurried away. He needed to warn Kariss. This camp was far too close to the Roman one. How on earth had no one realised how easily Taratus could slip away and pass their secrets to the enemy?

He had only just left the camp when he heard a cry go up, quickly followed by the siren call of the war trumpets. Every hair on his body stood on end - it could only mean one thing. The Romans were attacking, even before their own defences were completed. He raced through the trees, heedless of the sound he was making. It would not be heard over the clamour of the carnyces anyway.

He reached the open ground between the edge of the forest and the Brigantian camp. Everywhere he looked, men and women were scrabbling for their weapons. Tarnn, who had not long since arrived with his half of the cavalry, rode impatiently up and down the lines of warriors, harrying them into place and hurling orders to all and sundry. Dainarr was calmer, always ready for the unthinkable; he was unflappable in a crisis. Carrick raced past them, pausing only to hand Cloud's lead to one of the camp cooks, with the strict instruction to keep the dog safe at all costs. Then he was away, up the rise to where Kariss stood amongst her small group of advisers.

The stretch of moorland they had chosen for their battlefield lay bare before them but at the far end, in complete contrast to the Albion warriors, row upon row of legionnaires were now neatly lined up. The main force took the centre, with a small number of cavalry on the wings. Behind these knelt a smaller reserve force, waiting.

All thoughts of Taratus fled as the Roman army, not waiting for the Albion warriors to arrange themselves, began moving slowly forward. They marched in ominous silence, hoping to disquiet their unprepared opponents. Dainarr held his sword high and yelled for his warriors' attention. They dragged their eyes from the approaching legionnaires.

'For Brigantia,' Dainarr shouted. 'For our goddess and our land. For Kariss, for Lord Hightern, and for victory.' He brought down his arm and the warriors charged forward. Behind them, the carnyces blared.

By now the legionnaires were almost halfway down the moor; suddenly they broke into a screaming charge. It was the calculated opening manoeuvre that both Umar and Kariss had warned about. Fully prepared, the warriors lifted their shields in readiness. The legionnaires threw their pilia but many fell short as, alarmed by the sudden onslaught of warriors and noise, they threw too early. Most of the remaining spears were easily deflected by shields and swords. Only a handful actually hit their mark.

The legionnaires by this time had lost much of their initial confidence. They had thought to intimidate their foe into turning tail and fleeing but the Albion warriors were not so easily cowed. Still, the Romans pushed forward and the two sides came together in a clash of swords and spears. This initial burst of fighting was frenzied and brutal, though with mercifully few casualties. They began to disentangle, each pulling back to re-form and take some time to catch their breath.

Umar kept his eye on the centurions; they would be leading surges into the Brigantian ranks. Dainarr had been well briefed on this tactic and was busy shoring up the areas most likely to be targeted.

Tarnn kept most of his cavalry out to the west side, guarding their weaker flank. The work they had done on Spenny Beck had already deflected the Roman horsemen's first assault. Those that had managed to get through had found themselves cut off from the rest of their comrades. With no way of retreating, they had been cut down easily.

Kariss watched the action from the safety of the small hill. It was horrific. She had tried to brace herself for this moment but nothing could have prepared her for the realities of battle.

22

Umar swung his sword around his head as he roared his anger into the air. At his feet lay the crumpled remains of a legionary, his head almost decapitated. The druid had barely felt his blade connect with the man's neck. Battle rage had taken over his senses, blinding him to all but the next legionary heading foolishly towards him. He had no idea how long he had been in the thick of the fighting, and he had long since lost count of his tally of victims. To his side, he could see Dainarr and a group of Brigantians bearing the brunt of one of the centurion's latest surges. Already, three Brigantians were down. Umar lunged forward with his sword, dropping down onto his left knee as he did so. The blade powered into the belly of the oncoming legionary, finding easy access through a gap created by a missing bronze scale on the man's armour.

Thank you, he called silently to Belatucadros; only a god-driven thrust could have found such a mark. Umar swung around, ready to aid Dainarr, but Tholarg had already arrived with a handful of re-enforcements. Leaving them to it, Umar pushed forward. He dodged two men desperately hanging onto each other as blood ran from wounds too serious to allow them to continue standing to fight. Still, neither would back down as they pushed and clung with all their remaining strength.

A stone whistled close to his head and Umar turned in time to see the slingshot-user reach inside a fold in his tunic for another. The man's hand never emerged; Umar severed it from his arm at the elbow and charged on past. He could see a courier making his way behind a line of legionnaires, the feather tied to his spear making him instantly recognisable.

A flash of metal made him jump; he heard the jingle of an aproned belt and reacted without thought, slashing his sword towards the sound before flipping around to face the attacker. Umar saw blood flower under his sleeve; he had not felt the legionary's sword slice into his arm. The sight distracted him for a moment, giving the legionary time to step back out of the druid's reach. The Roman swung his sword again and this time Umar was ready. He blocked the thrust and finished the man with a stab to the groin, the tasselled apron no match for the force of his blade. He spared no more time on him. The courier was moving quickly; soon he would lose sight of him in the melee. Dodging through another bout of intense fighting, Umar hurried to follow. There was something in the courier's manner: a decisiveness to his movements; an over-confident slant to his head? Umar was not sure what it was but it was enough to be sure that the man must be stopped.

Before the courier had gone another handful of steps, Umar was on him. Wasting no time on questions, he sliced his blade across the backs of the man's knees, bringing him swiftly to the ground. Once there, Umar thrust his dagger into the man's neck just above his mail. The courier gurgled as blood flooded into his throat. Only the gods would hear his message now. Pausing to wipe the blood from the handle of his dagger, Umar felt the battle rage that had enveloped him since the fighting first began start to lift. He looked around him. The fighting was still in full flow but his protective shield was gone.

Belatucadros?

There was no answer.

Belatucadros?

As ever, during a skirmish, Umar's mind had been filled only by the next opponent and the next. Each sword-thrust and every parry. Fear hardly touched him; neither did rage, but now Belatucadros had removed the red mist of battle from his mind he was acutely aware of the reality surrounding him. To one side was Spenny Beck, framed by its muddy banks filled with sharpened spikes of wood. To the other side, men were fighting, screaming and dying.

He had never been this conscious in a battle before, had never felt the sheer terror of being amid such slaughter. The noise was deafening and the smell of fear and death was atrocious. A horse screamed close by as it plunged to the ground, blood streaming from a wound in its belly. The legionary riding it yelled out as his leg was crushed underneath. The Epidii warrior that had brought down the animal quickly dispatched it, uttering a quick prayer to Epona as he did so. Umar nodded to him, whispering his own prayer to the horse goddess.

He felt only coldness in return. Panicking, he called out to Brigantia, Maponus, Cailleach; to every god he could name, but not one answered him. Umar closed his eyes, feeling for the presence of any of the gods, but there was nothing - at least, not for him.

Someone shoved into him from behind and he jumped, swinging wildly around as a man fell at his feet, face hidden beneath blood and grime but clearly a Brigantian. Umar gathered himself together in time to stop the legionary who had killed the man from doing the same to him. Without his battle rage, though, his sword arm was much weaker and his responses slower. More legionnaires came at him and for the first time ever he saw his life flash before him. He charged at the Romans, fear driving him forwards. Like a raging bull, he ploughed through them. There was no finesse to his fighting now, only desperate, frantic urgency.

Again and again, he called out to the gods. The legionnaires fell back, not wanting to approach the madman in his rich madder robes. Time seemed to slow for Umar. He could see his fellow warriors being cut down; men and women he had spoken with only that morning, fighting for their lives, but he could not reach them.

The gods remained ominously silent. Umar was bereft. Never before had he felt such a cold, hostile atmosphere surrounding him. He was utterly alone. In his mind, he saw Nantosuelta raging at him from his father's deathbed and felt the emptiness that had followed her words grow. The lack of Belatucadros when he needed him most finally convinced him. He had nothing left. Everyone he had loved and held dear was gone. His wretchedness was complete.

Looking up, he saw the Augur, glaring at him from behind the Roman line. The priest's face was a mask of raw hatred. This was not the first battlefield that they had met on. The last time they had encountered each other, Umar had been in Raetia. Helping the Alamanni, a confederation of Germanic tribes, to break through the Roman border. That day had been Umar's first taste of defeat. A young boy had been with the Alamanni and Umar had taken him under his wing but as they broke cover and fled from the ensuing legions they had become separated. The next time Umar had seen the boy, the Augur was slicing open his belly to use his entrails in a reading. Umar had never felt such anguish. Was that why his god was deserting him now - because of his failure to protect his young charge?

Anger boiled up inside him, born of fear and grief. His father's face flashed before him, quickly followed by the young Alamanni boy. Maybe it was time Umar joined them? Life suddenly ceased to hold any meaning. Umar did not pause to wonder why. His life was over but he was going to make sure that he took the priest with him.

Somehow, he got through the throng of fighters and charged. The Augur stood his ground, lifted his hand and slashed a blade across the druid's face. It checked Umar's forward motion but did not stop it fully. His sword caught the Augur a glancing blow. Umar was not a small man, his stature was more that of seasoned warrior than faithful druid. The Augur, tall and slender, was more willow than oak. On the face of it the outcome of the fight should have been a certainty but the Augur had more strength than anyone could have imagined. He staggered as Umar's sword cut through his upper arm but without even looking at the wound he set his stance and prepared to fight.

'You killed my messenger,' the Augur spat.

'I could kill a thousand of your messengers and still we would not be even.'

The Augur raised an eyebrow. 'I could not fall far enough to make us even.'

The rest of the battle faded into the background as the two men fought. Umar's strength was undeniable but he had been fighting for a long time and with the loss of Belatucadros his control had gone. The Augur, on the other hand, was fresh and full of energy, his self-discipline, as ever, overcoming any possibility of his emotions getting the better of him. Even then it should have been no contest but for some reason Umar could not find an opening. Every move he made was preempted and blocked. He was driven further and further towards the treacherous banks of the Spenny Beck.

The Augur laughed. Umar lunged again, the handle of his dagger still slick with blood. The Augur squirmed his body sideways, the blade caught in his robe, and the dagger slipped from Umar's hand. Quick as a flash, the Augur stamped on it. The dagger disappeared into the wet mud. He rammed his other knee into the druid's stomach and fell to the ground with him, somehow managing to land on top. His hands clamped around Umar's throat.

'I am your death, druid. I will not stop until all of your kind are dead.'

Black spots mottled Umar's vision as he struggled for air. Suddenly, his will to live returned. He raked his hands on the Augur's, desperately trying to release the pressure.

'You are a plague, you all need to die.'

Umar bucked his body. He could hear drumming in his ears as death drew closer.

'Inida is helping me now,' the Augur gloated, loosening his hands slightly. He wanted to see Umar's eyes as his words sank in; to see the fear when he realised what was coming for his fellow druids. Most of all, the Augur wanted him to die knowing that there was nothing he could do to stop it.

'He found druids for me - Votadini druids. Men who, with a little persuasion, have now seen how wrong they were. You might have killed my first messenger but I will send more. They will set these assassins on their way. Who better to get close to you than your own kind?'

Umar strained for breath. The panic for his life was replaced by fear for those hiding out in the neighbouring nations. They would be waiting for word that it was safe to return to Brigantia so they would be sure to accept these Votadini men with open arms, thinking that they were terrorised druids fleeing the Romans. They would never see the slaughter coming.

The Augur pushed his face closer to Umar's. 'It does not even matter if Martaani loses this battle. The druids will still die, the Romans will still come. Inida will make sure of that.' He began to tighten his grip again.

Umar's vision was beginning to fade. From over the Augur's shoulder, he saw the shadow of Belatucadros. He thought it was an illusion but then a magpie called, loud and clear, incongruous amidst the madness of the battlefield. Umar needed no other signals. He hurled himself sideways, taking every advantage of the sudden surge of energy that Belatucadros gave him. The action dislodged the Augur and Umar was able to scramble away. At that moment, an arrow arched out of a nearby gorse bush and buried itself into the space between the Augur's neck and his collar bone. He dropped to the ground like a stone.

Umar staggered to his feet, gasping for air. He aimed a kick at the priest as he lay dying. The arrow was buried deep but still his eyes continued to mock him. With a roar, Umar plunged his sword into the Augur's chest and watched as those eyes went blank. Umar sank to his knees and looked around him. The skin on his neck was burning, he could barely swallow, and his head thumped with pain. Mud sucked at his robes and he longed to lay his head down and rest.

Umar.

The soft, lilting voice was familiar, though Umar could not place it. She called again. They were a fair distance from the thick of the battle here. He searched around him but all he could see was men fighting for their lives.

At the north eastern end of the battlefield, Martaani watched the Augur die with an impassioned shrug. There were always more priests. At least this one had not made as much fuss as the Pontiff had. He was still probably screaming in agony as the filthy poison his assassin had used raged throughout his body. They had left him in a tent a short distance away, far enough that they would be saved from hearing his death throes. Martaani had been looking forward to seeing the Pontiff get his come-uppance but she could still see to it that he would not be immortalised in memory as the paragon of virtue he had tried so hard to pretend to be.

23

The gorse did its job well; no one even suspected that anyone was up on the eastern hill. Torwain watched Umar stagger to his feet and give the Augur a good kick in the ribs. Naraic's arrow must not have finished him off fully because Umar leant over his body and plunged a blade into him. Almost at once, the air lightened, as the priest's contact with his gods was severed. A heartbeat later, Torwain heard the distant cry of an eagle. Something about it was not right. Keeping low to the ground, he led Naraic out of the gorse. The ground cover was good but anyone looking carefully from below would be sure to notice them. Once over the rim of the hill, they got to their feet and ran.

A number of waterways criss-crossed the land and they splashed through two before Torwain held up a hand in warning. They ducked low and waited. A stag broke from the cover of some nearby trees, running almost straight towards them before changing course at the last moment. Behind it they could just make out the sounds of fighting. They crept forward, easing through the trees with barely a sound.

In a small clearing, northern warriors were fighting legionnaires. Torwain soon found a sturdy oak tree for Naraic to climb. He should be safe up there and from that vantage point he would be able to pick off some of the enemy. Torwain passed up both bags of arrows. 'Be careful with the poison ones.'

Naraic nodded, he knew better than to touch the arrowheads. There was nothing Torwain could do to save him if the poison got into his body. Gingerly, he pulled the first arrow free and placed it on the string. Beneath him, Torwain unhooked the slingshot from his belt and searched the ground for suitable ammunition.

Naraic wasted no time getting a legionary in his sights. Adrenalin flooded his body, leaving no time for nerves. The legionary fell and Naraic had another arrow on the string in moments. He watched for another target. He didn't want to risk hitting one of the warriors. He thought he had recognised Galan but surely he was supposed to be with Loth and Uurad?

Beneath him, Torwain was letting fly with the stones he had found; he managed to get three legionnaires on the temples before Naraic had the chance to fell his second. The northern warriors may have been outnumbered but they had the element of surprise on their side and they were used to the scrappy fighting that such ambushes encouraged. The legionnaires were confused and in disarray. They had been caught unawares, expecting everyone to be concentrated down on the battlefield. Unlike the Albion warriors, they were not encouraged to think for themselves.

A number of the mounted legionnaires had managed to break away and escape the ambush. Torwain saw them disappearing into the trees. He called for Naraic and again they ran, tearing through the trees. They were just in time to see the legionnaires making their way through the last of the waterways. There was nothing they could do to stop them. Any moment, they would be seen from the battleground.

A mewing sounded from the sky. Looking up, Torwain again saw the eagle flying overhead. It was clear now why the bird had seemed different. This was a large, white-tailed eagle, not the more usual golden eagle, but that it was Bodach could not be in any doubt as he screamed overhead for all to hear. Corio would be looking for such a signal.

Torwain turned to Naraic, 'Hurry, I need you to send a message to Corio. Have you any arrows left?'

Naraic nodded, 'Only one.'

'Set it aflame and send it over into the valley. Corio should be looking up when he hears Bodach cry.'

Naraic nodded, already pulling the flints from his pouch. As he did, something caught his eye. There was a tent amongst the trees. It had been thrown up in a hurry, with scant care for neatness. He pointed it out to Torwain.

'Go, lad,' Torwain urged, 'leave this to me.' Carefully, he picked his way towards the tent. Hearing no sounds from within, he peered inside. The Pontiff lay curled in a ball, cold and grey. That his death had not been an easy one was clear from the strained look on his face. Naraic's arrow had hit him in the thigh. Someone had snapped off the shaft but the head remained buried deep in the priest's flesh. Monkshood was fast-acting. It would have become apparent almost immediately that the arrow was poisoned. The Pontiff's breathing would have become laboured and his speech would have faltered as his mouth became numb. His body trying to purge itself of the toxin would have caused him to vomit uncontrollably. Torwain was amazed that he had lasted long enough for the tent to be erected.

The priest had died here, that much was obvious. He had clawed at the ground as he struggled with his last breaths; grass was still entangled with his fingers. There was nothing of comfort in the tent, no soft skins to lie on, no water or food. The Pontiff had clearly been dumped here, the victim of one too many poisonings; out of the way, to die, frightened and alone. Torwain almost felt a moment of pity for the man.

24

The voice pulled at Umar, insistent and unrelenting. Every time his legs buckled, she called to him again; her voice all but dragging him from the moor. In the safety of the trees, she led him to a shadowed dip in the ground. Holly and rowan stood guard as Nantosuelta finally allowed herself to appear.

Umar was already on his knees, his exhaustion overwhelming. He cowered when he realised she was there and flinched as she reached forward to caress his cheek.

'Thank you, Umar, we have put you through so much, but you never failed us.' She smiled down at him, her eyes searching his face for a sign that he understood. He did not. Ignoring the dirt and the sharp, dry holly leaves that scattered the ground, she knelt before him. Taking his face in both her hands, she leant forward and placed a kiss on his forehead.

Warmth filtered through him, radiating from the place her lips had touched. His weariness lifted a little, the pain at his neck receding, and his mind cleared. For the first time, he was able to see the pain in her eyes. It was deep-rooted, echoing in the tired lines at the corners of her eyes. She had taken no joy in the task she had been made to undertake.

'You had to feel abandoned, alone and with no hope left. It was the only way you would overcome reason and challenge the Augur head-on. He would never have released his secret if he could feel any connection with us. He needed to see you at your most vulnerable, for only then could he allow himself to gloat. We now know his plans, and we can move to save our faithful druids. It is all thanks to you.'

A tear escaped and slid down her cheek. 'It was cruel to put you through this, but there was no other option. We never abandoned you, Umar. We just had to sever our connection for a while.'

Behind them, the noise of the battle began to fade. Umar turned his head, anxious to know what was happening, worried that he would be needed.

'Your role is complete now; you have no further part in the fighting.' Nantosuelta took hold of his hand, clutching it between both of hers. Umar felt his eyes close. He saw his father standing, smiling at him. Kel uttered no words but Umar could feel his father's pride and love washing over him in waves. He did not notice his own tears fall. Something cold and hard was sitting in his palm but he did not want to open his eyes and risk losing the vision of his father.

I love you, he told Kel. *I always have. I should have told you, I should have taken the time to tell you.*

Kel's smiled deepened; he nodded his head and slowly faded from view. Umar tried to hold on to him, to force the sight of him to remain solid even as it turned to mist.

'Your father is in the ether now, Umar. He cannot speak to you but he is always with you.' Nantosuelta spoke with her clear, soft voice. There was no trace at all of the harsh, cold woman who had chased him from his father's deathbed.

Umar opened his eyes and looked at his hand. There lay a clear crystal point, wrapped in a fine bronze wire. He had seen it before. It had been one of the objects in Kel's memory box; the box that had been destroyed as Stanwick burned. Twisted in amongst the wire were strands of fine, downy hair. Hair, the goddess explained now, that had once been part of the lock that Kel had cut from Umar's young head on the day they had been parted. Umar curled his fingers around it, squeezing tightly.

'You have been loved your whole life, Umar. Never doubt that. If you choose to walk away from us now, we will understand. We hope that you do not go. We hope that you will stay, even though your task is complete.'

At long last, Umar looked at the goddess. This time he was able to hold her gaze without blinking in shame. 'Why are *you* telling me all this? Why not Belatucadros? Am I dying?'

Nantosuelta smiled. 'You are not dying, Umar, but you are due a time of peace. Whilst Belatucadros is busy at the battle, I am here to take care of you. It is the least that I can do.'

Umar was too tired to think. The pain in his head was beginning to return, he could feel the marks on his neck again and his limbs ached so much that they felt too heavy to lift.

Nantosuelta rose, leaving him kneeling on the ground. With one swift wave of her arm, the sharp, dead holly leaves scattered. Beneath was a soft bed of dry moss.

'Sleep now, Umar. You will be safe here.'

He wanted to argue; his place was on the battlefield, not here in the tranquillity of the trees. He opened his mouth to speak but the words would not come. He could feel buzzing in his ears. The world was starting to spin. His vision darkened and he was asleep before his head had hit the soft ground.

Nantosuelta stood guard over him. She would allow no one to find him until she was satisfied that he would come to no further harm.

25

From their protected vantage point, Kariss and Anniel watched the fighting with sinking hearts. There was no doubt that the Romans were far superior. Their organisation and discipline were outstanding and far exceeded that of the unruly Albion warriors.

The centurions led surge after surge into the Albion ranks. The aim was clear - to power through the warriors' defences, separating the troops into smaller sections that could then be tackled from behind as well as from the front. Kariss was unable to see the other commanders further back, moving more legionnaires into place, and behind these the reserve force was still on their knees, waiting for their turn to fight. The centurion's lieutenant, the optio, paced up and down, making sure none of these waiting men got too excited by the fighting and rushed in before they were needed.

Kariss glanced towards her husband; she could see that he was torn. On the one hand wanting to join the warriors, on the other needing to keep his wife protected at all costs. A hand rested on her shoulder, making her jump.

'The others will not linger,' Cartivel told her. 'They know we will be outnumbered here.'

Kariss nodded, grateful for his advice and his presence. A battlefield was no place for a lame man but he had refused to listen to any arguments. 'You need me,' he had told Kariss simply. 'You need every man you can get.' She couldn't disagree. He had spent a long time that morning talking her through what she should expect. It had helped. After the initial period of complete shock she had found that, whilst the horror playing out on the moor before her was brutal, sickening and abhorrent, she could at least understand some of what was going on.

Just remember, they are not dying for you. They are dying for Albion. She heard Anniel's voice in her mind as clear as when he had spoken the words to her the previous night. She had doubted at the time whether she would really be able to accept them but now she could see the actual fighting her misgivings were gone. This was not a personal battle between her and Martaani. This was a battle for supremacy with neither side willing to give an inch.

Suddenly, she heard calls go up from the far side of the moor. The legionnaires at the back of the fighting turned, just in time to see Uurad and Loth charging in with all their men behind them. As planned, the Romans were sandwiched between the two forces. The optio leapt about, jabbing the second line of legionnaires with his staff of office, herding them to their feet to join the fighting. A great cheer rang out from the Brigantian watchers. Finally, it looked as if they would be victorious.

Only Corio remained unmoved. Verbia's words had not been forgotten. He had sent Torwain and Naraic to deal with the priests but he had no idea how they were faring. Only if they were successful would Albion's gods be able to see what was coming. Corio scanned the area, looking for the slightest signs of change. The arrival of the new warriors did not distract him from his search. This manoeuvre had been planned long before he had spoken with the goddess. It was not their actions that he needed to be aware of.

His eyes raked over the mass of fighting men and onto the group of Romans he could just make out on the far side of the moor. They were too far away to take in any details; only the sun glinting on the signam gave any indication that the group was an important one. The upraised hand that topped the heavily decorated pole was a strange sight to the druid. He could only presume that it signified something about the men who were fighting.

If he could have made out more he would have seen the smug look on Martaani's face as she watched the Albion warriors rally. That alone would have been enough to confirm all that Verbia had warned him of. Proculus was still by Martaani's side and a number of his men were also present, ready to defend Martaani should any Albion warrior get too close. The rest had been sent to join the fighting and it was clear to Proculus that those left behind were not happy with their lack of action. He moved over to one of them and snapped an order.

'Go check the horizon.' He flicked his hand eastwards.

Martaani's eyes did not leave the fighting; there was much to be learnt from the way men portrayed themselves on the battlefield. She was particularly impressed by some of the newly arrived northern warriors. She turned to the stout man next to her; Inida had joined them the previous day. With his wife, Claudia, gone, he was itching for a good fight. When the Roman re-enforcements arrived, he would join the legionnaires on the battlefield. It was far too dangerous to join in just yet - he was grief-stricken and angry, but no fool.

'Who is that man?' Martaani asked him, pointing to a tall, heavy-browed warrior. His dark hair was tied back in a long ponytail and his golden torc flashed as it caught the light.

'That, I believe, is Loth, King of the notorious Damnonii. I see the reputation of his warriors is no exaggeration. It is to be hoped that your friends arrive shortly or there will be few legionnaires left for them to support.'

Martaani studied Loth; she liked what she saw. He would make a good husband for her when she attained her rightful place on the throne of Brigantia. He would be just the ally she needed. She would never let Proculus go, of course, he was far too handy to have around, but a queen must marry, and marry well. She would not make the mistake of her ancestor, Cartimandua, and marry a man far lower than herself. Martaani's imagination drifted. The fighting was exciting but the thought of her future husband and what he would look like without all those clothes on was even more appealing than the death and slaughter going on before her.

Inida watched her, anger boiling up inside him as he realised the direction her thoughts were taking. He had risked all to show his support of the Romans so early. He would not have his position overshadowed by that of a northern rival.

Martaani might only have eyes on her immediate future but he was playing a much longer game. From the moment Julia Domna had first introduced them, Inida had seen the potential an association with Martaani could hold. Of course he had no time for her; the grasping, pretentious woman was merely a pawn. When Caracalla finally made his way to Albion, it would be Inida who stood tall as the most faithful ally of this new extension to the Roman Empire. If Martaani were to take up Loth as her husband, however, it would elevate the northerner way above himself. No matter that Loth had fought on the losing side and no matter that Inida was related to Caracalla by marriage. Caracalla had already shown what store he put in family ties when he had murdered his own brother.

The Votadini would be trapped between Brigantia and the Damnonii lands. It would make them vulnerable in a way he could never have predicted. He could not allow that to happen. He had already seen one of his other allies brought down in the fighting, another person who had only been using Martaani as a means to an end. He smiled to himself; did the woman not realise that she was not the only one here with ambition? He would miss the Augur's cunning but his loss was not a problem. Their plans were already in motion; maybe it was time to hurry them along?

A shout went up from behind Martaani.

'They are coming.'

Martaani's attention snapped back to the present, she looked eagerly towards the east. 'Send someone to guide them around behind us; it would do no good to waste their horses on those stakes.'

'Already done,' Proculus answered, returning to her side.

Everyone's attention was to the east when Inida slipped quietly away.

26

High up to his right, the great white-tailed sea eagle flew out from over the trees, catching Corio's attention the instant it appeared. It was rare to see one so far inland, with no tail wind to blow it off course. There was only one reason it was here. Almost immediately, a flaming arrow appeared over the edge of the hill. Torwain's warning. Corio's heart was in his mouth. He hurried to Kariss. Tarnn had just come to report on his cavalry's progress and the two of them finally sounded relieved at the way the battle was progressing.

'We have trouble,' Corio interrupted. 'Signals are coming from the east; I think Martaani may have re-enforcements arriving.'

Cartivel was sitting close enough to overhear. 'Surely not. We have had men out searching all this time; there was nowhere left for them to hide.'

'Did they check to sea?' Corio waved his hand abruptly, cutting off any further argument. There was no time; already there was a clear change in the atmosphere. Bodach circled the moor, swooping over the heads of the Romans as if he could pluck one from the ground.

Riders had appeared further along the eastern hill, heading towards the Roman camp and across the moor the cornicen blared on his horn. The legionnaires began to retreat.

Tarnn galloped across the moor, calling back the warriors. The carnage was terrible. Hundreds of bodies scattered the ground, life seeping away in red rivers that stained the earth and polluted the water. The sounds of men wailing and begging for help tore through him. He had to steel himself to keep going. He rode past a man he had known all his life who now lay crumpled on the ground, his right side torn open in a gaping wound. The man screamed his name, his eyes pleading for help. Tarnn left half his heart behind as he forced himself to keep riding.

Slowly, the last pockets of fighting stopped. There was even time to gather some of the wounded and bring them back to a safer resting place. The very worst of the injured had to remain where they were; movement would not aid them now. It was left to the gods whether they died quickly or were forced to linger.

Each side took the time to cook food and tend to their injuries. The Romans' supply lines were minimal and there had been no time for hunting or raiding. Even the newcomers had brought nothing with them, expecting their needs to be met by Martaani. They were tired, hungry, and not in the best of moods. At the other end of the moor, there was plenty of food. Camp followers set to work preparing more than enough for every warrior to have their fill. On the rise, Kariss was deeply engrossed in a meeting with her advisers.

They had always known that it was a major risk to meet the Romans in a set battle. Albion warriors simply could not match the superior Roman army in such a setting. It had only been the overwhelming numbers of warriors they had available that had convinced them that the risk was worth it. They still had a number of men in reserve. Those camping in the woods out to the west had not yet been brought in to fight. Loth also had foreseen problems and had arranged for Galan to remain out of sight with his Selgovae warriors.

Now they were discussing using those warriors as raiding parties, perhaps even sneaking men off unseen to join them. This was causing a heated discussion; as Dainarr pointed out, they had no idea how many re-enforcements had just arrived to support the Roman army. It would be far better to wait until the scouting party returned from spying on their camp before making any decisions.

Just as Anniel was beckoned away by a messenger, Uurad joined them; he had been busy helping tend to the injured men and women. His usual bluster was gone and his mismatched eyes were wet. He sat heavily down on the ground. 'We lost Enda.'

It was a blow. Not only because of the loss of a brave and gifted warrior but also because of the symbolism that she represented. Enda had been Kariss for weeks, and now she was gone; cut down on the battlefield in her prime. Maybe the legionary who had killed her had even believed he was killing the real Kariss.

Tholarg put a hand on Uurad's shoulder. 'She knew the risks and she was proud to do it.'

Uurad nodded slowly, 'Aye she was that, the lass. Fair made her day when Kariss asked her.' He smiled up at Kariss. 'You might not have known it, but she was honoured to play the part.'

Kariss was saved from answering by Anniel. 'Taratus has disappeared. He was at the camp all through the fighting, keeping his men in place and encouraging them to be ready for whenever they would be needed. Then suddenly he was nowhere to be seen. Whilst everyone's attention was taken by the new legionnaires arriving, he must have slipped away.'

'Damn it!' Kariss was beginning to feel overwhelmed. *Help me,* she thought. Her adrenaline was in overdrive. Just as she had thought they were winning, things had turned on their head and now she had no idea what to expect.

'How much does he know?' Tholarg asked.

'Not as much as he thinks,' Cartivel answered. 'He was put in the far camp to keep him away from all the action; it should have been easier to keep an eye on him there. All he can really tell the Viper is the numbers of warriors we still have hidden in his camp. He was never told about the warriors we had to the north so he has no idea that some are still out there. Neither does he know anything about Torwain and Naraic, or Kariss's own connection to the gods. He does not even know the true number of our forces.'

Cartivel had never stopped using Lord Hightern's nickname for Martaani. Volisios smiled, remembering how the old king had first thought of the name.

'She is sly that one, a real viper,' Hightern had said. 'She will always have a secret plan or a scheme to hand. We should ever be prepared for her to strike when we least expect it.' The words were poignant and Volisios lost no time repeating them. They rang around the small group, sounding more like a prophecy than advice.

As if she had pre-empted the words, Martaani was already riding across the moor, a ring of legionnaires surrounding her with their long shields held outwards to protect against any missiles that the Albion warriors might choose to throw at them. She rode exactly as she walked - tall, confident, and looking as if the world should be bowing down before her.

A cry went up, alerting everyone to her presence. Kariss felt her stomach lurch. She looked at Volisios, 'He was not wrong.'

'I will be at your side, my lady.' He nodded to Anniel and Garth, not wanting them to feel that he was trying to surmount their presence. Anniel clapped him on the shoulder in gratitude. It took a long time to grow a strong bond with a personal guard. Some people never managed it, yet Volisios had more than proved himself an honourable man. Anniel could not wish for anyone else to be protecting his wife. Garth gave him a brief smile; Volisios was a man he could respect. He clearly understood the hard line a personal guard had to walk sometimes. It was not the clear-cut, easy job some people assumed it to be.

They mounted their horses and the small group made their way carefully through the barricades at the bottom of the slope. Corio rode with them, alert for any further messages from the gods. Tarnn rode at their head, Dainarr bringing up the rear. Kariss could feel her insides turning to molten lead, as if every blood vessel were pumping liquid fire around her body; at the same time, here and there, the flow seemed to solidify into lumps of ice-cold dread. She tried again to speak with the gods but she heard no response. Whatever was happening, the gods were being kept busy.

They had not been deserted, of that she had no doubt. She knew all too well that even the gods had limits to what they could do. After all, it was not that long ago that she had been left stranded and all alone in London. She closed her eyes for a moment, feeling the steady rhythm of her horse beneath her. Memories flooded back: Neil Simons; the fire; the headlong race to the woods... the knife. She felt a hand cover hers and opened her eyes to see Anniel looking at her.

'You are not alone.'

She nodded, unable to speak. Nausea was threatening to overwhelm her.

'Do not let her see your fear. No matter what happens, keep that deep inside you, just as she will be doing with hers.'

27

The two groups stopped a few feet apart, guards fanning out on either side, shielding the two parties from the rest of the battlefield.

Martaani's face was steel; she had arranged her hair so that it sat high on her head, making herself appear taller and more intimidating. Beside her was Proculus, the centurion, and a cornicen. The centurion had clearly been in the thick of the fighting. He had not escaped unscathed; dark, crusted blood clung to his right forearm and his hand was bound up in cloth that may once have been blue but was now dark with blood. He held his reins lightly in his left hand and tried to hide just how wracked with pain his body was. He was the only one of their group to remain mounted.

As Kariss dropped from her horse, she felt a calmness come over her - Cailleach was keeping her strong. Overhead, the eagle let out a long cry, but whether it was in support or warning it was not clear. The rest of her group dismounted, coming to stand alongside her. The taint of the Roman gods in the air was much diluted now, Corio noticed. The priests had clearly lost their hold, Torwain and Naraic must have done their job well. He did not let his smile show.

Martaani stepped forward, closer than most people would have considered acceptable. She raised her eyebrows and directed her attention to Kariss. 'You think you have been clever, that you have me beat.'

Kariss said nothing. She had experienced such power games from her old neighbour, Neil Simons. He had always been looking for a response to feed off. Martaani looked over the people with Kariss, dismissing them all as irrelevant. She paused only to eye Corio up and down. She smiled, but there was nothing nice about the look. 'Your gods have failed you.'

She flicked her hand and the cornicen hefted the crossbar of his large curled horn further onto his shoulder and put his lips to the mouthpiece. The single melancholy note echoed in the stillness. Over at the Roman end of the moor, the ranks of legionnaires opened up and four men started forward. One person was cloaked and hooded, stumbling as two legionnaires pushed him along. The final man was Taratus; he held his head high and looked straight ahead, pointedly ignoring the gasps and insults coming from the watching Brigantes.

Kariss stared at him in disbelief; how could he betray them like this? He had fooled everyone, even the gods. She felt her heart sink. Beside her, Anniel swore under his breath.

'Why would you do this?' Corio demanded as Taratus drew near. 'Your own people - your own cousin!'

Taratus looked at the druid as if he were looking straight through him. Taking his place next to Martaani, he looked to Kariss and said simply, 'The rightful heir of Brigantia shall take her throne.'

Volisios took a step forward. Immediately, Martaani's guards reacted, lowering their pilia towards him. Martaani looked amused. 'One man! Against all my army?'

273

'Every person in our army will support him,' Anniel growled.

'But will Kariss?' Maartani said as one of the legionnaires pushed the cloaked man down onto his knees. Martaani swept back his hood.

'No!' Kariss darted forward. Volisios and Anniel caught hold of her before the legionnaires could keep her at bay with their spears.

Kariss's father, Cantigern, looked up at her, his eyes full of sorrow. 'I am sorry, daughter. You must let me go.'

Kariss's hand went to the hilt of her sword. She would have lashed out at Martaani had Anniel not stopped her. He was right; she would not save her father that way.

Martaani's face lit up with amusement. 'What a touching exchange.' She rested a hand on Cantigern's shoulder. He flinched at her touch. 'Now we must agree on another exchange.' Martaani paused. 'Brigantia, for your father.' She swept a hand around her. 'One simple exchange and all this fighting stops. No one else need die.'

'No, Kariss!' Cantigern pleaded with her, before she could speak, 'you must not even consider this. She is not a woman to trust. You know this. Remember what the gods told you, remember what I told you. Your blood does not come from me; it comes from your mother and her mother before her.'

'If you do not agree, your father will die right here before you.' Martaani ran a finger along Cantigern's jawline, in a strangely intimate caress. Cantigern snatched his face away and Martaani laughed. Power was such an exhilarating feeling. She cast a look to where the northern warriors stood watching. She was pleased to see Loth standing amongst his men, he appeared to be unhurt. She must remind the legionnaires that he must not be harmed. 'Will you really put all of them to the sword for one weak man?' She gave Cantigern a kick in the ribs. He grunted with pain but kept himself upright.

Kariss felt sick. Never before had she been so torn. All she wanted to do was save the man who had loved and protected her all her life. Yet the leader in her would not let her form the words. She had to consider her whole nation and the lives of those who had chosen to support her. Plenty of others had already known loss; who was she to throw away all that they had suffered for? She needed more time.

'Do not let me be the downfall of Brigantia,' Cantigern implored his daughter, 'I could not bear it. I am more proud of you than you could ever know. You can do this. We will see each other again in the next life. I will be waiting with open arms for you.'

Still Kariss hesitated, it was all too much. A tear rolled down her cheek. She felt dizzy and scared; more scared than she had ever felt before. Time seemed to stand still, her heart thudded in her chest, and she could feel the pulse in her neck and wrists beating out the rapid rhythm. How could she bear such a decision?

Cantigern tried one last time. 'One day we will be together again. One day we will see what a fine, strong girl you truly are. I will live for that day.'

Those words again.

Martaani made a noise of amusement, Kariss glared at her. As she did so, she noticed a snow-white barn owl fly across the moor. It was so pale that there was barely any of the tan colour to be seen.

'A male,' Taratus muttered. Martaani swung around at his words.

'What?'

Taratus shrugged. 'The bird,' he said. 'It was only a male, what use are they?'

Kariss gulped, the hairs on her neck stood on end. Anniel was pulling on her arm, telling her to step back and discuss their options. Corio and the others were agreeing. Their words faded behind her. Like the ripples clearing on the scrying pool, everything suddenly became clear. She shook her arm free and faced Martaani.

'Brigantia is not to be bargained with. One life does not come before a nation's.'

Behind her, Anniel exclaimed and tried to stop her. Again, she shook him free.

'Do what you will,' she told Martaani. 'But you will never have Brigantia.' She stepped back, her heart still hammering in her chest. Had she made the right decision?

Martaani showed no sign of surprise; it was almost as if she had wanted Kariss to make this decision. She turned to Taratus. 'Kill him.'

Taratus stepped away and pulled a bow from his shoulder. Ignoring the screams of abuse from those watching, he slowly set an arrow to the string. Kariss's heart plummeted. She closed her eyes and pleaded with the gods to intervene. Surely she could not have been so wrong? They must do something. They could not have led her to this decision without a plan to save her father - could they?

Cries rose all around them; excited cheers from the Romans and calls of horror from the warriors.

The bowstring pulled taut, Martaani laughed at the shock on Kariss's face. 'You did not think he would do it, did you? You stupid girl, of course he would. He has been my ally for months. He already has Brigantian blood on his hands, a little more will not matter.'

All eyes turned to Taratus. Kariss was frozen. She was going to see her father die, right here before her, and she could have saved him. She cried out just as Taratus let the string go. The arrow flew. It was a clean shot, straight through the heart. Martaani's face froze in shock, her laugh stopping mid-sound. She looked to her chest and saw the arrow protruding through her mail. Then her body crumpled to the ground.

Chaos erupted. Time suddenly came rushing back; Kariss dived forward and grabbed her father. The legionnaires next to Martaani thrust their pilia forward only to find themselves blocked by Garth and Volisios. Proculus lunged towards Taratus, who let off a second arrow which hit the praefectus in the shoulder, sending him whirling backwards. The centurion turned his horse and galloped back to his waiting men. By now, soldiers on both sides had joined in the fighting. It was disorganised and desperate.

The centurions tried to get their men under control but their sergeants and lieutenants had been scattered and were too busy fighting for their lives to respond. The warriors from Wendell, along with those from the Carvetii lands, came charging from their secret camp and hurled themselves into the action. They were fresh and eager and the tired legionnaires were no match for them.

277

Garth had given Cantigern a sword from one of their fallen warriors and the small party stood their ground. It was bloody work; they seemed to be the target of half the battlefield. Kariss could feel the adrenaline pumping through her body as she planted her feet firmly and made to defend yet another attack. The legionary coming at her was young and eager but he over-reached himself and staggered forward. Kariss killed him in two blows, one to the arm and the other to the back of the head. There was no time to think about what she had just done, or about the others she had already killed or injured. Another legionary was already bearing down on her. She recognised this one as the man who had stood to Martaani's right-hand side. His face was contorted now, in grief and rage. He had snapped off the shaft of the arrow that Taratus had shot him with but the head was still buried deep in his shoulder. Despite this, his movements were swift and sharp. He had lost the woman he loved and no amount of pain was going to stop him getting his revenge. He didn't care about the throne, about the Roman wish to re-conquer Albion. He only cared about the loss of Martaani and killing those who were to blame.

Kariss had no shield to protect her; she was fighting with only her sword and dagger. Proculus had his shorter Roman sword and his long shield that protected most of his body. The centre of the shield consisted of a metal boss which covered a handle on the inside, protecting the user's hand and enabling it to be used to punch into opponents. Proculus forced his shield hard against Kariss, all his weight behind it. The boss slammed into her ribs. As she recoiled, the top of the shield caught her face, splitting open her top lip.

Kariss could not get her sword around the shield's curved sides to cause him any harm at all. Proculus swung his sword.

This time, Taratus lunged in front of her and took the blow. It was unforgiving and he dropped to the ground. Taratus jabbed his dagger up under the shield and into Proculus's groin. Proculus let out an unearthly scream and buckled, landing half on top of Taratus. Kariss could barely breathe; Volisios grabbed her and pulled her behind him. Someone else dragged Taratus free.

Slowly, they managed to work their way back towards the relative safety of the protected rise from which they had watched the initial battle. Taratus collapsed to the ground, blood pouring from underneath his tunic. The wound was deep and beneath it his ribs were broken. Kariss knelt at his side as Corio tried to stem the flow.

'It is good to see you again, cousin. I am sorry you had to doubt me.' He sucked in air sharply as Corio pulled out a piece of broken bone. 'I was caught in the middle but I would have done anything to protect you.'

Anniel arrived beside them; he had become parted from Garth and had a small wound on his back but was otherwise unhurt. He took one look at the blood on Kariss's face. Her lip was swollen, white fat showing around the edges of the cut.

'You have never been more beautiful,' he told her, kissing her firmly on the forehead. He looked down at Taratus. 'We owe you a huge debt, my friend.'

'Can you tell my wife that?' He winced again as Corio packed his wound with moss. 'At least I will not have to feign such bad heads any more... it was the only thing I could think of to avoid hearing anything that would benefit Martaani. She had her ways of knowing when I was holding something back.' He winced again, rushing on to distract himself from the pain. 'Usually it was Kydas who paid the price. In the end, it became easier to make people distrust me; that way, they stopped saying anything important in my hearing.'

The fighting was still fierce but the Romans seemed to have lost heart. Finally, they decided to make a break for it. Those at the back broke first, led by Inida. They turned, running through the stream and up the slope, heading back towards the coast. They did not get far. Galan and his warriors were waiting for them at the top of the rise. A few legionnaires surrendered, Inida and the rest tried to fight their way through. The Votadini king was a traitor and a turncoat. He had opened his borders to the Romans, giving them a base from which to organise their activities and terrorise those nations loyal to the Albion gods. He knew there would be no mercy for him if he was taken.

The fight was over quickly. Inida was a small man; he was not built to wield a sword. His desperation to escape was no match for the anger of Galan's men. The rest of the deserters were dealt with just as efficiently. Those that surrendered were gathered together and herded back down the slope to join the rest of the captives.

In the end, only a little more than a hundred legionnaires were left alive. They hung their heads, bemoaning the shame of having to fight under a woman's command. At Kariss's insistence, these men were treated fairly. They were fed, watered and given shelter under the trees. If any of them considered that not all women could be counted equally, they kept their thoughts to themselves.

28

Anniel looked around at the dead and injured. There were so many. Legionnaires outnumbered the Albion warriors three to one but he could find no sympathy for the Roman losses. He wandered about the battlefield, wondering which of these men had helped to ransack his Vacumagi home. Which had held his mother as Martaani had scoured her back with the poison flagrum? He kicked a few of the more suspicious-looking characters. Maybe one of these had killed his little brother as he had tried to defend their mother.

The cries of the wounded filled the air, somewhere in the distance a female warrior was howling in pain. The sound made Anniel's blood run cold. He was no longer on the Brigantian moor; instead, he was transported back to Dun da Lamh and it was his sister wailing her desolation for all to hear.

His vision failed as tears filled his eyes; he stumbled over someone's arm and fell to his knees. Muddy water soaked through his trousers but he did not notice. He had thought he had done his crying. Now, all those buried emotions resurfaced. They were as raw as the day he had walked through the battered gates of the fort and found the devastation of not only his family but many of the Vacumagi who lived there.

His eyes no longer saw the corpse-filled moor around him. They saw the bodies of his brother, lying on the flagstones as his lifeblood flowed from his small body; he saw his mother lying so close that her outstretched fingers could almost reach her youngest-born, her breath so frail that it had been missed by everyone until Kariss had tried to cover her. He looked further away and did not see the Spenny Beck, flowing quickly past the horror of the moor, but his father's body, lying crumpled in a pool of his own blood. Sobs racked Anniel's body. There was nothing he could do to change what Martaani had done; no way he could turn back time and save his family. His father's old druid, Nectan, had told him that Kariss and her parents would be the only people the gods ever took through time. Anniel threw his head back and let out a desperate scream.

Kariss watched her husband from a distance. She longed to go to him but Volisios held her back. 'Give him time. He needs to get a few things out of his system. Trust me. It is enough that you are here, ready for when he needs you.'

A voice called to them from the far side of the stream. Naraic was running down the slope with Torwain close behind.

'You go,' Garth told Kariss, 'I will watch Anniel.'

For a moment, Kariss wavered. She wanted to weep for her husband, to be there when he had cried his last, and hold him in her arms. At the same time, she was so relieved to see Naraic safe and sound. She gave Anniel one last look and then she painted a smile on her face and picked her way towards Naraic.

Taking care to avoid the sharp stakes of wood, they met on the Spenny's bank, ankle-deep in mud. Kariss hugged Naraic close to her and surprisingly he hugged her back. 'You are hurt.'

Kariss touched her swollen lip. 'It is nothing, but it hurts when I talk. What about you?'

'I killed them both, the priests. And I helped with the fighting over the hill. I hid in an oak and picked off the Romans that Galan pushed my way.'

'He was outstanding,' Torwain added. 'His family will be proud of him.'

'What fighting over the hill?'

Word had not yet reached them of the events that had preceded Cantigern's arrival. Torwain quickly explained and, in return, Volisios told them what had happened on the battlefield.

'Has anyone seen Cloud?' Naraic was looking about him. The bodies of the dead and dying, the harrowing sounds of pain and grief, and the strange feeling of unreality was finally getting to him. Shock at what he had just been through was starting to hit home. His stomach was churning and his legs had started to tremble.

Volisios recognised the signs. 'Come on, let us go and find him. I think he is back in the main camp.' He turned to Kariss for her approval.

'I will be quite safe.' This time, he knew better than to doubt her.

She watched them go, thinking again how lucky she was with the people around her. Everyone looked out for one another, with none of the selfishness she had grown used to in London. 'I hope he is going to be alright. It is no easy thing to kill someone.'

Torwain agreed. 'There was not much time to think when the fighting started. He just got on with it. The priests were a little different but he managed just as well. The Pontiff is in a tent up there,' Torwain pointed roughly in the right direction. 'He died slowly of his wounds. It will not have been a pleasant death. The Augur died much quicker. Naraic got him in the neck by the Spenny and then Umar finished him with his blade.' Torwain looked about him. 'Where is Umar, anyway?'

Kariss swung around; she had not seen the warrior druid for a long time. Come to think of it, she had not seen him since before the fighting had paused. He had not joined them when the warriors had pulled back. Her heart sank. Had they lost another of the seven druids?

It took a long time to find him. He was carried back to the camp barely conscious. His face was peppered with tiny red spots; even the whites of his eyeballs were affected. Carrick had seen such a thing before and eased the top of the druid's robes down. Livid red marks surrounded his neck, intersected with deep scratches. He checked Umar's nails; sure enough, he found evidence of skin and blood. Whoever had tried to strangle the druid had almost managed it.

Torwain treated the neck wounds with comfrey and gave him soothing water laced with honey to sip. Umar tried to speak but his voice came out as a barely audible rasp. Torwain sat with him, trying to push away the hovering feelings of guilt. He had seen the Augur astride Umar, seen him with his hands about his neck. Torwain had never thought for a moment that the slight body of the priest could have had this much effect on the battle-hardened druid.

Kariss was exhausted. She had insisted on helping with the injured, ignoring all the protests from those around her. When she had finally sat down, she had found herself surrounded by people wanting to praise her. Without the northern warriors, they would never have succeeded. There were many who had doubted whether such an army could be gathered together. Many more had been unsure as to how such an army would perform with so many kings and war leaders, all used to being the one in command. It was a miracle that their old rivalries had been held in check long enough to focus on the task at hand.

'I couldn't have done it without each of you,' Kariss told them all. 'It is not my victory, it's Albion's.'

'You trusted the gods and you trusted everyone else,' Anniel told her. 'I really do not think you appreciate quite what a feat you have achieved. There is no one else who could have managed it.'

'But I didn't do it alone, you all helped. If it had been down to me, we would certainly have failed. I don't know the first thing about leading an army.'

'Exactly!' Anniel took her hand and kissed the palm. 'You never once tried to "rule" anyone. You told us all what you needed and let us get on with it. You never ordered anyone or insisted that they be friends, you just gave everyone the respect and the space they needed.'

His words were met with a chorus of agreement. He gave her a moment to let them sink in before continuing.

'You are the queen of the largest nation in Albion. You could have chosen to look down on everyone else, to see them as lesser men. Yet not once did you do such a thing. You looked to everyone for help and accepted it gratefully.'

Tholarg stepped forward. 'Is there a single person left on this field that you have not thanked? A single one you would not have helped?' He paused and inclined his head to her. 'I bow to your greatness. I only hope that I have learnt from it.'

As one, everyone else got to their feet and bowed to Kariss. She sat speechless, not knowing how to react. Torwain came to her aid. 'You are wanted,' he told her. 'You too, Anniel.'

He led them through the dusk to a small clearing in the trees, well away from prying eyes. No sooner had they arrived than six gods appeared in front of them. Torwain stepped back into the trees. This was not his meeting.

Brigantia stood at the centre of the group, her radiant skin glowing in the dim light. She held her arms out to Kariss, embracing her as a mother embraces her child. 'You have fulfilled every hope we ever had in you, my child. Because of you, Brigantia is safe once more and with it the whole of Albion. It will be many years before we have to fight for our rightful place here again. As soon as you return to Stanwick, call back the druids. We need them home again.'

Beside her, Verbia stood smiling. Around her feet, a pair of snakes coiled contentedly. She gave no discernible signal but all at once the snakes uncoiled and wound their way around Kariss's. Their touch sent waves of refreshing anticipation tingling up her legs and along her spine. 'This is the start of your new life, Kariss. Have no more doubts as to your ability to lead.' She stepped back and the snakes at once returned to her.

Cernunous tilted his head, dipping it so that his antlers came close enough for Kariss to touch. Upon them glinted a small golden torc. 'Take it,' his voice vibrated through her. She lifted the torc from the tines and slid it around her upper arm. It was almost a match for the one Torwain wore around his neck. Kariss was overcome. She had never knowingly stood in the presence of the great Cernunous before. He was the one god she had always felt an affinity to. The one she believed had taught her how to read the signals in the animal kingdom. She had kept that learning even throughout her time in London, always watching for magpies and black cats, heavily-laden berry bushes in autumn and early signs of life in spring. He was more of an emotion than the other gods; even his voice was felt as much as it was heard. He spoke again now.

'Yes, Kariss, it was I who stayed with you. You will not remember the young druid of mine, who used to visit you at Wendell when you were a child. He taught you all that you would need to keep your connection with us when you were gone.' His voice soothed the last of the fraying nerves inside her. She reached up and stroked the torc he had given her, feeling the same vibrations in the metal that she felt in his voice.

'Thank you,' she smiled at him, blinking as his face appeared almost stag-like, where only a heartbeat before it had been almost human. Only his eyes and antlers remained the same.

Beside him, Belatucadros rolled his eyes impatiently. Without waiting to see if Cernunous had finished, he stepped forward and bowed to Kariss. He did not smile but his face was full of respect. Kariss missed the surprised looks on the other gods' faces. Belatucadros did not bow to anyone.

Maponus gave both Kariss and Anniel a small, flint arrowhead. Each had a small hole worked into the shaft so that they could be mounted on a leather strip and worn. Anniel looked at his with watery eyes. Somehow, the sight of it brought back all his anguish in the aftermath of the battle. His voice broke as he attempted to offer his thanks.

Swiftly, Cailleach was in front of him, one hand on his brow and the other over his heart. Her eyes closed and she muttered something. Opening them again, she dropped her hands and beckoned to Kariss.

'There has been too much death and too much misery these last few months.' The old goddess shook her head. 'Anniel, I have taken away most of your pain, but I will not deny you all of it. You must mourn your family. Know that time will help to heal the wounds but their memories will live on for many years to come.

'Kariss, I could not be more proud of you than I was today. Forgive us for not telling you the truth about Taratus; he was too connected to Martaani to take that chance.'

Kariss stared at the faces of the gods; just how far did their involvement go? 'He has been acting for you all this time?'

Verbia nodded, 'A spy posing as a spy. Bodvoc has been his guide, giving him enough snippets of information to keep Martaani believing that he was loyal only to her.'

'Do not be hard on him for the information he gave her. He did it only to protect you and this land of ours,' Brigantia said.

'Bodvoc again.' Kariss should not have been surprised. It seemed to her that the older a druid was, the wiser he was, and far stronger in things other than physical strength. 'That man has been behind so many things.'

'Indeed my child, he has been very thorough in the defence of Albion. His frailty has been the perfect mask for his activities.' Verbia grinned, she was very proud of her druid.

'How did Taratus manage to gain Martaani's trust?' Anniel asked. His face was still flushed and his voice wavered a little but he felt happier and there was a lightness in him that had not been there for a long time.

'Kydas was taken to keep Taratus in line,' Maponus explained. 'Martaani threatened to kill him every time she thought Taratus was not giving her enough information. Taratus has walked a very fine line but he never once wavered in his loyalty to you, Kariss.'

The gods started to fade. They had risked much to gather in such an unprotected place.

'Wait!' Kariss called, reaching out to the now misty figure of Cailleach. 'What about my mother?'

Cailleach smiled, 'I am just on my way to fetch her, child.'

29

The following morning, the Roman prisoners were marched away. Loth was taking them to the coast, where they would be sent back to their boats. With them went the bodies of Martaani and the two priests. No one wanted their remains left behind to taint Albion.

Inida was placed in a cart and sent back to Dumpender Law, the Votadini capital where he'd had his home. Convention dictated that the bodies of royalty must always be treated with respect, no matter what the circumstances of death had been. It was far more than he deserved.

Another group left, carrying a bier upon which lay Uurad. The great man had been brought down at the very end of the fighting. With a heavy heart, Kariss placed a jewelled sword beside his body. It was the least she could do to honour his sacrifice.

She had grown fond of the big man with the strange mismatched eyes and deep, booming voice. His loss took much from the victory and for a time she struggled with her conflicting emotions. She felt the acidic taste of nausea in her mouth. It had been happening more and more over the last few days. The stress of the battle and the loss of so many good lives had taken its toll on her nerves.

'He would not have had it any other way,' Tholarg informed her as the horses trotted off. They were heading for the nearest Carvetii port, where they would board a boat to carry the Epidii king back to his beloved islands.

Tholarg was nursing his own injuries, the worst of which was to his shoulder. 'War wounds are a matter of pride,' he said. 'They show that we did not cower in the face of the enemy. Uurad would have rejoiced in our victory, have no doubt that his spirit will be joining in our celebrations with no regrets.'

A huge pit had been dug for the rest of the Albion dead. They were far too numerous for separate interments. They would lie in honour, their spirits guarding the place where Brigantia's freedom had been won. Brigantia herself walked the length of the grave, blessing the spirits of those who had given their life to protect her land. Everywhere, signs of the gods and goddesses could be seen. An eagle and a raven soared on the warm thermals; wrens perched on the nearest branches; hares chased each other through the long grass at the top of the slope; deer peered through the woodland and, everywhere, pure white feathers dotted the ground.

Later, the remaining legionnaires were piled onto huge pyres and burned, sending thick black smoke into the air, rising quickly where it could be blown away by the stiff westerly breeze. Proculus was amongst them. There was no separation between the leaders or the common soldiers. No one cared; they just wanted to purge the land of the Romans' presence once and for all.

Taratus asked to see Kariss when everything was done. His injury was severe; Corio and Torwain were unsure if he would survive. He lay on a roll of goatskin where the sun could keep him warm. Despite the glorious summer weather, he felt constantly chilled to the bone. Trying not to shiver, he watched her approach. 'I owe you an explanation.'

She knelt and took hold of his hand. 'It is I that owe you my thanks. You saved my father; I can never thank you enough. That means so much more to me than killing Martaani, though I owe you my thanks for that as well.'

'So like the Kariss I remember. Always fiercely loyal. You would take on anyone if you thought they had slighted someone you cared about.'

'Would I?' Kariss could not remember being so bold.

'Oh yes, you were quite the bossy girl at times.'

Kariss slapped his arm gently, in mock annoyance. 'I never was.'

He gave a weak laugh; pain threaded its way through his body. He tried to hide it with a smile then his face became serious. 'It was not easy denying your right to the throne, or causing you the pain of thinking that I had betrayed you. Had it not been for Bodvoc, I could not have managed it.' The effort of speaking seemed to be almost too much. Kariss tried to stop him but he still had words that he was determined to say. 'Somehow, Bodvoc knew that someone would be needed to get close enough to Martaani to kill her; someone who loved you enough to keep going even when the nation turned against them.'

'You love me that much? Still?'

Taratus closed his eyes and took a few breaths. 'I have never stopped loving you, Kariss. We are no longer children but we share a bond that has never broken. Our destiny was not to be man and wife.' He looked a little embarrassed. 'I see how happy you are with Anniel, and I have that same happiness with my wife, Shael. Though I am not sure she will ever forgive me for the way I have treated her lately.'

'You must not worry about that now.' Kariss squeezed his hand; she was starting to feel concerned. 'We will find a way to put it right. I will make sure of it.'

'Promise me.' Taratus tried to lift his head but failed. 'Promise me that you will tell her that I never stopped loving her.'

'You will tell her that yourself,' Kariss reassured him, 'Torwain will find a way to heal you.'

Taratus reached for her hand again, as if to reassure himself of her touch. His eyes were dimming now. 'My time is done. I will never see my precious children grow. I will not hold my newborn in my arms and rock him to sleep. I have left Shael with the burden of raising our family alone.'

'Hush, Taratus. You must not speak like this.' Kariss's voice caught in her throat. She could not lose him now. She looked about, frantically trying to catch the attention of someone - anyone who could shout for a druid. She clasped his hand between hers, frightened to feel that there was no strength left in his grasp.

'I love you, Kariss. It was an honour to help you.' He could no longer make out her face; even the bright sun overhead was just a blur of white. Sound was diminishing and Kariss's voice when she spoke seemed a very long way off.

'I love you too, Taratus.' Tears slid from her eyes and down her cheeks, splashing on the ground between them. She felt his hand go limp. 'Torwain! Corio!' On the grass beside her, Taratus's face went slack and his head fell to the side. 'Taratus… no…

294

stay with me, please, just a little while longer, help is coming. Torwain! Corio!' she yelled again, but she knew it was no good. Her cousin was gone and she would never get the chance to know him again.

30

Kariss was carried aloft into the Stanwick camp amid much cheering and singing. Garlands of flowers festooned every conceivable hanging place and multiple fires burned under large roasting carcasses of sheep and goat; everywhere people looked, there was food and drink aplenty. It had been arriving for days; evidently news of the victory had not been slow in spreading.

The feast was magnificent. It had been a long time since the people of Brigantia had been able to celebrate. They took turns standing and toasting those no longer with them, cheering their successes as much as mourning their loss. Tholarg looked over to where Kariss was sitting, Anniel's arm firmly around her waist. He raised his cup to her.

'I told you that one day we would meet in celebration and not by the side of the road.'

'You did that, though I distinctly remember you mentioning a large hall and a roaring fire.'

He threw his head back and laughed. 'Well, we have plenty of fires, and who needs a hall when we have weather as fine as this?' He waved his hand in the air. The sun was beating down in yet another brilliant display of summer weather; a sure sign that Bodach was pleased with them.

Cantigern watched the exchange and smiled to himself. It had been many years since he had attended such an event. He had missed the friendly banter, the fires and the freedom to just be himself. The time that

Cailleach had sent them to was not like this. It was filled with anxiety and apprehension. People had developed a way of living that was cut off from nature, isolating themselves from each other until you were lucky if you even knew who your neighbours were. He was still weak from his time in captivity. He had been beaten and ill-treated but most of all he had missed his wife. He would not stop worrying about her, until he could hold her as close as Anniel was holding Kariss.

The celebrations went on well into the night. The following day, when Kariss met with her advisers, there were more than a few sore heads present. Kariss's stomach roiled even more than usual. She vowed to limit her intake of ale in the future; it was clearly not something her body responded to well.

They were meeting to discuss the re-building of Stanwick. It had been suggested that they leave the old town to its demise and seek a new place to make their capital. Kariss, however, would not hear of it. This was the place where Lord Hightern had held his court, it had been one of the main forts in Brigantia for generations and she was not going to change that now. Besides, what good was a capital far away in the safe parts of the nation? Brigantia's main threat came from the Votadini. Inida might well be gone but the nation's links with Rome were too strong to be dissolved so quickly. The main source of their wealth came from trading with the Empire and whoever succeeded Inida would not want to let that slip through their fingers.

Only time would tell if the Augur's assassins would materialise and attempt to carry out his plans. Torwain was known to some of the Votadini druids, ones he was certain would never be part of such a plot. As soon as Umar no longer needed his care, he intended to travel north east and see what could be done. He was becoming restless; he had lived too long on his own in the wilderness to be comfortable amongst crowds for any length of time.

A new war leader also needed to be chosen. Dainarr had survived the battle only to die of his injuries the following day. His deputy, Brannall, was chosen to succeed him. He was a tall man, with tawny hair and blue eyes. He reminded Kariss a little of Viroco, and it made her feel safe. She would have liked him for a second personal guard but who could possibly expect a warrior to turn down the chance of being war leader, to nursemaid an inexperienced queen? Instead, she picked a young warrior, Callutagus, who had proven himself more than capable in the battle. Volisios was happy with the choice.

The northern warriors began to take their leave. Gartnet went first; Kariss was pleased to see him leave. Next went the Carvetii. Kinithu had not been well enough to attend but in his absence he had ensured that his nation was well represented. The Taexali, along with the Vacomagi warriors, followed shortly after. Anniel had made a point of speaking to every one of the Vacomagi before they left; he would miss hearing their accent and seeing their familiar faces.

The largest group to leave was that of the Caledones and the Epidii, once again travelling together. It was a far more somber group that made the return journey north. They had suffered heavy losses, being as they were in the thick of the battle. Tholarg left with messages to deliver to Mailcon,

Fayern and Tharain. Naraic was particularly anxious that Tharain should learn that his parting gift, the yew bow, had been the weapon Naraic had used to kill the priests. That way, it was as if Tharain himself had taken part in defending his families' honour.

Galan was the last to leave; he took the time to speak with Naraic before he went. He smiled when he saw the silver cuff on his arm. 'You wear it well, lad.' He bent to give Cloud a pat. 'Good to see you too, boy.'

Cloud thumped his tail on the floor. He was glad to be free from his rope lead and to be at Naraic's side again. Once he had got over the excitement of their reunion, he had pushed his body against Naraic's leg and refused to let more than a finger's length come between them.

A shout went up behind them and they both turned to see Carrick and Garth making their way over. A short man with greying hair limped along with them, using a stick for balance. Naraic felt his heart sink at the sight of him but at the same time his spirits soared. The contrasting feelings had him in such a state that by the time the three men reached them, he was trembling. He lowered his eyes to the floor, not daring to lift them and face his father.

Gildas had no such qualms; he pulled Naraic into a tight embrace. Tears washed clear streaks down his grubby face. 'My lad, it is good to see you again.' He pulled back and looked at his son, 'Why did you hide from us?'

Naraic's face was flushed, he stumbled over his words. 'My uncle, I... did not mean... I...'

Gildas held up is hand. 'No one believes that you had anything to do with your uncle's death. The

Romans had been causing trouble all over Brigantia, trying to stir up unrest. They do not know us well, son. We trust our own.'

'But I pushed him, I was angry… and then I left.'

'Did you see him fall?'

Naraic thought for a moment, he had always told himself that his uncle had fallen but…

'He staggered backwards, he…' His face brightened. 'He did not fall; he came up against the wall. He raised a hand to strike me but I was already on my way out of the door.'

'There were a lot of problems in Wendell that day,' Gildas explained. 'Strangers had come to speak with Taratus; they caused many problems whilst they were there. No one ever thought you were to blame.'

'But I heard them; I heard them say my name when they were carrying him out.'

Garth rolled his eyes. Was the boy so determined to be guilty? 'They were concerned for you, you young fool. Your uncle was dead, scuffles had broken out all over the fort, and you were missing. If you were not so headstrong you would have learnt the truth by now.'

Galan watched this exchange with interest. The family resemblance between Gildas and Naraic was obvious. He would have needed no telling that they were father and son. He stepped forward. 'I would be proud to have a son such as Naraic here,' he told Gildas. 'You are a lucky man. I know nothing of the trouble that has so obviously kept you apart. I hope it is now behind you. If you have any doubt as to the integrity of your son, know this. He has suffered greatly at the hands of the Romans. It will always be my shame that it happened in Selgovae lands.

300

Throughout all his ordeal, he did not once give up his friends. He honoured his gods and his queen. No one could have asked for more. He will always be welcome at my home.' He stepped back, bowed to them all and then left.

Carrick clapped Naraic on the back. 'You have made a friend for life there, lad. You have one in me, too. Your father here has a lot to learn about what has happened to you since he last saw you. 'Tis good that his hair is already white.'

31

It had taken quite a bit of manoeuvring to get out of the camp unseen. Even at this hour, some of the people were still awake and sitting at their fires. Sleep would not come easily for many of those who had been called to fight. Dreams no longer felt like a safe place to be. The times before falling asleep and just after waking were particularly hard. It would take time and for some the trauma would never fully go away.

The full moon tried her hardest to help, bathing the sleepless figures in cool, white light. Gradually, as she waned over the coming nights, she would take much of their pain away. Work re-building Stanwick would hopefully help, too; it would give everyone something to focus on, new plans to look forward to - a fresh new beginning.

For now, Kariss had no time for anyone else. She had heard Brigantia calling and was eager to get to Ioho. There had been no word from the gods since the battle and whilst Kariss had been kept very busy, she had nevertheless been concerned. To her right she spotted the shaky figure of her father, making his determined way down the long slope to the ceremonial grounds. She hurried after him, taking his arm to keep him steady.

He had never divulged exactly what his Roman captors had done to him but he was a shadow of the man Kariss had always known. It was hard for her to see him so broken. It had been two days since Cailleach had told her she was going to get her mother

302

- too long for her not to worry that something had gone wrong. A lump formed in her throat; she could not bear the thought of what might be coming.

Ioho stood in a pool of moonlight. Cantigern and Kariss approached with trepidation. They could not make out who it was that waited for them in the deep shadows beneath his heavy canopy. Then with a cry of joy Cantigern rushed forward and embraced the woman who had been waiting patiently with Cailleach.

'I told you I would bring her back,' the old crone goddess said. She stroked Kariss's cheek, her piercing green eyes shining. 'You have a perfect role model there. It is your turn now and I have no doubt that you will make just as good a mother.' She winked and before Kariss had chance to react, she was gone.

Kariss felt a fluttering in her stomach that was nothing to do with the excitement of seeing her mother again. In wonder, she put her hand protectively over the spot and knew exactly why she had been feeling so sick lately.

Before she had a chance to think, she was swept up in her parents' embrace.

'Oh, how I have missed you,' Lizzelle said. They stepped out from the shadows and into the moon-washed ceremonial circle. At last Kariss could see her mother's face. It was pale and aged but she could not have looked happier.

There was rain in the air. Before the day was out there would be a deluge. A heavy summer rain storm that would refresh all it touched. The parched land certainly needed it. Dust coated Kariss's bare feet. She had left her shoes behind, preferring to feel the connection with the warm, dry earth. Beside her walked Anniel and Corio, each lost in their own thoughts as they made their way down the path.

Are you ready my child? Cailleach's voice sounded in her mind.

Kariss felt her stomach do yet another flip. She had been nervous all morning and she was concerned that her pregnancy sickness would return and ruin everything.

She felt Cailleach laugh in sympathy. *Fear not. You will not disgrace yourself. Though how Anniel's child growing inside you could possibly cause you shame is beyond me.*

You try being sick in front of so many people.

Again Cailleach laughed. *You will not be. I promise.*

There is one thing I still don't understand.

What is that, child?

Brigantia told me that Anniel still had an important part to play in everything. Is there something that I don't know?

Anniel has always been your strength and your reward, just as you are his. What could be more important than that?

Before them, the path led onto the ceremonial area in front of Ioho. Crowds of people were gathered, waiting to see their new queen appear. A cheer went up as they saw her. She felt Anniel's reassuring squeeze on her hand and smiled; Cailleach was right, it was so good to have him by her side.

Your people await you. Never forget that you deserve this honour, Kariss. You have earned it. You are far from that fearful young woman I spoke to all those moons ago.

That was certainly true. Kariss thought back to her life in London, all those years in the future. Progress was not such a brilliant thing when you stripped everything back. Yes, she missed certain things - writing, reading and the ability to communicate with people many hundreds of miles away just as easily as speaking to the person next to you but, really, that was all.

Life may be shorter, and medical care nothing like as advanced, but the people of Albion packed so much more into their lives. Everything felt more real, more connected. She did not miss that modern, lonely life, cut away from everything around her by layers of concrete and plastic. She needed her gods around her, to feel the life force of every living creature and know that the same need was shared with everyone else. She would put up with any amount of hardship for that.

She stepped forward to where she could see Brigantia and Verbia waiting beneath Ioho. Cailleach appeared beside them and the Great Goddess was complete. Kariss could feel the other gods around her and though she could not see them she knew without doubt that they were there. All had come to see the crowning of the new Queen of the Brigantes.

The End

Author's Note

I had always wanted to write novels but the timing had never been right. When I developed ME and became too ill to continue with life as it had been before, writing became my outlet. It allowed me to escape the confines of my home and be free. Through my characters, I could be anyone and do anything. No longer was I a prisoner in my own failing body.

Kariss, as I have said elsewhere, is named in honour of an old woman I knew when I was a child. She was the bravest person I have ever met. I will never forget her telling how she had suffered her umpteenth heart attack. Collapsed on the floor, unable to reach the telephone or shout for help, she had lain alone all night, knowing that in the morning someone would arrive. She knew the heart attack was massive and might be the one to finally kill her, but she remained calm and probably saved her own life by doing so.

That woman was such an inspiration; she did not let health or loneliness stop her from living her life. I needed bravery to keep going when everything became too hard but I struggled to find it myself. I do hope Mrs Elsie Carris does not mind me borrowing hers.

I cannot tell her how much she has meant to me over the years and how much of her determination I put into the character of my Kariss, but there are a number of other people whom I would like to thank for all their help and support during the writing of The Albion Chronicles series:

First of all, Katharine Smith, of Heddon Publishing, my wonderful editor who puts up with all my nonsense and a barrage of questions; Katherine Willis, for taking the time to beta-read each book and give her valuable feedback; and my fellow members of the Alliance of Independent Authors, without whom these books would never have made it into print, for all their help and support.

Special thanks go to my family, who never once told me that I was mad to try to write a book, let alone a series. They have stood by me throughout this massive learning curve and given me all the support I needed.

Previously in The Albion Chronicles...

Queen of Betrayal

(short story prequel)

The Girl of Two Worlds

Seven Druids

for news on these and other titles by Nelly Harper visit:

www.nellyharper.co.uk

www.goblinhouse.co.uk

Also by Nelly Harper:

The Jet Necklace

A POWERFUL SPELL, ONCE UNLEASHED
WILL NOT STOP UNTIL ITS WORK IS DONE.
~ However long it takes ~

Centuries have passed since the jet necklace was
made and imbued with a magical calming spell capable
of stopping even the strongest hate and hostility.

Oonagh is forced to flee the invading Vikings,
hiding the necklace from them as she runs. With
everyone she knows dead, she builds a new life far
away from the troubles.

When an act of ultimate betrayal brings the past
crashing back, her daughter Bethoc, must return to her
mother's homeland and try to retrieve the necklace
before it is too late.

33456001R00183

Printed in Great Britain
by Amazon